THE
CURIOUS
EAT
THEMSELVES

THE CURIOUS EAT THEMSELVES

JOHN STRALEY

SOHO

Published by
Soho Press, Inc.
853 Broadway
New York, NY 10003

Library of Congress Cataloging in Publication Data

Straley, John, 1953-
The curious eat themselves / John Straley.
p. cm.
ISBN-10: 1-56947-412-5
ISBN-13: 978-1-56947-412-9
1. Detectives—Alaska—Fiction. 2. Alaska—Fiction. I. Title.

PS3569.T687C87 1993
813'.54–dc20   93-8883
                              CIP

Manufactured in the United States
10 9 8 7 6 5 4 3 2 1

For Rachel Straley
and that first, most satisfying meal.

THE CURIOUS EAT THEMSELVES

ONE

I KNEW THERE was no escape from what was coming. A storm blowing up from the North Pacific, off Vancouver Island, would soon soak all of southeastern Alaska in a hard-driven rain. I wanted to think of a family somewhere far from here. They would be sitting down to a breakfast of scrambled eggs flecked with pepper and ripe berries served with cream. Sitting in a sunlit kitchen set back from the beach, they'd smell a warm ocean and the fresh coffee. A small girl would be itching to gulp her juice and run out to play, pestering her father by banging her knees under the table until he, in his kindness, released her into the sunshine. But that was a long way from this cement gray morning, waiting for a young woman's body to rise from the water under Creek Street.

Creek Street is a row of wood frame houses built on pilings over an estuary. Late in the year the salmon run up the creek to spawn by the thousands. A hundred years ago the street was Ketchikan's red-light district, where miners, sailors, and the curious were offered all manner of sport: booze from Canada, opium courtesy of the Chinese cannery workers, and whores who were mostly women from Scandinavian or Eastern European countries, occasionally a Negress. People say that every third week you could find a man's body floating with the tide out to the bay. It was lucky for everyone that the police didn't ask many questions. During the red-light era, it was said to be the only body of water where men and salmon went upstream to do the same thing.

The houses are old and weathered and the wooden siding seems damp even if it hasn't rained in days. A young man was watching from a third story window. He probably had his wrestling letter jacket in his closet. He was naked to the waist standing by the window ledge, rubbing his eyes and waking up to go to the swing shift where he'd worked for fifteen years.

Hannah and I were watching the bubbles of the Alaska State Trooper Tactical Dive Team, next to the pilings of a boarding house where two weeks earlier they had found an empty pocketbook on the deck outside room 23. They were looking for my client, Louise Root.

The water was chocolate brown from the rain, and the salmon were flashing like slices of silver near the surface. Occasionally one would flop up, slap the surface, and then disappear into the murk. Louise Root would never finish paying me, but I guess I didn't begrudge her that, since it appeared that within the first days after she hired me she had taken up residence underwater.

We had lost daylight-saving time and the days were short enough so everything seemed to happen in a twilight gloom. Or at least that was my mood of the season. I was waiting for the body to rise beneath the pier. The salmon were swimming upstream near the pilings and the woman who used to love me was standing nearby crying like a child lost in the woods. I had eaten breakfast but I was still hungry.

Hannah's crying was snotty and hiccuping, but she bit down hard on her lip. Her eyes had a distant, wild look of anger.

"I sent her for help, Cecil. For Christ's sake, I sent her to you for help."

I couldn't think of anything. My mind was a dirty sponge wrung out tight, the last of the smelly water dripping out.

They brought up her body tied by a loop around her shoulders. She was naked, and her skin was smooth and shiny white, like a marble statue being pulled from the mud. Her brown hair dangled in spiky wet curls around her brow like a young maiden's garland. She had been weighted down with scrap iron laced into a piece of trawl net and tied to the wrists. Her throat had been cut deeply so that the trachea flopped out like a rubbery white radiator hose.

Hannah jerked away from me and away from the body being pulled from the water. She had her elbows cupped in her hands and she was looking angrily out at the harbor. The halyards on the sailboats were clicking against the hollow aluminum masts. One late-season cruise ship stood at the dock where in busier summer months the tourists come off to buy film or popcorn or fudge or totem poles made in Taiwan, or soapstone whales made in prison. The creek was sucking out to the inlet.

"What do you ever do, Cecil? She needed your help. Do you ever get anywhere in time?"

She was right. I'm a defense investigator. I'm hired by

people in jail to help their lawyers beat back the prosecution. No one really hires me to find the truth. They hire me to imagine their innocence, then go out to the world and try to bring it to life. It happens often enough to make it worth doing but in the end I'm a storyteller with no authority, no badge, and no flashing blue lights.

"Another satisfied customer, Younger?"

George Doggy stood on the other side of me at the rail, looking down into the water. He was wearing a warm-up jacket from the Seattle Mariners open to the waist, except oddly, the top button. He had his trooper's shield stuck in his shirt pocket and this kept his coat cocked out at an odd rake.

"Satisfied," I said, and let it dangle while I flicked a piece of cinnamon roll off my collar and down to the water. A salmon flopped languidly onto the surface and away. The salmon wouldn't bite at bait anymore. They were single-minded on their way to the gravel beds upstream where they would take care of their reproductive mandate and die.

A small tourist lady in a plastic raincoat stood undaunted next to the barrier tape and took a picture. Then she looked up sadly at Doggy.

"I hope you get whoever it is, Officer. Imagine doing such a thing to an innocent girl."

Doggy kept looking down at the water and grimaced like someone who was reaching for a particularly hard spot to scratch. He turned toward me and, resting his elbow on the rail, whispered, "Innocent," and smiled. Then he started yelling at a cop who was having trouble with the casing on his underwater camera.

The young cops were wearing black jumpsuits and baseball caps and were running around communicating in snappy affirmative directives: "Isolate search area." And

6

"That's a go." Gear was everywhere: cameras, video players, radios, lab kits, diving tanks, and even a two-man sub. Everything, except the sub, had been in expensive cases that were stacked neatly like a kid's blocks on the corner of the boardwalk. These were the best toys bought with Alaska law enforcement's oil money. The whole scene was making Doggy a little sad, like a bad, small-town parade where there are more guns than band instruments.

Of course it was big oil that paid for almost everything in Alaska; nothing had changed that over the years. When the *Exxon Valdez* went aground on Bligh Reef in March of 1989 there were people who said something was broken in the north that could never be put back together. Of course, some said the oil would just sink into the ground where it came from but the others believed that if you dug a hole deep enough and waited . . . eventually the black stuff would begin to rise.

"Christ, Younger, I hate to think it, but maybe my wife is right."

"About?"

"About giving this up. It's just not as much fun anymore. I even find myself telling war stories to these kids. She says I'm getting to be a grouch and a bore."

"This is boring?"

"She thinks so. Garage sales—that's what she's into. Garage sales and banana giveaways at the market. She called me last night to say that she'd found a set of cast-iron owls for the fireplace. She was excited."

He stopped talking as the hoist paused and Louise Root's body swung in the air above the rubber sheet of the coroner's area. Her head hung straight down over the incision across her throat and her arms dangled loosely at her sides.

The motor of the hoist throbbed briefly to build power. They lowered Louise slowly, and the young men in jumpsuits reached their gloved hands up to ease her onto the dark green blanket. Gently, almost reverently, they laid her down, and her colorlessness glowed as pale as the sun on a foggy day. They stood silently for a moment like children with their heads down being told their parents were going to die someday, shifting from foot to foot, waiting for the inevitable joke that would bring them back to their work.

"I hope she paid in cash, Younger."

"No. No, she paid by check," I said, absently, not thinking of where I was or that I was involved in a joke.

Everyone laughed too loudly, and the youngest of the cops almost swaggered in place, knowing, once again, that they were on the inside of the joke, and safe.

I think George Doggy's job description read "Special Assistant to the Commissioner" because he wasn't a fully commissioned trooper anymore. He was supposed to be retired. He had given his service to the territory and then to the state. But they kept him on because they hadn't found a way to input into a computer all of the dirt this guy had swept up over the years. There have only been six governors of the state and all of them had kept him close. When they wanted to be briefed without having to read all of the bureaucratic butt-covering, they still sent for Doggy. I had known him most of my life. My father had been the presiding judge in Juneau for many of the years Doggy had been stationed there. They had been hunting partners. After the judge's death, Doggy made frequent trips to Juneau to help my mother with house chores. She preferred having him fly over and never thought for an instant that I could have managed.

8

He turned and looked at me, then led me away by the elbow. "Well, that's about it for you, Cecil. I wouldn't worry about it anymore."

By now the cops were snapping photographs and the dive team had set up a grid on the bottom to search for other physical evidence. There wasn't much hope because of the tidal action and the flow of the river, but still they followed the procedures if for nothing else than to be able to shut up some smart-assed defense attorney years in the future.

Doggy turned and looked back at the scene and it was clear he was involved in some way and wanted to talk and get rid of me at the same time. Hannah stood off to the side looking down blankly into the water, watching the salmon struggle against the current.

"The thing that bugs me most about these kids, Younger"—he stood close to me alongside the rail and spoke almost conspiratorially—"is that they're so damn . . . professional."

He let that hang. Doggy had been born well before Elvis Presley and before young men were under the injunction to invent themselves. He was part of the old Alaska and he accepted who he was as easily as he accepted the climate. Yet he had a hard time with me, whom he thought of as some exotic creation: the ne'er-do-well son of the famous judge, who lived with an autistic man and ran a private investigator's service in a town with no business. Eye contact with someone like me was hard enough. Asking a favor was pushing him to the edge of some kind of seizure.

"You need to stay clear of this, Cecil," he muttered.

"Doggy, what is going on? Louise Root came to me and said she had been raped up at the gold mine at Otter Creek. She said the company didn't do anything about it and the police wouldn't help. She wanted me to interview some of the witnesses. We hadn't gotten too far along—"

"And you're going to get no farther." Doggy spun me around and sent me across the street toward a little construction shack the cops had taken over as the crime scene headquarters. He motioned to Hannah that she was expected to come along. She gazed at him and stood flat-footed until he stared at her with his own look of patient authority that lifts most people to their feet. Hannah followed us across the street.

The shack had a makeshift drafting table that was pieced together from scrap plywood. There was a radio, a kerosene heater, a phone wired into the wall, and two chairs against the wall near the tall drafting stool. Doggy sat in the low chair nearest the door. I sat opposite him and Hannah excused herself and sat on the drafting stool.

"Now . . ." Doggy rubbed his hands together, looking at them briefly, then he looked straight up into my eyes. "I want all of it. I know you two know something about this. I want it all." He was speaking to me but Hannah answered first. She didn't look at either of us sitting below her but looked out the window to the parking lot of the old federal building and spoke.

"We were old friends. Years ago she cooked on a fishing boat out of Craig. She got me a job. She had been to college and we liked to talk about books we were reading. We would talk late at night, sometimes all night. We drank together and tried to hide out from all the men off the other boats."

Hannah was wearing her rubber boots folded down and her canvas pants tucked loosely inside. She had on a plum silk shirt and wore a black beret with a silver Tlingit killer whale pin on its crown. Her pile coat lay folded on her lap. She turned from the window, flicked her straw-colored hair off her shoulders, and looked at me as if she were swallowing rancid milk.

"She got sober before I did. I loved her a lot. She was tough and funny and didn't take shit from anybody." Hannah looked back out the window.

Doggy looked at her. He didn't have a notebook but asked his questions slowly as if he were going to memorize her answers. He was known for not taking contemporaneous notes. He had a phenomenal memory, and the absence of notes made him the toughest of cops to cross-examine.

"When was the last time you saw her?"

"Three weeks ago. I've been working up in Juneau and she came to see me. She told me about the rape down at the mine. She said no one was looking into it." Now Hannah looked hard at Doggy and he held her eyes longer than I ever would have been able to.

"She said that the troopers and the police told her they couldn't make a case so they were not going to do anything. I did . . . I did the only thing I could think of doing. I sent her down to see Cecil. It was stupid, I guess, but I knew the troopers wouldn't stand up to the company men. Isn't that true, George?"

George Doggy looked at her and his eyebrows curled with some sympathy but his mouth stayed flat. "This is a murder investigation. I know about the rape allegations. I also know the men denied it. I'm only interested in the murder. Did she say what she was going to do?"

"She said she wanted some evidence. Even if it was only

for herself. Even if it was only for her family. The company men said she was a slut. They said she was asking for it. She wanted the words of the men telling the truth on tape. The word of a woman isn't evidence enough."

Doggy looked at me. "Is that what she wanted? She wanted interviews?"

I moved uncomfortably in my chair. "Yeah, she wanted me to talk to some of the men but at the last minute she backed out."

"Why?"

I raised my hands in a gesture of ignorance: palms up, shoulders slumped. Doggy smiled. Then he looked up at Hannah. Her mouth was stretched down tight and her breathing was getting deep, as if her chest were pumping the tears to her eyes. Her voice quavered.

"She was a good . . . good person. She loved working in the woods and on the ocean. She loved to read early in the morning and drink lots of coffee. She loved me and I didn't do much to help her. I just palmed her off on someone else." She raised a shaking hand to cover her eyes and her chest heaved. I looked down at the floor of the shack, scuffed the heel of my shoe along the coffee stains on the plywood floor. Doggy got up and stood next to Hannah. He put his hands on her shoulders and looked out the window to where a gull was sitting on the rail above the harbor. His voice was lower now as he spoke.

"I know we didn't do enough to help her when she came in from the mine. The local cops sent me a copy of the reports. There wasn't enough there for a case. But that doesn't mean it had ended there. I can't tell you everything. But . . . we were still working on it."

Hannah reached up and took his hands off her. She

turned around. "Well, if it wasn't too late then, it must be now. Are you going to arrest the man who did this to her?"

Doggy spread his hands much the way I had. "We've got nothing right now. We've got to make a case before we make an arrest."

She walked past me and out the door. I had to work my knees around against the wall to let her pass. She was gone and the door slammed as Doggy stood above me.

"You better keep her under control, Cecil. I've already got enough trouble with this case without her running around mucking up the evidence."

I stood up, but Doggy's index finger pushed me back down. "And I want everything you have on Louise Root. You got it? That's your job. You give me everything. You keep out of this investigation and you keep her out of it. Cecil, I got people looking over my shoulder on this. I don't need the Hardy Boys messing up the scene. Clear?"

The gull hopped off the rail and Hannah was storming across the street. I had been given a complex assignment that involved not doing anything and I thought I had better get cracking on not doing it.

"Yeah, Doggy, it's clear," I said, "and as soon as I don't know anything more I'll let you know." But I was speaking to his back as he was already out the door.

I followed Hannah down the street and into the Gotham Hotel. It was one of the few transient hotels left on the street. It was a cheap and fairly discreet place where the loggers and fishermen could flop when they came off the ferry.

There were bathrooms down the hall and telephones on the landings, and the flooring was decaying and spongy under the cracked linoleum. The windows were beginning to rot in their frames and a quarter of them were either stuck down or stuck up, with cardboard jammed in the openings to keep the rain off the bedspreads. As we walked in and I took my first breath of mildewed carpet pads, leaking fuel oil, and cigarette smoke, I was flooded by a memory that came up like a fish to the surface.

It was after my father died and before Hannah had moved out. I was looking for a stevedore, a Lakota Indian, for a lawyer in Wyoming. I had come to Ketchikan and gotten caught up in a wild party of Indians, loggers, and cokeheads that rolled through town like a steam-powered thresher. It wasn't until I walked in that red door with Hannah that I remembered that the party for me had ended in a room in this hotel. I remembered the impression of the short shag carpet crushed into my forehead and a cigarette butt pressed against my eyelid. I remembered looking up and seeing my shoes leaning against the door next to some corked work boots, with the supple leather of their lasts drooping over my leather slip-on romeos as if my shoes were somebody's little brother. I remembered the powerful urge to both drink more and throw up. I vaguely remembered having kissed a woman who was wearing a girdle, and the taste of lipstick on my teeth.

Hannah stood at the door of 23. There was no police lock on the door but there was yellow police barrier tape across the door frame. She turned the knob, ducked under the tape, and we went in. There was a double bed with a mustard brown spread, a night stand, and a clock radio with the numbers flashing at twelve o'clock. The gooseneck reading lamp coming out of the wall above the bed was broken, with wires dangling from the flexible metal, but someone had wired an electrician's bulb that hung bare and shiny as a skull. The room was tidy. On the bed was a backpack, an expensive internal-frame traveler's type designed for either airports or trails. Hannah picked up the pack and began walking out.

"What are you doing? That's evidence. You can't just walk away with her pack. Doggy is going to send some of the troops down here to process this room."

"No one is going to do anything to help and you know it, Cecil."

She turned and ran out of the place and I felt a gust of disinfectant whirl in her wake. I followed her out helplessly and stood in the doorway of the hotel. It was only raining lightly. I thought to follow her, but then I thought of just going for a walk. I could go along the creek upstream and walk the streets that were like streets in other mill towns all over the west.

The rain was increasing. There were pickups blocking traffic, the drivers in their work clothes with their forearms out the windows and their hard hats sitting next to them on the seats. Most of the drivers are still sober this time of day. The cars behind don't honk. Girls cross the street in front of the trucks and the air glistens with perfume, exhaust and gum. And it all mixes with smells from the dumpster and the cold air that rides the surface of the creek from upstream, from up the steep-sided mountain that takes off like a staircase behind the ball field.

Holding on to the plane ticket in my pocket, I wondered

how in the hell I was going to get a ride to the ferry to take me across to the airport, when I heard the tinkle of a braceleted arm and smelled the light lemony perfume of a complicated life.

"C. W. Younger, my favorite dick! Short and sweet."

I turned to face the eyes I knew were casing my butt. "I can't believe you said that and with officers of the law present."

"Hell, Cecil, they know you're sweet." And she smiled, not the way Doggy had, in a tight grin that tried to push the humor away, but in a deep buttery smile that seemed to travel up her pelvis, spiraling up into the red hair that framed her wide face. Ketchikan has the reputation for having more women who have more fun on more nights of the year than anywhere else in the north. If this is true, the list would have to begin with Lolly, the proprietress of the Gotham.

She was almost six feet tall, and we stood eye to eye. Her left eyetooth sported a gold cap. She wore a loose-fitting silk blouse and a purple jacket with padded shoulders over tight stretch pants. And as we stood in the doorway of her hotel, the hem of her blouse fluttered onto the inside edge of my coat.

Lots of lawyers had tried to call her, but Lolly was a rotten witness because she told everyone exactly what they wanted to hear. Every guy in jail wanted to be released into her custody and she had tried it a couple of times for some of the boys who were the most fun, but the light in her eyes, her hair, and the way she cocked her head and parted her lips when she smiled could make almost anyone violate the conditions of their release.

"Cecil, put that bag down. Come inside and have a drink.

I've got beer and smoked black cod and some of those nasty oysters you like so much."

I looked down at my romeos, and, for a second, saw them walking into Lolly's room and kicking themselves off next to her overstuffed chair by the radiator. I saw them under the bed in the morning. I set the pack down, as if to throw out an anchor.

"Listen, Lol, I can't do it. I mean, I could, but . . . well, it's like this—I can't do it—"

This was her opening for the smile. She put her hands up behind and under her blouse, then stretched back slightly as if her lower back were tight. She smiled and laughed easily like steam rising from a coffee urn.

"Younger, I'm not going to do anything. I just figure we should have a little drink . . . and visit."

There is something so self-aware about Lolly's desire. This is not a kind of flirting that comes from any lack of confidence. It is simply for the pleasure in it, like trying on silk underwear and wearing it under your work clothes. If I didn't eat the oysters it would be someone else and that made me want to eat them all the more.

"Well," I said, "it's like this."

"Don't tell me you're on the wagon again."

"Have you ever known me when I was on the wagon?" I asked, truly concerned, because I wasn't sure.

"If it wasn't you, it was somebody—somebody I didn't much care for." She gave me a lesser version of the smile as she sensed I was passing out of range and there was no sense wasting any.

I shrugged. "The truth is, I've got to go back to the airport, to the ferry. I mean, I've got to."

"Forget it, Cecil. Listen, say hi when you catch up to her."

She gestured up the street where Hannah had disappeared like a storm squall.

"Yeah. I will." And I tried to turn my feet north. I hate being on the wagon. It's like getting my life back but losing one of my senses.

"Lol, what do you know about Louise Root?"

"She was an odd one. Kind of mousy. Friendly enough but not much fun." She curled her fingers through her hair and stared down at my shoes. "I think she told me she was waiting for somebody." She looked down the boardwalk to where the cops were loading a stretcher with a black body bag on it into an ambulance.

"Did she say who she was waiting for?"

"Hey, you know, I don't talk that much about who my customers are waiting for. It gets too drawn out and—ah—wistful for me. But she told me she was waiting for a man and he had something for her."

"Did she pay cash?"

"I think so. She paid up and was around for at least three days. I don't know. We . . . spent a little time together, you know, just talking, but I didn't get much out of her."

"Did you feed her?"

"No, I was saving everything for you."

With the possibility that I was moving back in range, she kicked her heel out of the back of one of her pumps and shifted the weight of her hip out to give the small of her back another stretch in my direction.

"Do you remember anybody coming by? Any visitors at all?"

"The last day I remember seeing her around, there were a couple of guys that came by. She just missed them. They said they would come back. I don't remember anything other than that one said he was looking for this girl, Louise Root." Another smile. "And don't start with me on, 'What did he look like?' and that shit. I don't know. I just remember there was a guy here. He wore something pimpy. I don't know."

"Pimpy?"

"Don't start, Cecil. I don't remember. It was just some god-awful piece of jewelry or something. The other guy was weird-looking too."

"Weird?"

She looked at the cuticle of the middle finger on her right hand. "Christ, this is boring. He looked different than the little pimpy guy. Rich or something, like the little pimp worked for him. He acted in charge."

"What do you mean 'in charge'?"

"Like he was the one giving orders. Even if he wasn't giving any."

"The police already talked to you?"

"Hell, they started to but then Doggy said that he would interview me himself. I guess he hasn't gotten around to it."

She looked at the boardwalk and the crowd of cops. Doggy was writing in his notebook. His jacket was fully unbuttoned now and his gray hair was blowing back from a wind that was probably pushing rain ahead of it from the southwest. Doggy looked up at a young cop and then sneaked a look at Lolly, then quickly back at the cop. He was faking his attention to the cop and was aware that we had seen him looking at us. Lolly laughed softly and stared down at him. She was balancing on her one shoe and was visibly leaning toward Doggy.

"How's your retarded roommate?" she said, almost absentmindedly turning her gaze toward me as if she were waking up from a dream.

"He's 'emotionally and intellectually challenged.' I've got the papers."

"Take a pill, Cecil. I'm teasing you. You don't have to tell *me* about Toddy. I knew the boy after he watched his mother die. Hell, it's been thirty years and the old man is still drinking it off in the bars."

Todd's father had been a logging mechanic, but after his wife died he took to drinking hard and his work got sloppy. A chain hoist crushed his hip under a camp generator's diesel engine. He sleeps on a friend's boat and drinks up his workers' comp money. Whenever I saw the old man I ignored him and he didn't recognize me. He always wore a faded canvas jacket and a greasy ball cap covered with various enamel bird and fish pins. He'd hold his beer glass and cigarette in the same hand and cover his pile of change with his other hand, staring down into the bubbles of his beer as he spoke to everyone in the bar. No one nodded or even looked up in his direction.

A trooper car drove up and the young woman in the jumpsuit leaned over the passenger seat and called out the open window, "I was told to get you to the ferry so you can go over and check in for your flight."

I looked down the street and Doggy was staring at me, his finger pointing north toward the airport. I was meant to go and he was not smiling. I got into the back seat, where there were no inside door handles. The window was open and somewhere up the valley fish was being barbecued. I looked back at Lolly and she waved. I imagined the pockets of warmth under her blouse, and I thought how her red hair would cling to the curve of her throat as she lay down that evening.

Gulls circled above Creek Street and dipped down toward the water where the body had been sunk. A salmon carcass was lodged on the slick rocks of the riverbank and a raven took the eyeball.

TWO

I LIKE TO think Hannah had been deeply in love with me, even during the years we lived together, and I tried to win her over with my drunkard's melancholy joie de vivre. But I was never a heroic drunk nor a particularly poetic one, no matter that I thought I was. I first read her Ou-Yang Hsiu's "Drunk and on the road I am bound in the floating threads of spring" lying on the floor of a hotel room in a backwater fishing town and for years we tried to match its eloquence by dancing into our own dream states.

Now, of course, Hannah is a professional person and a sober Christian. She still dresses like a fisherman but I've had to get used to the appearance of the silk scarves and the delicate perfume, the barbarous olive green suit coats with the dulled metal accessories. She's a social worker up north in Stellar. But her life's work is traveling and leading workshops for others in "the recovery movement" and that is what she had been doing for a while now in Juneau.

Companies and state agencies pay her big money to lead workshops and counsel groups of executives. She goes from airport to airport, and checks into her room early, then stretches, goes for a run, and showers. Before leaving for the lecture she will lie on the bed wrapped in a towel and read from a book of current poetry, thinking and stretching, fingering each page as she stops and lets the images from each poem rise. She reads women poets mostly, and often those who engender some reverence for "journey."

We had met ten years ago in a bar in Craig, back when Craig was like a logging and fishing version of Dodge City. She'd walked in with a skiff man off a Bellingham seine boat. She was wearing a black tank top and had on skintight jeans with a bandanna around her knee. She had the skiff man's baseball cap on backwards. The tank top draped down, almost exposing her nipples.

He was supporting her with his forearm as they eased into the bar. She had the wobble-necked look of a self-aware drunk who fully understands reality is basically an ironic joke that no one else gets. She looked around at the early morning crowd and announced: "I need a line of cocaine as long and as fat as my arm and I'll do anything to get it!"

I have since learned that in the terminology of the recovery movement this is called being "really fucked up."

She had her head bent back and scanned the room, passing over me and briefly considering the skinny kid in the corner who worked as a choker-setter. Then she retreated into a thousand-yard stare out the door. Her jaw was jutted out and slacked loose, as if it were just too much trouble to keep it shut. The skiff man set her at the bar, propped her on her elbows, and put a small stack of cash in front of her. He motioned to the barmaid to come over. He explained that she had a ticket to Ketchikan and she had some bar money. His skipper had told him to get her on the plane but he was pulling out before the plane did. Would the barmaid mind just steering her to the float plane in three hours?

It was arranged. He took his ball cap and said goodbye. Hannah looked up from the bar and when she understood that he was leaving, she slapped him, hard enough for his face to redden and for him to clench his fists. Several of the old-timers shifted in their chairs, the barmaid reached for her shortened ball bat, the skiff man looked around and eased. Even in Craig, hitting a coked-up girl in broad daylight could provoke some sort of chivalrous reaction.

When he said goodbye, Hannah grabbed hold of him and French-kissed him long enough for the barmaid to shift on her feet and look out the window. The skiff man broke the clinch and headed out the door. Hannah called for a beer and started to cry. Then she sputtered about "cheap bastard seiners." I sat down next to her and commented on how beautiful the day was.

She looked up at me with the glittery smile of an ocelot and said, "Fuck the weather, let's get high."

Now she considers this her dark period. Her forty days in the desert. Now she's giving talks and running workshops, and she recounts this phase of her life to roomfuls of self-conscious men and women all drinking watery coffee. She always starts off nervous and moves awkwardly into the confessional tone. She always begins at the bottom, the pivotal point of her recovery, the moment that brought her to the inescapable truth. I've heard the talk, I've tried to walk the walk too. But somehow in this personal mythology, my place is somewhere in the desert traveling with her other discarded demons.

That first night she and I got a room in the hotel above the bar. We drank and snorted cocaine and watched TV every night until dark and then went dancing briefly. After the band shut down we would go back to the room and take long showers to get the smoke off, then lie naked on the bedspread and watch sword-and-sandal epics, lay out lines of coke on each other's bellies and snort them off during commercials. We'd send out for food and had plates and plates of french fries and greasy steak sandwiches. It piled up by the door in drifts with the food half-eaten. After a couple days of cocaine, food only has an abstract interest. Eating is a great idea that you never really develop. The cocaine is like frozen gin icing down your brain. It primarily affects your vanity. So much so, you think that the world, the maids who will clean up your mess, the cops who are planning your arrest, and your friends who shake their heads and frown at your shortsightedness, that all of these people are held in the thrall of your hip purity of thought.

The TV off, she read to me from Tu Fu and Ou-Yang Hsiu, and we tried to rise with the words, just like we tried to have sex, but it never worked. We clutched and kissed and tried to gain a purchase on each other's skin, but we couldn't. Our minds were too light, our bodies too distant.

Before the cops came, we made it down to another seine boat and gave the skipper what was left of our stash to take us to Ketchikan. We drank whiskey and lay on the back deck atop the webbing. The sun was hot and the engine throbbed below the steel decking. While the rest of the crew watched like vultures, Hannah curled in my arms and sang into my chest. We drank from the bottle. We slept. Seven years.

I think when I kissed her that first time and tasted the weird flavor of bourbon, lip balm, and halibut gurry, I almost laughed out loud with the recognition of wanting someone without restraint. Later, after her recovery, she became a dignified, rather mystic Christian; no telethons or handling snakes, but strength that cupped the wildness like a lake bed. I used to bait her with talk of snake handlers and mean comparisons to the Christian hucksters on TV. She would smile but never rise to it. She would only say that I could never understand as long as I stayed drunk. I couldn't understand her because now she was both vertically and horizontally connected. She was right. I didn't understand her.

Now Hannah was sitting at the table near the snack bar at the upstairs gate of the Ketchikan airport, waiting for the flight that would come north from Seattle two hours and take us on the thirty-minute hop further up to Sitka.

She was going through Louise Root's pack. When she saw me walking toward the candy stand, she looked down at a bundle of letters she was holding.

I work out of my house on the waterfront of the old Indian village area of Sitka. For the last eight months Hannah had been in Juneau working on an alcohol treatment project for the state's Department of Social Services. Louise Root had sought her out by asking advocates at the women's shelter. In turn, Hannah had recommended me. Following Hannah's advice, Louise Root had taken the ferry for the twenty-four hours needed to buck the tides through the passage west, and ended up on the outer coast near Sitka. She walked the five miles from the ferry to my house in town. That was only two weeks ago.

Louise Root was soft-spoken and had that young aristocratic look of a modern wilderness adventurer with expensive water-repellent clothes. They were black and gray with accents of vibrant lavender. She had on soft shoes and a Norwegian sweater. But her hands were large, deeply creased with callouses, and she had pale crescents of scars over the front edge of her left hand. I think she told me she nicked herself while chopping food.

Her voice was flat and had no accent or drama to it. She was blunt, if not truthful. Occasionally, when she made a point, she would reach up and comb her fingers through her hair, and then she would look quickly down and fold her hands onto her lap.

She had been raped. That was about as clear as I could get it. A birthday party up at the mine. She would start into details, her throat would constrict, her hands clench tightly, and she would stop. She wanted me to find witnesses. She wanted me to interview them and suggested I wear a wire and secretly tape their statements. One hitch—she didn't want to give me their names. It was as if naming them gave the men power she would never acknowledge.

I hate wasting time in the opening consultations. Wasting time comes when I start charging by the hour.

"Ms. Root . . ." I leaned forward and tried to soften my eyes and my voice so I could create the atmosphere of a sealed confidence. "I know this is hard for you but . . . you're going to pay me thirty-five dollars an hour to answer some questions for you. I would like to help you, but I'll need a place to start and an idea of what you want to end up with."

She let out a long breath and raised one hand in a distracted gesture, then traced the veins down her slender wrist with the tip of her index finger.

"I don't think you really understand." She smiled weakly. "The men don't care, and the police don't care. . . ." Her voice trailed away. "And for a while, you know, I was tempted not to care. But not now. Not anymore." She looked out the window at a wooden troller going by my house out in the channel. She narrowed her eyes and set her jaw in a position that willed the courage of anger and refused tears.

Out in the wind, a full sheet of newspaper twisted hopelessly like a spineless kite and settled on the water, then was washed by the wake of the troller and sank. A tear formed at the corner of her eye.

"They can't be allowed to deny it."

"Can you tell me their names at least? It would help."

All she said was "No," and got up to leave. "I will think about it some more, Mr. Younger. Maybe it was too soon for me to come and bother you."

I stood too, and held out my hand. She placed a folded check for a hundred dollars in it. Then she was down the stairs and gone. Now she's a corpse, still connected to the earth by her body but lost to everything else.

I was alone in the middle of the terminal waiting area, thinking I was still in line, and for a moment I felt her leaving like a flight of geese in the dark.

I walked over to Hannah's table in the bar area and sat down. She didn't look up at me but started in, her voice trembling slightly.

"What do you want to know? She was born in 1959 and she was thirty-four when she . . . died." Hannah paused, still staring at the sheaf of papers from the pack. There was a passport, some letters. She cleared her throat. "She had a college education but she wanted to work as a cook at the Otter Creek gold mine south of Sitka." Hannah's hands trembled and she handed me the pack.

Our plane was not on the ground but they were starting the security screening. I set the pack between us and opened the flap. Louise Root's expensive outdoor clothes were folded and rolled neatly into the pack. A toilet kit appeared, made from brushed leather, a bag with a brass clasp, and a wooden hairbrush with boar bristles. I leafed through a couple of loose books and found a package of letters wrapped in plastic and wound with a rubber band. The edges of the envelopes looked well-worn and the creases matched the edges of the entire stack as if they had been bundled for a long time.

The letters were addressed to Steven Mathews at the Early Winters Institute for Environmental Ethics in Mazama, Washington, and had been returned to the sender, Ms. Louise Root. The letters were in light blue legal-sized envelopes that had a stamp on the back fold that showed they were made from recycled forest products. The ink was a pretty flowing blue that looked like it came from an old-fashioned fountain pen. They had been originally sent from the Otter Creek mine through a post office box in Ketchikan, and had been returned unopened. I slipped out the top one, and slit open the envelope with my finger.

Dear Steven, I'm here at last. My gear was lost by the airlines, wouldn't you know. But I had my small pack (with your books in it) with me all the way so at least they arrived safely.

It is beautiful here if you look past the gash of the mine. From the back of the cookshack I can see up into the alpine, and most mornings there are smoky clouds curling down the valley. I haven't added to my bird list. Mostly it's gull, raven, and eagle. There were deer above us but of course they keep their distance as long as the equipment is running and that is most of the time.

I have two prep cooks and one scrubber. They are Filipino: a husband, wife, and a cousin. They are good people and are such a relief from the sullen thugs up on the slope. With those guys I thought I needed a whip and a chair, but Angi, Javier, and Teo are so great. They can sing and tease me out of my bad moods that usually come on after break-fast. I hate lunch with this group. That's different from the slope too. These guys aren't getting the bucks like some of the oil boys so they gripe more and are belligerent if they don't have the full offering of fifteen thousand calories at every sitting. I know it's their only homey comfort but they're just driving earth graders and front-end loaders, and still they want to eat like they're putting up hay by hand. Well, you've heard it all before from me. Roast beef, potatoes, gravy, and peach cobbler. It still breaks my heart in a way. They're good guys all in all. They just tell themselves a crazy story about their lives. I don't even think they see this ghetto of cables and mobile homes, where the company makes them live.

I'm sorry, I'm a broken record. I've dug out the material on the cyanide process. I think you are right. Even though they say everything is okay, there is a lot to be seen.

Much love, Lou

Another:

Dear Steven, I guess you must not have time to write . . . but I understand. I have the galley of your essay with me and I just read and reread it at night, pretending that it is a letter to me. I don't understand it all but I love the descriptions. The science and the politics are all pretty heady stuff—especially for the boys around the bunkhouse. I keep the title covered up under my sweater so I don't have to listen to the teasing. But after the last dishes are done I make myself a cup of tea (almost my last pleasure left) and I sit on the back landing near the washhouse and read. Thank you, it feels like a gift of sanity.

Your letters and your thoughts would be such a relief to me if you could find time to write. Sometimes I think I am in jail, serving time by dishing out beefsteak and macaroni salad. When I hear that the mail has come in on the plane I let Javier finish whatever I have started and I head for the loading area. I get more mail than anyone else and even that is the subject of teasing, as if literacy was a threat, which, sadly, I think it is for most of these guys.

But I'm not trying to make you feel guilty. Really, I'm not. I just suppose I'm trying to stay in touch with you. Who was it that said their poems were like letters to the world? Maybe my scribblings to you are just letters to the world too.

Listen, take good care and thanks for whatever time you can spend reading this. I don't think my letters are being opened and I think your last suggestion about the telephone calls is pretty preposterous. If you want to send information to me, just send it via good old air mail and I will respond. No sense being cloak-and-dagger about this stuff. What do we have to be afraid of?

Much love. Lou.

I stopped reading for a moment. She had been good with words. I wished she had told me more when she had been in the office. Hannah was looking at some of the other papers and I went back to the letters.

Dear Steven,

You are very thoughtful. Your birthday gift arrived right on my birthday and I am rushing this note so that it will make it on the plane out. I love the Abbey, and I am working on the Simone Weil . . . but I particularly love the candied ginger and dark chocolate. You are a gem. Something is up. This is a dry camp, but the boys snuck a couple of gallons of whiskey off the plane, and there is scuttlebutt about a party. Word's out it's my birthday. I'd love to have a drink but I've been going so good on my program while I've been up here. Being sober has made me think so much clearer. We'll see. Maybe I'll get that ride on the chopper to the summit yet. See ya . . .

Hannah came back from the bar with a beer and she did not offer me a thing. She stared at me as if I were a rotting bag of meat. The next letter in the stack was different in appearance. It was in a white standard envelope from the City Moose Motel in Anchorage.

Steven,

I regret how our last telephone conversation ended. It was not a veiled threat. I suppose it was a no-win situation for you. I am disoriented. You have to understand. . . . Your acknowledgment of my pain is just that—your acknowledgment. It does nothing for me. I'm sick of this male sensitivity shit. It's almost as dishonest as the vulnerability of women. I'm sorry, your suffering does not interest me at this point. And I don't care what your plans have been up to now. I'm going to take care of this myself.

I stayed in the shower until the men from Global security came. They told me they would take me to a clinic and I ended up in Anchorage. It took me three days before I could talk to a woman from a shelter.

They were wonderful but the cops would do nothing—a jurisdictional problem, they said. But everyone, even the high-powered alcohol counselor they brought in, knows it has to do with Global. It's all about that long straight line of authority. Fuck them.

Sometimes I think that my anger is the only thing that seals my skin. Without it my blood would come out through the pores. I've showered for hours and I can't get his feel off of me. I used to love to take a bath after the last of the dinner was cleaned up. Long, hot baths. And I would towel myself off slowly with the window open, looking up at the sky with the steam rising through the transom. But now (and I've tried it only once) I ease into the tub and the surface of the water feels like their hands stroking me. I get out. Fuck them. Not in their imagination and not in mine—never again.

You were my friend so I tell you these things. You may want to know how I am different. We have so little in this life. I'm not going to waste any more of mine on anyone else's plans or expectations. The body holds the soul and so must give it some shape. My body is horrid to me now and so my soul is shapeless.

I put the last letter back. There were other papers: copies of reports from the mines, lists that looked like bills of lading from tankers, with off-loading times and schedules. There were some tank inspection forms but I didn't know what I was looking at and just passed my eyes over the numbers and the columns. The only thing that stopped my eye was that there was a log marked DRAWDOWN timed for entry Christmas Day.

A 737 pulled up to the jetway. Hannah took the pack from me and passed through the security area. She carried the pack onto the plane. I would not see her again until we arrived in Sitka. We very definitely did not have adjoining seats.

The weather was cloudy and the wind from the south. The 737 didn't reach full altitude on the half-hour flight north from Ketchikan to Sitka but we did get our nuts and juice at sixteen thousand feet. A flight attendant with thick blue mascara just smiled at me and gave me orange juice even when I cheerfully asked for champagne. She did not let on that she recognized me from one of my infamous in-flight binges but she must have. For a time I'd been allowed on the airline on a strictly provisional basis because of past disturbances. Not much fun for the flight crew: bad jokes, loud arguments, blood, and the cops meeting me at the jetway. But I was nice as pie on this trip back to town.

I looked out the window of the plane to the steep-sided islands of southeastern Alaska. Here it's rain forest, and the water sluices down the rocks, carving steep, fast river channels. The towns cling to the sides of the islands on whatever flat land the river silt has piled up. Further north the rain dissipates and the mountains run out to the flat plain where the rivers slow and meander. Looking down from the plane I thought of all the thousands of square miles to be lost in. I thought of Louise Root, hopping south from Juneau to Sitka, down to Ketchikan, looking for some answer. I looked north to the Fairweather Mountains above Glacier Bay, and further to the subarctic haze of the interior. Even at sixteen thousand feet the different worlds of Anchorage, Fairbanks, and the north slope of the Brooks range are beyond the curve of the earth. The distances in this state are so great the land almost seems like an abstraction. Again I thought of Louise Root, traveling by boat and plane, following the channels, trying to keep from being lost.

Sitka is north of Ketchikan, south of Glacier Bay and on the open coast of Baranof Island. Unlike Ketchikan, which has that close feel of a waterfront boardwalk town, Sitka leaves you feeling more exposed. The North Pacific swells travel long distances across the gulf to collide with the rocks in front of the grocery store. Sitka Sound shelters a dozen or so islands that huddle like feeding gulls before the land juts out along the capes and the points into the stormy distance of the Pacific. You can watch the weather come from the west but it doesn't do much good because most of it comes from the southeast or the north.

I love Sitka. There are eight thousand people, twelve miles of road, and two main streets. It had once been the capital of Russian America. To me it's a town full of mystery and wildness. It's so crowded by the wildernesses of steep mountains, thick woods, and ocean that a person can have the sensation, on the same afternoon, of either floating away or taking root.

Great upwellings of ancient basalt and three-legged dogs are on the streets. There are gulls and murrelets. Cormorants lift their wings to dry their inky black feathers in the sunlight. Puffins with colored tufts like Gypsy scarves. Humpback whales feed on the herring that are feeding on the effluent from the pulp mill. Pickup trucks and Subarus. Everyone on their way to a meeting or softball practice.

Four kids with canvas jackets and earrings, with their

hats on backwards, standing in the doorways near the Russian cathedral looking bored. An old man walking outside the Pioneer Home in the middle of town, wearing pistols holstered on the outside of his pants. Occasionally a brown bear in the cemetery or a deer swimming in the harbor. The cathedral and the jagged, ancient mountain like a background for all of our arguments. Priests, tourists, loggers, bureaucrats, fishermen, even an amateur whore or two, and one full-time private investigator.

I got off the plane and Dickie Stein was at the baggage belt to meet me. It was fifty-five degrees with misty fog that was keeping the air cool and wet, but Dickie was wearing baggy shorts and green high-top sneakers. He had a new haircut that made his head look vaguely like a toaster, and his T-shirt read U.S. OUT OF NORTH AMERICA. Dickie is my lawyer. He graduated from Harvard Law when he was nineteen. He wanted to be a lawyer because he hated authority but didn't want to give any up. Both his parents had died when he was young and he never talked about his upbringing, but he dressed as if he had been raised by teenage wolves. He was twitchy, looking over the crowd getting off the plane as if he were going to have a hard time recognizing me.

"Listen," he said. "I know you've heard, but I just want to fill you in. He's been gone since Tuesday. A guy out by the ferry terminal thinks he may have seen him going up the logging road on Wednesday. But I don't know. The guy was drunk up at the shooting range that day and maybe the rest of the week and I don't trust him. Anyway, Gladys is up there looking. I got the cops to promise me they would tell the duty officers to make a point of keeping an eye out. The ads are running on the radio and we've got flyers on the poles around town. By the way, you're offering a two-hundred-dollar reward."

"What the fuck are you talking about?"

"Come on, man. Nelson! Toddy's dog, Nelson? He's gone."

"Two hundred bucks! That's almost more than I made this month. Christ, Dickie, Nelson will be back. He's a Labrador, he can't live without human contact."

"Yeah, tell me about it. We had a kid break the same black dog out of the pound three times trying to get the reward but, hey, you're a generous guy. I gave the kid fifty bucks to keep trying."

Hannah came up beside Dickie and eased her shoulder between us to talk directly into Dickie's face. "Nelson is gone? Todd must be frantic. What can we do?"

Dickie backed away from her slightly, not comfortable with her in his personal space. "We can look for him and we can start calling around. Yeah, Toddy is upset. But, you know, he's holding it in."

I looked at the luggage that was starting to move down the belt. "Jeezus, I mean, I've only been gone two days. How lost can Nelson be?"

"Hey, how lost do you want him to be? He's not around and Toddy is freaking out. He wants you to find him."

Hannah snorted, tossing back her hair, then took her bag.

"Ha. Yeah, right. Cecil will find him. He's an investigator."

I hate it when people start a sentence with, "Well, you're an investigator, why don't you . . ." And I've heard almost everything: Why don't you—find my keys, know where my wife was last night, discover what the cops have against me. It's all the same question. Why don't you know what I don't know? I hate to break it to them.

I waited a few minutes, hoping Hannah would either get back on the plane or disappear with someone else. But soon Dickie offered her a ride across the bridge to town and she lugged her stuff out to his car, double-parked in the tour bus zone. When I slammed the door, pieces of the car flaked off like a rare manuscript. He was driving an old Japanese station wagon with a body so eaten by rust you could watch the pavement scroll by through the floor.

I was riding with this manic, high-powered attorney to a low-power town across the bridge so I could head up the incident command network that had been established to find a Labrador retriever.

"Why don't you find my dog?" I said.

I'm only allowed to remain as Toddy's guardian as long as I stay sober and he stays relatively sane. The first part is fairly easy. The Social Services people document my movements pretty closely. People in town keep an eye out for Toddy. If I were to fall off the wagon these days in Sitka, the Social Services switchboard would light up and melt down from the heat. So I'm seldom seen drinking in Sitka.

But the sanity stuff is a risky business. Toddy is a smart boy in a man's body who speaks as if he's trying hard to imagine what an adult might sound like. Every two months Todd has to go in for an interview to determine if he is "stable and free of any delusional ideation." We have to cram for it:

"Okay, what do you tell them if they ask if you talk to your mother?"

"I tell them she's dead, and she doesn't want to talk to me anymore."

"Wrong. You tell them she's dead and can't talk to you anymore."

He looks down through the thick lenses of his glasses and begins to rock, twisting a napkin into a tight little spike. "Relax, buddy. Just tell them the truth. Just relax. . . . Tell them you don't talk to her anymore."

He rocks forward slightly and looks up at me with that nervously unhinged look, like a kitten that knows you're going to bathe it.

"Last time they asked me what would happen if you died."

"What did you tell them?"

"I told them when you died you'd become invisible."

"That's okay. What else did they ask you?"

"They asked me what I would do if you died. I told them that I had things to choose from if I looked into all of the available assistance from churches and service organizations. I could continue to be a custodial engineer at the community schools and I could apply to the group home for their subsidized residency program."

"Very good. I know we worked on that."

"Yes. When I tried to explain that you weren't ever going to die really, she started frowning and writing stuff down and I don't think she liked it."

"Don't worry, buddy. It just takes time for them to understand."

Toddy has a theory that everyone always gets what they want. When I die I'll become invisible, or so he says, because that's what I want to be. When he dies, he's going to be a black Labrador.

39

Of course the ideal Labrador is Nelson. The walls of our house are speckled with photos of Nelson. Nelson at the beach. Nelson on his tenth birthday. Nelson standing on top of the car. It is as if Nelson, or at least his image, were some sort of ubiquitous elfin spirit that pops up everywhere in our environment. Sometimes I get a picture of Nelson in my lunch box if Toddy thinks I'll be lonely at work. Todd takes Nelson to birthday parties at the old folks' home and they make special cookies for him and set them at his place. Every fry cook in this town has a scrap bucket next to the garbage marked for Nelson. As a result, Nelson, it might be safely said to anyone other than Todd, is at least twenty percent overweight. He has a swayback and his front feet turn out like an old milk wagon horse's. His muzzle is gray and after he eats one of his three meals a day, which are always topped with oil and a raw egg, he inevitably plops his head into your lap and will not remove it until his ears have been thoroughly scratched.

This posture is not my idea of communing with nature. In fact, it's my opinion that dogs were domesticated partly because they were too stupid and emotionally dependent to survive in the wild. Once, when I got the raw-egg-and-slobber nuzzle, I actually raised my voice to Nelson and Toddy took him into his room. They stayed there for two days, only emerging for supplies of cinnamon toast, raw hamburger, and cream soda, and only when I was out of the house or asleep. It was like living with two nocturnal frat brothers.

The car stopped in front of my house. Dickie didn't park, he barely slowed down.

"Go inside. He's in there and I think there is a phone tree that will show you who to call."

"Thanks," I said without much enthusiasm. Hannah

rushed in ahead of me while I shut the car door. What was she doing in Sitka? She should have stayed on the plane for the next short hop over to Juneau.

I walked across the street and looked up at my house. It's built out on pilings over the channel and is in need of paint and a serious look at its supports. Home. It sags a little but it's mostly dry. The flower boxes on the window clung to the last evidence of summer; the sweet williams hung down sadly. I made a note to get a fuchsia if any were left. I was picking out the colors for the new trim when Todd came to the door. He just looked at me, his squat body sagging so that his muscular bulk looked wilted and turned down like a weathered pumpkin. His hair had grown out somewhat since his last crew cut and his glasses were taped at the bridge from when they were broken years ago. He slid his glasses up. He started to speak and then stopped. He was tapping the tips of his fingers against his thumb rapidly as if he were practicing the guitar.

"He'll be back, buddy," I said. "He hasn't been gone that long."

"He's been gone twenty-six hours, Cecil. That is a long time."

"Maybe he's in love." I shrugged.

"You had him fixed after that deal at the gas station with the rottweiler."

"Well, that doesn't mean he can't be in love."

"Do you think he may be up in the woods strangled on his collar or something?"

"No."

"Do you think somebody may have just picked him up and put him on the ferry? They may have wanted to steal him, he's a good-looking dog."

"No, I don't think so, Todd. I think he's just out running around."

"Maybe he swam out to one of the islands and he's out there and he needs food or something. You told me that bears and deer and all sorts of animals swim over to the islands. He may be out there, huh?"

He was twisting his hands in a tight wringing motion. He stared at me intently, almost pleading. A kid on a bike with training wheels pedaled by and, without stopping or looking at either of us, reported, "Nothing behind the hotel. I'm going to check the garbage cans at the dock."

"Okay, Louis, thank you very much." Toddy waved and the kid rode off in a flurry of knees and elbows.

I said, "I don't have a lot of time to help you look, Todd," and stupidly waved in the general direction of my upstairs desk. "I've got a new case and I've got to work on it. Lots of reading at first, you know."

"Maybe you could make some calls?"

"Has anybody gone out the road by the ferry terminal?"

"Mr. Stein went out that way but he was driving and I think he had his windows up so he probably couldn't hear all that much anyway. You know, maybe Nelson fell in a hole up in the woods and can't get out. Maybe he's hurt and he can't walk so well."

His eyes widened, he took long breaths. I could see his eyes brim with tears.

I touched him lightly on the shoulder. "Don't think of that stuff just yet. I'll take a run out there. Let me get my rain gear and grab a sandwich. Will that be all right?"

"I made you a sandwich. I've got it in a plastic bag. Smoked salmon and cream cheese. I also put in an apple and some peanuts."

He looked at me, smiled, and rubbed his eyes.

The phone rang. He bolted inside and answered it downstairs. I took my bags and walked in the door. I kicked off my shoes and sat down and looked at my rubber boots. It was starting to rain and that only made the darkness seem to come on faster. I listened to Todd's conversation.

"No . . . no . . . he got back just now. He said that he was going to go out down the road. I made him something to take with him so that he wouldn't have to take time to eat dinner. Yes . . . yes, I will. Thank you. I certainly hope so too. Do you want to talk to him before he leaves?"

He turned to me and held out the phone. "It's Mr. Doggy."

The sun was moving behind the islands, and the light had that late look caught between gold and silver. A float plane taxied away from the dock and a glaucous gull stood on one leg on top of a piling watching the surface of the water out in the channel. I imagined that George Doggy wanted to talk to me about things that would require me to either squirm or lie.

"Tell him I'll call him back."

I grabbed the rubber rain suit that was hanging on the hook behind my front door, took the bag of food that Todd offered, and squeezed past him out the door.

I walked past fish plants and the harbors. The refrigerating units rumbled and traffic slowed as the last of the shift's trucks pulled away with a freezer van headed to the airport for a delivery of silver salmon. I walked past the big red Forest Service office and turned north up the road. I was going to check the ditches. The image of Louise Root on the end of the hoist line, dripping onto the rubber sheet, was burned into my mind like the afterimage of a flash.

As the sun broke from the mountains and clouds and the moisture in the air fused with the light, the atmosphere became dense, filling the distance between the road and the horizon. There is a quality of light that helps a person understand distance and sometimes that light floods the mind, and causes you to forget. Understanding distance is another one of a drunkard's important jobs.

I'd walk the ditches for a while and maybe come home and make a hot dinner. I sampled the apple, biting out big chunks, and tried to hold off thinking. It had been raining off and on in Sitka for four days and the ditches were running with brown water from the muskegs. I paused at several spots along the road where the culverts were plugged and small ponds had formed. If Nelson had been hit he would have made it into one of the ditches.

I rummaged around in the upper slope of a ditch and happened to find a broken-off pike pole used to pull the ropes of a docking ship. The piece I had was about four feet long and had a barbed spike on the end. I could probe the deepest part of the ditches with it. It wasn't something I wanted to do, but they were the most likely spots to look.

I got to Halibut Point Road. The cars drove by on the slick pavement and their tires sounded like tape being stripped off the floor. With each one that passed I felt a little grimier. At the surface of the ditch rotted fireweed stems, bent by the rain, crisscrossed the water, along with pop cans, paper bags, and broken bottles. One wheel of a red tricycle stuck up from the mud. Forgotten things.

I thought about Toddy and became more and more sad. I was catching a chill and considered turning back and taking the skiff over to the island to sit in a hot sauna. As I hunched my shoulders, I imagined the wood heat and the perfume of cedar burning my nose, then the numbing plunge into the forty-three-degree water. I shuddered and then stuck the end of the pike pole into the brown water and pushed it into the soft mud until it struck a rock as hard as bone. Nothing . . . thankfully.

The Otter Creek mine was controversial from the start. After *Exxon Valdez,* the energy industry had been under siege. Exxon paid out millions to anyone with a claim, the thinking being that there wasn't any problem that enough money couldn't fix. It may have started off as a crime or as an accident. But it resulted in the most damaging oil spill in history and then, quickly, became a carnival of greed. Anyone with a pulse could make thousands of dollars either cleaning up oil or talking about it.

Some in government, and in the energy industry, saw it more as a public-relations problem than an environmental catastrophe. They were concerned about the plans to open up more of the Arctic and were deathly afraid of what might happen to gum up their schemes because of this one ship hitting a charted reef. Their resolve was strong and clear: never again with our pants down. Long public discussions about prophylactic contingency planning for the future would distract citizens away from the oily ducks on TV.

Global Resource Exploration and Recovery had big holdings on the North Slope and wanted to expand into gold recovery down in the southeastern panhandle. They wanted to use the cyanide recovery process, which was safe and effective but suffered from bad press. These gold mines weren't tunnels into the mountains but were processing centers where ore was mixed in a slurry of cyanide and water so that the runoff carried microscopic pieces of the gold into controlled "pregnant areas" where the heavier gold settled out. As long as the solution was dilute enough and the containment structures didn't fail, the process cleanly and efficiently recovered gold that would otherwise be too tiny to bother with. Of course it took a lot of rock to get an ounce of gold. And in southeastern Alaska, which could get as much as two hundred inches of rain in some drainages, there was a hell of a lot of water flowing everywhere. This was a problem—getting just enough water through the system without having the overflow carry high concentrations of silt or cyanide out of the controlled areas.

Global was dancing through hundreds of hoops to get the water quality regulations to their liking. In the skeptical post-*Valdez* era, when every regulatory agency wanted plans and promises in triplicate, Global had spent more money on lobbyists than most mining outfits would ever spend on building a site.

Everyone in the north knows that gold makes people crazy. Even microscopic gold sluiced out in a weak solution of poison will make men salivate. Oilmen talk about the good their product does and, even in the most jaded company, oilmen think of themselves as team players. But the pursuit of gold is more like a lone treasure hunt: Whoever gets there first can get the most gold. There is nothing much simpler than that.

Otter Creek was shut down now. It must have been closed shortly after the night of the birthday party when Louise Root got caught up in a gallon of whiskey and some boys who thought they were having a little fun. The company said that out of an "abundance of caution" they wanted to retool some of their monitoring equipment to guarantee the purity of the groundwater. Everyone knew the state had been heavily monitoring the outfall from their drainage pipe and apparently there had been some problems but they were scheduled to reopen in the spring.

I was out past the city shops and decided to look in at the pound just to get some relief from the chore of walking the ditches. A weary black dog—probably the one who had been sprung by the enterprising kid—looked at me and perked up. He sat panting and his nose worked the air in quick breaths, his tail tapping a light greeting. The rest of the kennels were empty. A plastic collar and an empty bowl sat on the concrete floor. I went back to the ditches.

A raven followed me above the road in the alder trees. Occasionally he would drop down and pick up a piece of something I had stirred up. He would look at me as if I were crazy for being there and then call in that weird, angry rattle like grinding rocks. I pulled out a deer hide and something that looked like a sea lion skull, then a plastic bag of clothes. I stuck the pike pole in the muck again.

Judging from her letters, Louise Root had been up to more than just cooking for the boys. I knew the name of Steven Mathews. I had read some of his work and followed his career. He had been a tramp, a Beat poet, and a Yippie. Now sixty, he was in Alaska and was mostly a humorless environmentalist. I could imagine Louise Root as one of his devoted students in his now defunct Institute for Environmental Ethics in eastern Washington State. He had never received her letters, the forwarding order must have expired. But he had to have been in some kind of communication with her. I decided to go through everything in her pack again, scatter it out on the floor of my office. That is, if I could get the pack away from Hannah before Doggy or one of his troops confiscated it.

The end of the pole eased into the unmistakable softness of flesh. A pickup full of kids drove by with the radio thumping, and the rain fell like needles. I stood without moving. I could look out to the coast and see the swells that had come from a thousand miles out to sea. I could hear their breath rising and falling against the cobblestones on the shore.

With inexplicable certainty, I knew I had found him. I didn't want to pull the dog out, with the same weight of certainty that I knew I would in fact do it. I thought of Toddy and the searchers calling Nelson's name up in the woods. I knew they were only out in the wet evening because of hope. I hated to be the one to end it.

I reached into the ditch up to my shoulder and dragged Nelson to the side, then laid him on my lap. His shoulder and the side of his skull were shattered. Gravel was ground into the thick matted hide all along his back. A voice came from over my shoulder.

"That your dog?"

"No. Well . . . yeah."

The voice belonged to a skinny old man who was wearing his house slippers out in the rain. He had a highball glass in a Styrofoam cover and a cigarette in his hand, and was wearing a flannel jacket with nothing on underneath. It looked like he had cut himself shaving late in the day. He had the thin reddish skin and narrow eyes of a mean drunk.

"It's too bad about him, but he was getting into my garbage. I ran him out of here a couple of times. Got hit by a truck yesterday. You know, if you kept him tied up like you were supposed to, this probably wouldn't have happened."

"Yeah." The wet carcass was heavy in my lap.

"Damn. I get sick and tired of having to clean up my garbage every morning. You don't know what it's like."

I felt sorry for the poor dumb bastard and his garbage. I felt sorry for the kids driving past with their lives caught like little bubbles inside their cars. I even felt sorry for the pop cans and the tricycles in the ditch. It's always been a problem for me. I read once that foolish sentimentality was loving something more than God had loved it, and that had made some kind of sense when I read it. But here I was, sitting in a ditch being soaked by this ancient rain, with Nelson on my lap wondering how much God loved this black dog, or this old drunk, or me least of all, with my crazy desire to find things I never really wanted.

I wasn't going to take Nelson's body back to Todd. Not on a bet. Never try to talk about sex or death with an autistic adult. Sex gets too abstract and death gets too literal. It always comes down to trying to explain love or describing bodies decomposing. I wasn't in the mood for either. I lugged Nelson out of the ditch and put him on my shoulder. I gave my sandwich to the raven in the alder overhead.

Dickie Stein drove past and pulled over hard. I would take Nelson to the house of a friend. I'd let the search go on for a while longer. I'd think of something.

We dumped Nelson in the back of his car and drove over to Jake's. Jake understood why I wanted to freeze Nelson but he didn't know if his girlfriend would like having him next to the frozen venison chops and open bags of peas. I told him to say the garbage bag contained evidence of a crime and had to be secure. If she opened it she would be committing a felony. He didn't like it but he bought it. He had purchased a huge freezer thinking he would live off hunting and fishing, but he found that he hated both hunting and fishing so he survived on what friends gave him in exchange for freezer space. In a way it worked well. I jammed Nelson into the back of the bottom shelf. I stood up and swore both Jake and Dickie to secrecy, then turned to head out.

Dickie stopped me. "A couple of adults showed up at your house. I think they must have been on the same plane you were on."

"What kind of adults?"

"I'm not sure, but I think we're talking money."

"Money. You mean like a job?" I said. I'm never ambivalent about money but I often am about work.

"They're from Global, I think. They have the look."

"I don't know why, but I think you're right."

I patted the freezer, thanked Jake, and headed out the door to keep my date with Louise Root's former employers.

THREE

HE WAS TIRED. I could tell from halfway down the street.
He was wearing a camel's hair coat and a flannel shirt and
he sagged into them as if he had been sleeping in his clothes
for a week. On his feet were low-cut rubberized shoes that
bulged out with some sort of synthetic insulation. The guy
next to him was twitchy. He was looking up and down the
street like a lost tourist while fussing with his silver lighter,
banging it against his thigh and then sheltering it from the
wind and against his cigarette.

I felt like driving by, but Dickie pulled over and let me
out. As I approached, the shorter one in the camel coat held
out his hand and extended it with the leading edge of his
little finger.

"Mr. Younger? I'm glad we were able to catch up with you."

I shook his hand. The taller one gave up on his cigarette
and looked at me with a dull bulldog stare.

"Yeah, I'm sorry I wasn't around when you got in. Boy, I'm
bad with names too. I can't remember yours."

"We've never met. I'm Lee Altman. This is Charlie Potts.
He's a consultant with us."

It was dark and raining, although I hadn't noticed. The bar down the street had its door open and two men in coveralls were in the street talking to an Indian woman with long black hair who carried a bag full of groceries. I could faintly hear the sound of the bar's large-screen TV and it made my stomach tighten. I mourned the day they put that TV in.

"Can we go somewhere?" Altman said, scanning the place.

He avoided looking at my front door. I noticed that his hair was starting to mat against his skull. Potts was in his late thirties and appeared to be wearing a yellow cardigan sweater under his raincoat; his leather shoes had tassels on them. He took in the puddles forming around his feet and worked up a dry spit.

I spoke up. "Yeah, I'm sorry. Let's go in."

Dickie beeped his horn and I waved as he pulled away.

I walked in first and took my coat off in the mud room at the foot of the stairs. My two visitors bumped clumsily behind me. I kicked my boots off and they started to unlace their shoes. Todd was at the top of the stairs.

"Anything?"

I paused and took a breath. There was never going to be a good time to tell him but there were bound to be lots of better ones.

"Yeah. Listen, Todd, I didn't find anything but I talked to a kid. He said he thought he saw a black dog swimming over to one of the islands in the harbor. He said he was swimming strong. This was out north of town. He might end up on Middle Island or the Chaichi's."

"Really?" His eyes widened, shoulders straightening. "Really! Do you think we should call Mr. Stein and tell him

Nelson is almost home? Do you think we can go out in the boat tonight?"

"No, no, I don't think we should do either. We can go out tomorrow as soon as the weather looks good," I said.

"Should I pack a day outfit? Maybe get some food together for Nelson?"

"Yeah, that would be okay."

"I'll get the tide book."

"Good."

"Do you know what time sunrise is?"

"No. Listen, Toddy, we've got some company. Do me a favor and put some hot water on, will ya?"

Todd moved in a flat-footed march to the kitchen as we walked up the stairs and into the living room. I gestured to the couch by the woodstove. Altman looked around in a three-sixty. Potts was still shaking himself and made his way straight for the stove. Altman ducked his head awkwardly and peered out the window to the channel. There was a long yellow skiff passing by making its way to the gas dock, a blond woman in an orange float suit standing at the wheel. Altman turned into the room in an almost dramatic movement.

"It's been years since I've spent any time in Sitka. Always on the airplane on my way to Juneau. I get off and have a slice of pie like all the rest, but it's been years since I walked around."

He had slightly graying hair and pale blue eyes. His face was creased as if he had spent a large part of his early years out in the sun and the wind. There was something about him, the way he hung his shoulders sitting forward on my couch, something that made him seem sad.

"You haven't been here all that long, Mr. Younger. How do you like it?"

"I like it fine."

"I've heard it takes time to get established."

"People are a little standoffish for the first ten or fifteen years, I suppose."

"You had quite a reputation in Juneau. What made you come here?"

"Mr. Altman, I'm kind of wondering just how I can help you." My father had taught me never to give out information before the meter started running.

Altman rearranged himself on the couch, took a deep breath, and stared up at me almost balefully. "I'm not sure, but I hope you can, Mr. Younger." He sat forward with his hands stuck down between his thighs. "Mr. Potts and I work for a large energy resource company. Oil, mining, solar. And we have a very important job that needs doing."

I stayed still for a moment and when he didn't speak I pushed ahead: "Is it about who killed Louise Root?"

He sat up straight, winced, took in a breath, then, as if I had disappointed him, frowned.

Potts was flipping through one of Todd's *National Geographic*s and he just lifted his eyes up slightly to flicker a look at Altman. Mr. Altman was pausing a little too long, so I started to worry that he was going to get up and go. I felt like I might have played my puny two pair too soon.

Altman said, "No, it has nothing to do with that. It is a completely different . . . area."

"But you guys were just down in Ketchikan, weren't you? I mean, we were on the same plane." I was guessing because I didn't recognize them.

"Yes, we were in Ketchikan, but only briefly. You see, we're making some arrangements to take depositions and we need to locate a witness."

"Are you sure this has nothing to do with Louise Root? The rape at the mine? Or her death?"

Potts lowered the magazine slightly and looked directly at me. His hair was still damp and slick from the rain and his eyes sparked with temper. I could see his eyes narrow as he squinted over the edge of the pages rich with color shots of Indonesian blowfish.

Altman glanced at Potts with apprehension. He gestured with his hand over to Potts's knee and missed touching it, leaving his hand dangling as he turned to me.

"I'm sorry, Mr. Younger. I am. You can't believe how suspicious this Otter Creek thing has made me." He wiped his forehead with his handkerchief and tucked it back into his inside pocket. "You know Global is a progressive resource development firm. We've always been in it for the long haul. You can't believe how this thing at Otter Creek has set us back."

I nodded. I knew I was in for the whole presentation.

Altman's face took on a leadlike sobriety. "The original company was a pioneer in alternative energy. It was founded in northern California and was issued all the most promising patents for the development of solar potential. When it was purchased as the flagship company of the mining conglomerate in '82, we saw its potential to fill the needs of the communities in the west. We never were in it for the short term. Really. No 'wham bam thank you ma'am.' We were going to bring sustainable industry to the west and to the north. Oil, mining—everything for the long term. I mean, it's like the Global commercial—'We're your new neighbors.'"

Toddy brought them some tea and Potts looked as if Todd were asking him to pet a snake, but he took the tea. Altman looked kindly at Todd and said, "Thanks," in a soft tone, then turned back to me. "And then this . . ."

He set the tea down and shook his head sadly, including the death of a young woman in his helpless gesture. Then he reached in his breast pocket, pulled out a packet, and set it on the table in front of him.

He said, "This should get you started."

The money sat there like a rare volume of unpublished poetry. It looked to be maybe fifteen thousand. But I didn't count it. Apparently, this would be the kind of fee arrangement that was measured by weight. So it seemed sort of thoughtless to start sweating the details.

"How do I start?" I asked, feeling a little sunnier.

"We want to know everything there is about Steven Mathews."

"You want to depose him?" I said.

"Perhaps. But first we need to know everything about him."

"I'm going to ask you again. What does this have to do with Louise Root?"

"Mr. Younger, I'm going to talk about this with you only one time." Altman's voice was even more slow and buttery. "It was an awful thing. But I don't know what happened to that girl. I think whatever did happen, she knew what she was getting into. You may find out more and that is fine, but I'm telling you, I don't know what happened."

Potts was back at his reading and the tip of his tasseled shoe was bouncing to the rhythm of some interior tune.

"Business can't be too good in this little town. There can't be enough trouble to keep you busy. Why not look into some of our trouble?" He smiled, leaning back and casually sipping from the top of the mug. "In fact, I know your business isn't good. Before we came to you we had a back-ground done. Suborning perjury. Possession of cocaine. You can't even drive a car any longer. Even in the best of times you were not in great demand. You've had several lawsuits against you. One involving a shooting?"

"That was settled."

"I know. That's nice. But still . . . allegations. You can sympathize. Anyone can make allegations and there it goes. Your whole reputation. It must make it tough to get clear of your drinking."

He let that hang. He was good at this. Showing me how much he knew without having to make threats.

It was a crazy idea to run an investigative service in this small town on an island, and business was never good. Still, I had a following of lawyers all over the state who would give me a tumble because I was cheap and relatively reli-able. But the phone was not ringing off the hook with clients who could pay. I was running around serving papers for hire and begging for one-case contracts from the public defender.

Altman picked up the brick of cash and fanned it, then let it plop back on the table between us. "We don't want any written reports. We don't want any documentation: no bills, no tapes, and nothing on record, you understand? We want a clear and reliable report that we can trust. Your word is good enough as long as you report orally, consistently.

"We're not avoiding our responsibility in any way. It is just that we are being hit with hundreds of lawsuits and each one has a discovery phase where we have to turn over docu-ments. So we don't want documents. It's pretty usual these days."

"I don't suppose this policy is written down anywhere?"

He exhaled and ran his hand through his wet hair, then grimaced and looked as if he were going to lose his temper. "No." He smiled. "It isn't."

I felt stupid. This guy could not be needled into any snappy repartee. I tried to think of some sort of glib retort but all I came up with was, "Sorry."

"It's a pretty romantic lifestyle you've got for yourself, Cecil. I suppose it's easy for you to feel superior to guys like me and Mr. Potts. You've got family money and you don't have to get your hands dirty."

He glanced around the room and rubbed the back of his neck as if he had a cramp. "I . . . I apologize. I didn't mean to go off. Would you have anything . . . could I get a drink or something to warm up?"

I held out my hand palm up. "I'm sorry. I've been on the wagon."

He stared at me with horror as if I were doing some kind of rude parlor trick. "On the wagon? How long?"

"I don't know. Some time."

He took a deep breath and I felt like I should offer him a place to lie down.

Finally he spoke. "That's okay. I mean, the booze can kill you." Then he looked around some more. "I didn't mean to insult you. That was out of line. I just feel like I've been on the defensive for a couple of years. Lots of criticism of development. Lots of complaints. But people want the money, schools, and services. They want the arts, they want the books and the theaters, the writers' conferences and the chamber-music festivals. And all of that money comes out of the ground."

Potts threw down his magazine, stepped past Todd, and poured himself a glass of water. I could see that he had heard this lecture before. Todd was listening intently as he does to all strangers.

"I'm not saying you don't have to put anything back in. Sometimes I think it's like a bank account. The earth, I mean. You get what you put in, and a little interest."

"Mining gold with cyanide gets you quite a bit of interest."

"Miners have been using cyanide for years. Cyanide breaks down the minerals and lets us recover smaller and smaller amounts that would have gone to waste. It hasn't killed anyone. It's not the technology; it's the language. Cyanide *sounds* bad. People hear the word and there is no reasoning with them. There is no compromising. For them it's poison and that is the end of it."

He was becoming flushed and his hand trembled slightly as he lifted the cup to his mouth. He saw me watching and he broke into a calming smile. "Boy, don't get me started." He chuckled.

"Too late." I said as we all stood up.

"Anyway," he looked over to Potts, "we've got some other appointments. Then we are headed up to the slope on the evening flight. We just wanted to stop off and get you squared away."

He looked down at the stack of money. Under the rubber band that held it together was a slip of paper with a telephone number typed on it.

"If you need anything, just call that number and ask for me. Then I will get back to you. Stay in touch and don't be afraid to ask for help."

"Give us a line on Mathews." Potts spoke up for the first time and his voice was surprisingly deep. "And stay clear of this Louise Root thing. Don't show up in the papers, for any reason, or all bets are off. . . ." He let these last words hang as if to imply a seriousness that I might otherwise ignore.

"Any problems?" Altman said cheerfully, trying to lighten the mood.

I looked down at the surface of the table and the money, then up at Toddy, who was sniffing the air like a blind terrier.

"No problems."

He started towards the stairs and backtracked, reaching into his pocket. He pulled out a photograph. "I almost forgot. I can give you this."

It was a picture of Mathews taken from a book jacket. Along with it was a brief biography that looked like it came from the publisher. Stapled to that was a computer printout of a criminal history that had been run by the Alaska state troopers, certifying that Mathews was clean.

Altman and Potts brushed themselves off and Altman put his cup on our kitchen counter, whispering "Thanks" to Todd.

At the head of the stairs, Altman turned.

"Mr. Younger. Please—and I know you will—but please keep this confidential. You were involved with the woman whose body was found in Ketchikan. I know you were talking to the police. But you have to remember that you must stay out of the limelight."

"I'll be careful. I'm not much for the bright lights either."

He smiled and shook his head tiredly. "I know. That is partly why we came to you."

Then he was down the stairs. Todd stood looking at me with a panicked expression on his face. Once the door was closed Todd spoke up.

"Cecil, I think he may have misunderstood you. You forgot to tell him you were going out to the islands to find Nelson tomorrow."

I looked out the window and I could see the rain coming down hard but there was a lightness in the sky over the western islands. The storm was stalled off the coast. A Coast Guard cutter was under way and easing out of the channel under the bridge to the airport.

I turned to Todd and said, "I'm going to work tomorrow . . . for them. Hell, Todd, everybody in the state has got some of that money except us. And we've got bills."

"What do they want you to do?"

"Christ, this is big business. They want information on their enemies. It's nothing."

"What about that girl? What about Hannah?"

"Will you leave it alone!"

"When are you going to take me over to the island to get Nelson? You said you were going to take me out to get Nelson."

I looked down and my fists were clenched. I was thinking about Hannah, the pack, and the girl lying on the coroner's green blanket. I felt the words bubbling out like vomit. "Leave it alone, Toddy. The whole world doesn't revolve around you and that goddamn dog!"

It got very quiet. Todd bit his lip and I could hear the rain hit the windowpanes as a gust of wind blew down the channel. The teapot sitting on the woodstove rumbled softly, and Todd went to his room. I went out and stayed out all night.

The morning wind had begun to blow in off the edge of the storm. It rattled the rigging of the trolling boats moored in the harbor. The remnant of a blueberry danish lay crushed in the gutter by the café, and a small raven, along with several pigeons, was hopping on and off the curb vying for the biggest piece. The wind that reached the curb ruffled their feathers and curled under their wings, lifting them in awkward hops. One pigeon ducked into the gutter and out of the gusts, getting the biggest share of the pastry.

Since I quit drinking I feel like eating all the time: doughnuts, popcorn, chocolate malts, even the ugly wrinkled hot dogs on the spindles in the corner of the bar. They all sing to me through my nose and through my eyes and I want them.

I had walked most of the night in a circuit, up and down the roads. I was stiff and it felt like the hinges of my joints were rusting. I turned the corner and walked west, down the main street past the dime store and the cabstand: popcorn and hot dogs, the acid of perfume and cigarette smoke. A Chrysler Le Baron with a rusted-out side panel slid by with the radio on and the wipers going. The driver was hunched over the wheel looking in the doorways, looking in the windows. The rain fell in drops as big as marbles, and the woman who washed dishes in the café stood out under the eaves. She had the back of her apron undone and it hung loosely so she could fish her smokes out of her jeans pocket. Her rubber gloves were tucked in her armpit. She stared out at the storm coming on, bathed in the light that cut in front of the black clouds. She lit a cigarette and pulled her hair net off and stared out to the channel. Breathing in and breathing out: the wind and the light and a squall passing over her in each moment of her ten-minute break.

Just past her, two men were unloading a mirror from the side rack of a van. It was the size of a standard piece of plywood and they jostled and coached each other as they applied the suction cups and lifted it out toward the bar. The closer I got, the more of the conversation I could make out. A drunk had broken the mirror above the bar the night before; a usually docile drinker had taken offense at some comment about the president of the United States and had thrown a shot glass at the bartender. I got closer. They crouched, carrying the mirror, and walked awkwardly under the eaves where the water fell in streams. The men from the glass shop were in their full rain gear and they had their hoods up so I couldn't see their faces but they yelled to each other to watch the top of the door frame. They stopped for an instant and I could tell something was wrong. A stream of water from one of the eaves ran down the glass and onto one of the suction cups.

It was that awkward and inescapable moment before calamity. The mirror wavered only slightly and jerked into just the right angle so I could see my reflection down the street, the crows, the dishwasher, the cathedral, and the mountain behind me. But in the foreground I was startled by myself, reaching out, thinking I could help, the reflection off the mirror swirling into my tired brain: my pale skin, my red eyes, my flat clumsy stance. It was a very bad likeness of myself that I instantly recognized. I was reaching out and then the suction lost its grip. As the mirror fell I sensed the men swearing and the backdraft of air as the plate fell against the wind, taking my breath. I saw the mirror shattering like a flight of sandpipers rising. I blinked. I had seen myself and the dishwasher, whose eyes had widened with a startled interest. I had seen it all shatter, replaced by the old post office, by the fuel dock at the end of the street, and the weird light coming in off the Pacific. The workers swore, the old birds in the bar craned their necks and turned on their stools and one even walked to the door and commented, "That's a lot of bad luck coming." Then he laughed and went back in and ordered a drink.

I apologized and walked self-consciously over the pieces of mirror, stupidly trying not to break some of the bigger pieces. Then I moved on down the sidewalk. I shook, I was hungry, and I wanted a drink.

The Chrysler passed again and the dishwasher stubbed out her cigarette on her heel and put the butt in her pocket, then walked back through the doors of the café. The wind blustered into my ear, feeling like it wanted to lift me up. I rounded the corner and went into the bar with the biggest windows on the waterfront. Drunks don't drink in the daylight. I ordered cognac. Drunks don't drink cognac. I stared down at it, looking at the amber curve of the surface tension all around the glass.

One storm squall was behind the other and in between was this brief respite. The sun eased into the bar. The barmaid was wearing a Lycra running suit under her baggy sweatshirt, and as soon as the sun came out she sat in the booth by the cleanest windows, working on her receipts. The light glinted off her long eyelashes. When the door opened, the wind filled the bar, riffling the napkins like a storm filling a library and clearing out the dusty pages of the books. I eyed the glass of cognac and then ate a candy bar, then a bag of chips and a pickled egg.

Anything is an excuse to get drunk when you live in a world bound by chance. Anything is a pretext to tell yourself a bullshit story about your life. To sit in a bar spinning out the most solid version of heroism or victimization is preferable to the alternative. Like any drunk I knew that this bar stool was the center of the universe and that nothing important ever happened outside the pull of its gravity, nothing but randomness, stupidity, and bad luck.

Just as I lifted the glass to my lips I saw Toddy standing by the door next to a clean young police officer, pointing. The kid came over and his uniform creaked with leather and the hiss of his radio strapped to his side. He took me by the elbow.

"You're going to have to come with me, Mr. Younger. You're under arrest."

FOUR

THE CHIEF OF police was looking over the top of his reading glasses. "I'm supposed to start with tampering with evidence, and work up from there. Doggy is really upset, Cecil."

I was in the interview room at the Sitka jail, I had missed dinner hours ago and I was hoping to miss breakfast. There was a pile of Styrofoam meal containers in the trash: meals picked up in a squad car from the hospital. I watched the gravy dripping down the edge of the plastic bag. A tuft of mashed potato from what was once alleged to be a hot turkey sandwich curled like spring snow around the edge of the chief's shoe.

"What'd you do to get him so excited?" he asked.

"Beats me."

"You want to talk about it? I bet we could get this all worked out today. You could go home and sleep in your own bed."

"I want to talk to my lawyer."

He let out a long breath and smiled patiently at me.

He had the look of a tired day-care worker who wanted to slap the snot out of a kid but knew the parents were watching.

"'Course you have the right to talk to your lawyer first, Cecil, but we got a warrant and we already found the dead girl's pack in your house. It's been gone through. Doggy wants to make sure that everything is there. He's been on the phone and said if everything is there it will all be okay. But if anything is gone, or destroyed—now these are his words—he said he'll put your nuts in a vise." He held up his hands in a gesture of mock protestation. "Not me, you understand. He said that, not me."

The door to the interview room opened a crack and the dispatcher's small red nose appeared. She was timidly trying to keep someone else from hearing. "Mr. Younger's attorney is here," she said in an agitated whisper.

The door banged open and Dickie Stein stood behind her in the doorway with his surfer shorts pulled up high on his waist and his red high-top sneakers unlaced.

"Hi, Carl, I've seen the warrant. It's shit. Let's get out of here, Cecil." Dickie lives for moments like this. There are so few opportunities for drama in the law, he jumps at every one he can get.

The chief looked crestfallen, not at the news about the warrant but at the fact that Dickie was on the scene at all. Everything about Dickie depressed and irritated the chief. It was the basis of their professional relationship.

"Dickie, you know you will get your chance at the warrant. But we're still going to hold him."

"Chance at the warrant? Chance at the warrant? Some chance. It's based on the affidavit of one Lucinda Music a.k.a. Lolly." Dickie was rolling and he spit out the a.k.a. like mouse turds in the soup. "She said there was a pack in a certain room. No description, no nothing. Then she said it was gone. What the fuck is that? Chief, you know the informants used in a warrant have to be reliable. Re . . . li . . . able. Now. Lolly has many fine attributes. She may be charming, witty, gay, and even . . . exotic."

The chief was sitting down and now was cleaning the mashed potatoes off the rim of his shoe. He was rocking slightly with the cadence of Dickie's rant.

"But she is not, by any stretch of the imagination, reliable. In fact, I talked to her on the phone already once this evening and will tell you that her affidavit was not filled out by her but by the police, and she was under some type of duress when she signed."

The chief looked up, and waited a full five seconds in silence. "You done?"

"No. How much is bail?"

"We're getting the magistrate, which, by the way, I don't have to do. He should be here in a few. We're going to ask for ten thousand in cash."

"Get the fuck out of here! You can chop your wife into crab bait in this town and get out for five."

"Mr. Stein, you can talk to George Doggy. It's his case, he's the one that is upset. We'll have the hearing and call it a day. I don't need this."

Dickie slapped down the brick of money that Altman had given me. The chief stared at it and then groaned.

Dickie was still wearing his U.S. OUT OF NORTH AMERICA T-shirt with a wool halibut jacket on top of it. He slipped his wire-rimmed glasses out of the front pocket and stared at the chief.

"This will cover it. You start on the paperwork, Carl, and Cecil, you shut the fuck up."

I was not all that sure I wanted out of jail, but I was in the system and I had asked for my lawyer. That was the last anyone would hear from me.

The sun was out as much as it was going to be and I'd given up on the temptation to go on a bender but I wanted some sleep. I had put up ten thousand dollars but that left me about five sitting in the inside pocket of my lawyer's coat. My conditions of release said I couldn't leave the state, break any laws, miss any court dates, or else I'd be back inside with the screamers and the cold milk gravy.

We rounded the corner to the main intersection of town and turned towards the Russian cathedral: a wooden structure with a dome and bell tower. A raven sat on the cross, his head pulled down, his hackles up, as if he too were waiting for the storm to blow through. Gum wrappers and paper cups blew in a swirl with the grit from the street. Dickie turned to me.

"So how come you took the fuckin' pack? That was stupid."

"You're not supposed to ask me that."

"Fuck you. We're talking hypothetically. It's not the sworn-truth until it comes out of your mouth on the witness stand. How come you took it?"

"I didn't take it."

"Well, are you going to tell me?"

Just as he was finishing, the wind sucked up his words and Hannah rounded the corner of Jake's street by the apartment house. She had her own satchel and was walking quickly. She saw us, and like a deer bolted, staring quickly, maybe hoping she was invisible and considering her next jump, in case she wasn't. We walked closer and her body eased into a studied casual slump.

I said, "They got the pack. Did they get everything?"

"Most everything." And she sniffed the air as if she were lifting her head away from my scent.

"I'm sorry you got arrested." She sailed the words over her shoulder.

Dickie looked at me and smiled. "She's sorry you got arrested. That's nice."

She turned around and stared at me in a way that reflexively made me want to duck. But I held my ground, for a moment at least. She returned my stare and then something in her expression softened and I hoped she was thinking about me.

She cleared her throat and muttered, "I'm supposed to meet Toddy and get something to eat. You want to come?"

Dickie shrugged and gestured toward his office.

"I gotta go. Listen, Cecil, talk to me later in the afternoon and we'll get this money thing figured out." He was mumbling too, trying to shuffle away with all the rest of the money.

I walked over and put my hand out and said nothing. He reached into his inside jacket pocket and gave me the remaining cash, reluctantly, as if I were taking him into custody.

"Okay," he said. "We can talk about it later." He turned and walked back toward the middle of town.

Hannah and I walked over the crest of the slope past the

refashioned block house that used to be one corner of the stockade dividing the Indian village from the Russian compound.

The pale light barely warmed the air. We walked down the narrow dirt street to the back of a café near the fish plant. Hannah walked next to me, our shoulders nearly touching.

She didn't look at me as she spoke: "You should know better than to try and keep a secret in this town. I know Nelson is in Jake's freezer. When Toddy was looking for you he found out about it too. He's pretty upset."

I saw an immature eagle land and bend the branch of a spruce tree in the cemetery up the hill, behind the fuel tanks. I thought about Nelson and Toddy chasing birds on the beach.

She bumped my shoulder and smiled halfway. "But hey! At least you found him."

We walked in the back door of the café and eased past the freezer unit and around the prep cook slicing off chunks of halibut for the fish and chips. Todd sat in the corner next to the steamy plate-glass window. He was sitting with his encyclopedia opened to the section on dogs. His eyes were red and when he looked up at me, he quickly looked back down at the pages of color paintings of dogs of all breeds.

We stopped short of his table and Hannah touched my arm lightly and said, "Wait a second, Cecil. We can talk over here. I don't think he wants to talk right now." She walked over to him and he looked up unwillingly, thinking, I suppose, that it might be me. But when she reached out and touched his hand he looked up and smiled, gratefully.

The café was a hiss and clatter of steam, running water, and dishes being stacked. I couldn't hear what they were saying but I saw her put her hand to his cheek and he nodded as she spoke softly to him. He held one of her fingers as a small child might. She spoke seriously to him in a low voice that carried love and authority, without the syrupy tone of condescension. I knew his heart was broken but he looked up at her and he smiled. She spoke to him, he nodded his head, and as the waiter came with a cup of hot chocolate and a pecan roll, she bent down and kissed his forehead. He closed the book and ate, without looking over at me.

She walked back over to where I was sitting. I watched her move easily and in one quick gesture she took off her beret and pulled her hair off her shoulder. I remembered making love to her. I remembered her smell and her laughter that would curl under my neck and seem to lift me off the bed. But it was a memory, like steam rising.

She sat down across from me and smiled. One strand of her hair still clung to the front of her throat.

I nodded toward the direction of Todd in the window. "Is he mad?"

She smiled and looked quickly behind her and then at me. "I guess he's like me. We don't have enough energy to stay mad at you. Being mad at you is too much like being in love with you."

She poured some water from the plastic pitcher on the wobbly table and took a sip. "But Todd, he has a higher capacity for you than most."

She looked up at the chalkboard above the counter and read the menu. The kitchen people were just getting the grill warmed up but we talked them into making us some eggs and shrimp. We drank black coffee and she laid out what she wanted to do.

"I just want to know what happened, Cecil. I want to find out the names of the men who were in on the rape and the coverup."

"Why? What good will it do her now?"

She looked down at her plate of eggs. "I knew her family, Cecil. Her mom worked at the university outside of Portland and her dad had been a merchant seaman. We grew up playing together, and her mom used to make us sandwiches in the morning. We sat in the cherry trees pretending they were rocket ships. The blossoms were asteroids falling all around us. We wore those funny pointed glasses and long pigtails down our backs. We would spend all day in those trees, looking up into the sky and pretending we could fly. I went to Alaska first and she followed. I got drunk first, then sober, and she came with me almost every step of the way. I lost touch with her only in the last few years. When I was living with you."

She stopped here and, looking at her fork, prodded the cold scrambled eggs. Her eyes narrowed. She almost seemed to be looking into the distance.

"Her parents waited for her to get Alaska out of her system but she didn't. They need to know it wasn't her fault, Cecil. I've known these people all my life. I want them to know that Lou wasn't wrong about this place. She didn't make a mistake. The cops are saying she was asking for it. If she had just stayed in the kitchen this wouldn't have happened. That's not true. She was vulnerable and kind and . . . she wasn't asking for it."

Hannah's voice had the resolution of a granite slab falling across the mouth of a cave. It was a voice I had heard before.

I reached over and with my fork took some of the eggs she was fiddling with and ate them.

"Hannah, how are you going to find what you want? Even if these guys talk to you, they'll lie. The company has shredded their records and the cops won't give you anything."

"I don't know. But I'll find something."

"Even if you make it up?"

"I won't make it up."

"I think you will. I think all you'll find is closed doors or dead bodies. Because whoever did this to Lou is serious. They're not going to come clean with you. She's dead, that ends it."

"It doesn't end with death. What do you care? I'm not asking you to do anything. I know you don't want to get involved and that's okay."

I let out a long breath and thought of the girl on the sheet with her throat cut. I wiped my mouth. It might be over but I was still curious about how the story was going to be told.

I drank some of my coffee. "Okay, she didn't tell me much. What do you know?"

"Lou called me right after the company flew her out of the mine. All I know is, there was a party. They had some drinking contest and the winner got Lou as the prize. Lou knew none of this, of course. It was a surprise party. Anyway, the winner took his prize and the others cheered him on. After it was over the winner was hustled out of camp by the company and the others got their story straight and stayed on. They were all friends and worked the same shift in the water-monitoring station."

"Do you know their names?"

"I've got the name of the winner. There are lots of names in the rest of her stuff. The only one I recognized was Alfred Tom. He's a Tlingit guy who lives down the street from you. I don't know the rest of them. I don't know if Tom was at the birthday.

"Who were those Global guys who were talking to you? Did they tell you anything?"

"A guy named Altman and his partner, Charlie Potts. They paid me a lot of money to steer clear of Louise Root and to find dirt on Steven Mathews."

Hannah's hand trembled as she lifted it up, pulling her hair next to the side of her face. She was not angry but her voice was flat. "Where did they say they were going?"

"They were headed to the North Slope. Flying to Dead-horse on the night plane. Why?"

"No reason." I saw that her hands were clenched and her voice was tighter now. "Are you going to do some work for them?"

"They want me to do a background on Mathews. They gave me the bail money . . . sort of."

She looked over her shoulder to where Toddy was reading his encyclopedia and turned back to me. "It might not be a bad thing to know more about Mathews. He wasn't there at the mine, but he might know what Louise was planning to do after she left you."

She reached out and touched my hand.

"Hey, Cecil, you don't have a handgun, do you?"

"You know I don't have a gun." I looked at her puzzled.

"What kind of private detective are you, man?" She scanned the café. The graveyard shift of workers was start-ing to come in. Her long blond hair was lifted by the wind that gusted through the open door. The underside of her chin was a soft concave valley and I wanted to lift my hand and smooth her hair.

"I don't know, Hannah. I just don't want to shoot anybody."

"What if somebody wants to shoot you?"

"Then they're going to have to bring their own fucking gun."

She pushed back from the table, curling her shoulders and putting up her collar as if I were a draft of cold air. She gave the cook the money for our eggs.

"Well, listen, I've got to go. I guess I'm going to see Jake about something. Then I'm headed out."

She walked over to Todd and he got up. They were turning into the open door, moving past two guys in rain gear with bandannas around their foreheads waiting to get in.

I held my hands up almost helplessly. "The weather is kicking up. Might be a long time before we're able to get out to the island. Do you want to take a sauna before you . . . have to leave?"

She was holding Todd's hand and he was looking at his shoes. She leaned away from him and tried to whisper to me. "You do what you want, Cecil. I guess that's the best way. See ya." Then she was out the door. I waited a moment, watching the door swing shut and was about to leave by the back door when she reappeared suddenly.

"Give me the day. Maybe we can go out tonight if the weather holds. Maybe I do want to sweat some of this out." Then she was gone.

I walked down the street past one of the bars set back from the water. The bartender was hauling garbage cans out and though it wasn't officially open I peaked in.

The light in the bar looked like it was meant for catching bugs. The four people sitting up at the counter were hunched over their beers. One Coast Guardsman, two loggers, and a white woman who was Alfred Tom's ex-wife, fingering the ice in her drink. The loggers were arguing about the herring that were prematurely schooling and the killer whales that had been recently sighted out on the coast. They were talking in loud blurting phrases about whether a whale would attack a swimmer or not. I tuned them out and walked over to Nanny.

She was skinny and her skin was tightly drawn over her face so that her hairline seemed to pull her eyebrows up. She was smoking nervously, sitting in the center of the bar. Her thinning brown hair was matted down so that it clung to her skull. She flicked her teeth with her thumbnail between drags on her cigarette. The bartender stood down at the far end chatting up one of the barmaids who looked like a weather girl. He was leaving Nanny's glass empty.

Nanny had been out of jail for a week. She was breaking the conditions of her probation just by being in the bar. Maybe that was why she was nervous. But more likely she hadn't had a drink in a couple of months and after the taste of the first one she was facing a decision. The first one was for the taste and for getting out of jail. The first was an obligation. The second . . . that was what she was considering. Her most current husband had gotten out of jail a month before her. He was supposed to be working in a camp out on Prince of Wales Island. He had completed all of the programs in jail—alcohol and anger management. He had taken some courses and made it out without any write-ups. He had kept it cool. Cool.

Nanny had some problems. Three write-ups and some lost good time. "Bitches," she murmured, and she watched the shadows on the sidewalk move past the smoked glass. "Bitches."

I took the stool on her right side and rapped the wood to wake her up out of her cell space.

"Nanny, hey, you're looking good. I thought you'd be all pumped up and beefy, coming out of the joint."

"Fuck you, Younger. I don't know why I'm even here. I mean, if my probation officer even gets an idea that I'm here—with YOU, no less—I'm fucked . . . royally." Then she ducked and looked around sheepishly, smiled, and then looked at me.

"Well, hey!" I said. "It's great to see you too. Let's get out of here then."

"Not so fast. I might need another drink." She gazed at her glass and then down at the pretty-boy bartender who must have asked his girlfriend to cut his hair like one of the Bee Gees. Then she looked back at me and her face relaxed with a sad recognition.

"Fuck it. Let's get out of here. Nothing good ever happens in here."

"You want something to eat?"

"Buy me a steak, Younger, and two pieces of cheesecake, and I'll tell you what you want to know."

"It's morning—breakfast, Nan. I just had some eggs."

"Well, good for you. I just said I wanted a steak. I didn't ask the time, did I?"

I figured we had to go down the road for the steak so we

needed to walk back to the cabstand to get Artie, the driver, to run us out.

The streets are narrow and even in the dark the mountain behind the town seems to press in, making them seem tighter. The night was grudgingly giving way to morning and the kids were huddled under the eaves by the hotel and the café. The music drifted out onto the street near the cathedral. We walked by some of the other bars and the smell of sour beer, vinyl, and cigarette smoke seeped out along with the laughter. Cars drifted by slowly and kids gawked back and forth at each other, watching but not paying any particular attention. Above the streetlights, the sky showed black clouds that were rimmed with the silver of a moon somewhere. A gull sat on a dock rail, and an oil barge moved out through the channel making way for Seattle.

"You know, there was a time I thought I could never go to prison. I thought I'd just die if I ever had to face being locked up. I don't know. But you go in for a while and the scary thing is . . . not how bad it is but—it's not good, don't think I'm telling you that—but at least it's orderly. I don't know. I kissed everybody's ass to get out. I went through my release plans and my employment plans and all of my positive growth scenarios, all of that shit. But it's always the same. It's like, what do you do? All of those plans were just talk to get out of jail so I could live without them on the outside. You did a little easy time, Younger. What was it like for you?"

"Well, Nan, we're different, you know. I completely rehabilitated myself. In fact, I'm being considered as the poster child for the Department of Corrections."

She looked up at me with that stunned Labrador look of disbelief. "You are so completely full of shit."

"But I'm not a recidivist."

Artie didn't want to take us to the bar and grill down the road, knowing quite rightly that we'd stiff him for the fare. But I showed him a couple of bucks in advance and he begrudgingly let us in his cab. We drove out of town past where I found Nelson and past the beach, where there was a nice swell running in. There was a man in a wet suit with a boogie board paddling out into the surf break. Whenever the people in the houses see him come down to the beach they call their kids in from playing outside but they let them stand up on the window sills and watch him paddle out and ride the short choppy waves back into the beach.

Everything was closed up at the steakhouse but I knew the cook and he was one of the only people in town who actually owed me money, so he let us in the back and agreed to make us some food. Nanny liked being in the kitchen. She craned her head into the stainless steel coolers like a horse nosing through a wire fence. I told her I was already full and she wrinkled up her nose. She didn't offer to forgo the steak. She just said she'd eat it fast. She drank one water glass of red wine by the time the cook flopped down her "Alaskan"-sized steak in front of her. She talked about how she was going to get her kids back from her sister down in Blaine and how her husband was going to get on steady somewhere and they were going to get a house here in Sitka. She kind of liked her probation officer here in town but Nan had heard that she was going to move up to Kenai. She was complaining about having to get rid of all of their guns and what a hassle it was because they couldn't even have any contact with weapons so they had to leave the guns to some idiot nephew to sell and he didn't know a thing about what a gun was worth. She was going on and on about how long it had taken her to find "this pretty little nine millimeter semiauto pistol" when the cook poured some coffee and asked if we wanted more wine. We declined and I used the momentary sadness in the pause to start asking questions about Alfred Tom and the scene up at Otter Creek.

"Well, Al and I were divorced before he got that job up there. You know, he was a good guy to be divorced from. I liked him, I mean. He was just . . . Heck, Younger, he's an Indian, you know?"

I nodded, not really knowing, but not wanting to interrupt the flow.

"He never had that much of a temper when we were married but the older he got, the madder he would get about this 'Indian' stuff. We broke it off before we got mean. We stayed pretty good friends and he's tried to talk to me about it but I never understood all that well. Anyway, I found Russ and he had a steady thing working for a logging outfit and that seemed better, but look . . ." And she gestured with her hands, pointing toward her face as if it were painfully clear to everyone in the world that she had just gotten out of jail.

"Did Alfred ever tell you about what happened up at Otter Creek?"

"Only that they were assholes and treated him like a child. Man, he would go off about that."

She chewed her steak methodically as if she were counting the bites, then stared out the window as an eagle flew low over the beach and toward the dumpster.

"He did talk a lot about the cook."

"Which cook?"

"Someone named Lou." She nodded her head awkwardly. "Yeah, at first I thought he was talking about a man and I was thinking this is getting really weird. But it was a woman, I guess."

She put down her fork and knife and leaned back and stared out to the water.

"This Lou would set the boys' teeth on edge. She was good-looking. Some of the guys would nose around but she was kind of cool to them. Kind of cool, but according to Alfred she was good people, just a little strange, you know?"

"I'm not sure."

"Well, I guess she would talk to the boys but kind of tease them just the same. I mean, I can picture it. I had a girlfriend in Bozeman like that."

The busboy who had just come in for shift cleanup cleared away the plates.

"In the kitchen sometimes she would only wear her robe. She would start each shift by sharpening each of the cutting knives until they almost jumped out at the food they were so sharp. Al thought it was kind of weird. She would spend hours sometimes sitting out on the back porch by the landing sharpening the knives, and then when the knives were sharp enough she would put her nose in a book and just—I don't know—read for hours. It was always the same. First the knives got sharp, then the books. That's what Al said. She would even shave the hair on her arms to test how sharp the knives were. It got a little loopy, I thought.

"The guys used to come in and stand by the sink and, you know, use their best 'Joe Cool' voice or something and ask, 'Is there anything I can do for you?' thinking they were being studs, and I guess she would sit there, right out of the shower with nothing but her robe on, strapping her favorite carving knife, and say, 'Men only like to fuck and kill things. I don't really need either right now. But thanks for asking.'

And they'd stand there looking stupid and she would laugh and then give them a little hug and go off to the next thing. These guys just didn't get it. I'm not sure Al really got it."

"Did Lou have any weapons up at camp?"

"Like guns or anything? No, she hated guns and used to throw fits when she saw guys plinking with their twenty-twos around camp. She would chase them off. She had some lecture about guns."

"Did anything . . . happen to her up on the mountain?"

"Al said the boys raped her. He felt bad because he had seen it coming. I didn't talk to him much about it because he got mad and we didn't talk much when he got mad."

"You know she was raped?"

"Shit, Younger, I don't really *know*, I guess, but that's what I heard."

"Did Alfred rape her?"

She shook her head sadly as if this world were too complicated to explain to a goof like me. She let out a long impatient sigh.

"No, he didn't rape her, Younger. He was in love with her. Okay?"

She looked at me and her eyes were wet but her face had not broken out of its tough set.

"I guess some of that crap with the knives was an act because she liked to talk to him about books and stuff. And she asked him about the stories his grandma told. She liked to know about that Indian stuff. I guess she was smart. No, he didn't rape her. It hurt him when she left . . . and made him crazy mad."

A tear fell on the tablecloth and she flicked at the wet spot as if it were an ash from her cigarette.

"Fuck it, Younger. Let's get out of here."

83

We hitchhiked downtown, slamming the car door of the kid who had given us a ride. We walked down the street toward her hotel. She was going to try and find someone to take care of the guns in the morning and she was going to fly out to camp. It wasn't a family camp but she knew the boss and she could sneak a couple of days in the bunkhouse. Her husband had written her about maybe getting together in Sitka but he ended up not coming because he didn't want to have to check in with the probation office just in case something went wrong with the paperwork or the gun situation. It was better to be out at camp and making some money than fooling around in town anyway.

We were walking slowly up the street and there were two couples standing on the sidewalk. They were weaving in place, noticeably drunk. Their voices were raised. Nanny walked closer to the curb. One of the men was wearing his hat backwards and had on a dirty hickory shirt under a blue bar windbreaker. His hair was long and stringy. He narrowed his eyes to focus, then he hit the woman and she fell, slapping the sidewalk like a wet paper sack.

"You fuck!" she shrieked.

He was swaying and standing over her with his fists clenched. "Fuckin' pussy, man. You are on your way down. All the fucking way down."

The other woman leaned over her fallen friend, the man squared his shoulders and stood on the balls of his feet the best he could. The two women were crying now and the man with the squared shoulders moved in and pushed the fighter in the chest.

"Hey, mellow out, man. Whattaya go slappin' the girl around for?"

The fight began like most fights in real life. Pushing and yelling, all elbows and awkward, loopy swings, and then one of them threw the other into a parked car. His head hit with a sodden crunch. The first woman was leaning up against the side of a hotel door and blood was dripping onto her lap.

"You fucking guys! I started talking about my life. And you start this shit!"

I could smell the salt off the ocean and just faintly I could hear a swell that climbed the seawall down by the government dock. I imagined that that swell had been generated hundreds of miles out at sea by the storm that might have been holding off the coast or by now was over, sending along the swells. A raven hopped in the gutter and picked up a burned-out paper match in its curved beak.

"You fucking guys. I'm talking about my life. I'm talking about my life and you hit me and you fight and shit. . . . You fucking guys!"

She was rocking her head back and forth against the wall of the hotel on the main street. The men were rolling in the street and fighting, their arms flailing and their fists clenched. Rarely did a punch land, rarely did a bite find flesh. Every once in a while a swing went wild and they would hit the pavement hard, sounding almost like a kid breaking pebbles with a claw hammer.

Nanny walked over to the woman crouched on the sidewalk. She held the woman's chin up so she could look her in the eye.

"Baby, I'll take you somewhere. You got somewhere to go?"

The woman swung her hand and slapped Nanny's hand away. She spit her words out.

"Fuck you. Stay out of this. This is my husband. I didn't ask for nothing and I'm not your fucking baby!"

Nanny held her hands in front of the woman's face. Then in a quick gesture she banged her fists together and showed her empty palms like a dealer clearing the table in Vegas.

"I'm gone."

Nanny knew the police were on their way and she motioned to me that she was heading for the hotel. The cops came in a flurry of sound and lights as she rounded the corner. I followed her up to the landing of her hotel room. "Ain't love wonderful?" I asked her.

"Yeah." She smiled weakly.

She turned her back to me and put the key in the door. "Listen, Younger. I think Al may be in some trouble with this girl up at the mine. The cops came around asking about him and he told me not to say anything. I don't really care about anything but . . . I don't want him to know I talked to you. And . . ." Her jaw was set. Her eyes were red and she would not look at me. I stood next to her without trying to force the next words.

Finally she let it out. "Will you help him out if you can?"

I could hear the doors of the police car slamming on the street below and I heard the sizzle of their radios squawking out incoming calls. She pushed open the door to her room and the hall smelled briefly like disinfectant and cigarette smoke. I leaned into her and gave her hard shoulder as much of a hug as it would accept.

"I'll help him. You need anything?"

She looked down at the cracked linoleum on the floor. She looked hard as if she were trying to read her fortune. "No. I guess not. Russ's working. He says he's stopped drinking. I guess I don't need anything else. I'll see ya."

The door shut. By the time I was downstairs the men were in the back of two separate squad cars. The women were propped up against the wall and a cop was writing in a notebook as the two of them talked at once.

I cut across the street and walked around the corner past the bars, down to my house to get some sleep.

FIVE

WHEN I WOKE up, what sunlight there had been was gone.
The room sagged in darkness. I heard footsteps beneath my
house in the boat shed and I got dressed quickly by the light
of the street lamp cutting through my window.

Hannah stood by my skiff and she had a towel rolled
under her arm and a daypack slung over her shoulder. She
didn't say anything but nodded to my boat and put the pack
in the bow.

My aluminum skiff is only thirteen feet long so it was nice
that the storm was far enough from shore to bring only the
easy swells and rain. The squalls were still swirling through
but the water had laid down flat on top of the swells. The
darkness came down to the water once we escaped the lights
from town. We could hear the broken whistle of eagles flying
in the dark. It seemed like there were more eagles this year.
Ever since the *Exxon Valdez* people had been looking more
closely at the coast and there was some speculation that
what was going on at Otter Creek had thrown off the pattern
of the eagles. We passed several small islands that dotted

the sound, shaggy humps in the dark rain. As I neared the beach I saw the silver flash of phosphorescence and the clouds of herring under the boat. There had also been talk that something had thrown off the herring cycle. They were starting to school near the beach in the fall and not in early spring as they were supposed to. There were even some reports that they were starting to spawn. This was crazy and made people anxious, in the way that a series of storms or bad luck can.

I pulled the skiff up on the gravel beach near the sauna tree. There were two dead gulls on the beach, their feathers matted and splayed out, making them look like rags. Ravens had taken their eyes and sand fleas were working into the crevices of their chest cavities. Hannah nudged one with her foot, paused briefly to watch the movement of the sandfleas, and then continued up the beach.

We lugged some gear in plastic boxes up to the lean-to. It was more or less a permanent tent I had hidden in the trees in case I needed a landfall when coming in late off a storm from the outside. The lean-to was made of heavy plastic and netting I had beachcombed and tied to poles I'd cut in the interior of the island. We tucked the ends down, laid out our emergency gear, and took towels out to the sauna.

The sauna is half-buried in the hillside under the roots of a Sitka spruce at least eight hundred years old. The door was a solid slab of red cedar milled from a log that floated up on the beach on the outer coast. The planks of the walls were rough-sawn yellow cedar with beachcombed hemp rope battened into the seams. There were two small windows on either side of the door and the roof was tin. The stove was a barrel that sat inside and took up much of the floor space. It was fed from the outside so it would not create a draft drawing the cold air in. On the inside there were two levels of benches curved to the form of a back made from red cedar two-by-fours. As the fire in the stove caught and burned, the benches warmed with fragrance to fill the head and chest.

Hannah took her clothes off and hung them on pegs outside under the eaves so they wouldn't get wet. First her sweater and then her turtleneck. Kicking out of her slippers, she pulled her jeans and her underwear off at the same time. She shivered quickly and started for the door, then turned and looked back at me. She stood against the tree whose bark was brittle, shell-like scabs etched with globules of pitch. Her skin was the smooth white of a porcelain jar disturbed only by the rippled impression of the underpants that had rimmed her waist, and the bra that had tracked faint red lines across her back and shoulders. She had scars on her knees that marked her several operations.

I was supposed to be undressing but she caught me watching. She smiled, then spoke.

"You got a knife?"

"A knife?" I almost laughed.

"Yeah, I've got to whittle down the candle that's on the window. We may want some light."

I watched her for a moment and tried to consider what she was saying but I was still struck by the whiteness of her body. Naked people in the north seem so vulnerable. When she stood in front of me I found my hands reaching up as if in a kid's game of levitation, and I wanted . . . not to stroke her, not even to touch her, but to cover her with something.

Her skin seemed so thin in this world of slick gray stone and green wood.

She tossed her hair, loosening it from a rubber band, and on her shoulder I saw a tattoo. It was nicely done in purple and black—a brown bear with its head resting on its front paws, eyes staring intently outward, not menacing but watchful. Under the bear, written in script, were the words THE CURIOUS EAT THEMSELVES.

She turned and saw me floundering around in my vision of her. "Better check that fire," she said.

"I like your tattoo. When did you get that?" I pointed stupidly.

"Yeah." She grinned. "I just got it in Seattle. You know where the words come from? It's one of your favorites."

"Roethke. I think. . . . 'The Far Field.'"

She smiled even more broadly and her eyes now held mine like some thug's grip. "No. 'Straw for the Fire.'" And she pulled the towel out of my hand and turned her back so quickly that her hair brushed my chest.

She disappeared into the opening and now her voice came through the door.

"Could you bring some more water when you come?"

I was naked now and I walked gingerly on bare feet to the chopping block and lifted a round of cedar and split three pieces off. I placed them one by one through the opening in the barrel stove. The fire rumbled through the vents. The rain fell steadily on the tin roof. I looked down at my own silly body: white and exposed in the darkness, scarred knees, scarred shoulder, the ridiculous penis retreating as far into my abdomen as possible, like a rat in a hole. I hunched my shoulders and shivered, then danced to the door.

"Don't forget the knife. This candle is all melted down and I need to dig out some of the wax to get to the wick."

I got the penknife out of my pants pocket and opened the door to the steamy cedar heat.

Inside, my body loosened and my flesh seemed to ease away from my bones. The heat and the smell came in through my nose and my mouth, into my chest, my stomach. In the corner above the stove Hannah sat with her knees up to her chest, her arms encircling them. The stovepipe was glowing red and it was rusted through in several places. There was the briefest flicker of orange light on her skin, which was glistening with beads of sweat.

"There. It's in the corner."

I took the melted candle and scooped a channel for the wax and stripped down the outer layers to the wick. She handed me a wooden match and I held it to the surface of the stove and it lit without friction. The sulfur mingled with the cedar and drifted toward the holes in the stovepipe. I sat on the opposite end of the bench.

"You think you know all about me, don't you?"

I could see her eyes in the brief light from the stove. She grabbed her knees tighter, then tilted her head forward and scooped her long hair off her neck with her palm and her forearm, piling the fine blond hair on top of her head. She leaned back and rested the loose pile of hair against the wall. She exhaled and wiped her palms on her neck, her chest, in a slow tired motion. She spread her legs slightly. A track of sweat curled down the inner surface of her thigh. She turned and looked at me, holding herself stiffly, not yet eased into the heat.

"You know that I loved her, don't you?"

"Yes."

The fire popped, and I could see a creamy bead of wax ease to the base of the candle and puddle out onto the bench. The rain kept up outside and I could hear the water on the beach below.

"Do you have some faith left in me, Cecil?" Her body relaxed and she acted as if she might come closer.

"Yes. Sometimes I think that's all I have."

She leaned toward me and stretched out her back. She threw her hair forward and pulled the sweaty strands away from her neck. She shook her hair loose and worked her fingers through it. I took a sponge from a bucket of cold, fresh water and squeezed it down my neck. I felt the pores of my skin open with new sweat. I poured a cup of water on my hair and a cup on the stove. Steam hissed up and the hot vapor stung my eyes and the inside of my nose. Hannah did not look up but she held her hand out to me, her arm slender and arched in a pretty curve like a painting of an almond branch in bloom. She wanted water and I dipped from the bucket, giving her some. We sat in silence for several minutes.

She threw her hair back with her forearm. She looked at me and her gaze was hazy with the heat. She poured the cup of water down her chest. The water ran down the curves of her body and what was not soaked up by her skin splattered down onto the plywood floor.

"I will do anything to protect myself." She looked in my eyes as she spoke, the skin of her cheeks flushed, her breathing shallow.

"I know that."

She sat up straight and twisted her hips in an odd

shuffling motion, arranging her bottom on the bench and rubbing the sponge down her arms, down her legs.

"Do you ever do anything to help your luck, Cecil? Anything to protect you from danger?"

I leaned back against the side of the sauna wall. I stared at the glowing red stovepipe, listening to the rumble of the fire pumping. "I made vows when I was a kid with my friend Edward. He said they were Eskimo rituals, but I think he was bullshitting me. But we swore oaths and he said that those oaths would protect us always. Blood oaths."

She moved next to me on the bench and her voice was in my skull and the reflected heat off her body made me sit up straight.

"What were those oaths?"

"I don't know. . . . For some reason I just don't remember . . . ," I sputtered.

She moved the candle and my penknife next to me. As she leaned over, her hair brushed against my waist. She took my palm and leaned close to me, her cheek on mine, her lips against the lobe of my ear. She whispered: "Don't look."

And she pulled the penknife across my palm. I jerked back in a muzzy spasm of pain and held my hand up: Two-inch slit, bone white and then warm sticky red.

"Jesus!"

She held her own hand to the candle and pulled the knife against it and the drops fell on the shiny skin of her thigh. Then she grabbed my hand and pressed her cut against mine. She put her lips to my ear and her breath was cool going into my skull.

"No matter what you do, no matter what you think you do, you will not betray me."

She leaned away. She was smiling but her eyes had the urgent stare of a marten trapped in a cabin.

The heat and the blood were causing my head to spin and my mind was unhinged. She thrust the cut edge of her palm into my mouth. My teeth felt the edge of her skin, the dense salty taste of blood; my tongue touched lightly on the cut. Blood speckled my ankles crossed beneath me, blood on my penis, stunned and lazy. She cupped her bleeding hand behind my neck and kissed me on the lips and her tongue tasted her own blood inside me.

I kissed her several times and I reached for her shoulder and my hands clasped around the small of her back and I lifted her to me: salt and slick skin, our cool breath mixed in the smell of the burning cedar in the tight pressure of heat, the rain on the roof and the Pacific Ocean hissing on the cobbled beach as the tide began to rise.

I stood off the bench and kept kissing her, teetering off balance, leaning forward. We broke away for a moment and I stood up straight. She lay down on the bench and reached for me as I moved as close as I could. My hands skimmed her wet skin. Her throat bowed up slightly and she turned toward me, her breathing now more measured and urgent. I pressed the sponge against our cuts and she poured a cup of cool water over our heads. My lips sputtered with the sweet-tasting water and I shuddered. She guided my good hand down her stomach and her thigh. I felt my head reel up and out into the air as she grasped my penis in her palm and pulled me toward her. Then her voice in my ear: "It's hot enough. Let's swim."

We walked on tender feet into the dark water and kicked away from shore. The rain fell in percolating drops, breaking the tension of the shiny black surface. The whole earth rose and fell like even breaths. She swam out ahead of me. My body a furnace of stored heat, my mouth filled with the taste of salt and tideflat, the stones and mussels on the shore. I kicked down, but was in deep water now and could not stand up. My skin was numb but clamoring to find its senses. I was breathing hard. She turned and treaded water, then rolled on her back like a seal, her whiteness slick and vivid. Her breasts, her hips, her legs curled away from me, and I swam toward her. Then the water was alive with silvery fish fluttering against my skin like an electrical current. Herring. Billows of herring that flickered with the phosphorescence. I felt I was either being lifted out of the water or dragged down. The numbness was giving way to icy needles of pain: the herring surrounding me in a cloud. She surfaced and held me by the hands, pulling me out to deeper water. Pulling me and swimming beneath, her hair trailing like the garlands of kelp that roll onto the beach, trailing like Chinese dragons dancing in the streets. Her breasts moving gracefully with each stroke. Her legs kicking beneath me, strong and loose, the herring fluttering against our skin, my chest, my throat, her thighs, my penis numbed and stupid with sensation, but long and curled out into the milky water.

She stopped and kissed me, biting my lip as my teeth chattered. We treaded water together and my penis bobbed between her legs, growing softer as the cold rushed the barriers of our skin and began to curl into a painful ache in our joints. She looked at me and her glance had that strange sense of distant life that you see sometimes when a seal watches you from the water. "Taste this water, Cecil."

And I did. There was the salt and the faint muddy flavor of herring milt. She hugged me tightly and her chest was heaving. The tone of her voice was changed as something was seeping in with the cold. "This is all there is. Don't ask for more just yet. Time . . . all we need is time." And she cradled my head with her bleeding hand, kissed me again, and swam hard for shore.

SIX

AS MUCH AS I hated to admit it, Nelson had been the center of our daily life. For Toddy, he was like water from the spigot: the reliable source of good things.

"Listen, I really think he can hear my thoughts. Look at his head and his eyes, Cecil. I know he can."

Todd would sometimes sit on the beach with Nelson next to him and the two resembled an old couple on a park bench. They would watch the sea birds and together their heads would bob back and forth while the gulls moved off the shore and swirled in a motion like a mobile in the wind, never tangling a string, until they would circle and land in the shallowest water of the sand. Finally Nelson would turn his blocky head and stare into Todd's eyes and beseech. Please . . . Please . . . Todd would let him run and call out, "Catch a bird, Nelson. Catch a bird, Nelson." And even as he said it, he knew he would be heartbroken if Nelson ever did catch one.

The refrigerator door was covered with photos of Nelson. Some in costume and some not. I had one photo in my room taken of him and Toddy on the beach. It was next to the only shot I had of Hannah. In it she was standing next to my father.

I went out to the kitchen where Todd was putting some books into a huge cardboard tweed suitcase. I put my arm around him. I apologized. I didn't comfort him. I didn't make promises. He blew his nose on a paper towel and he wiped his glasses on the tail of his shirt.

We didn't talk about Nelson. Toddy knew he was dead. He knew about Nelson's being in Jake's freezer behind the bait herring from last summer. Nelson was gone and he wouldn't be coming home.

He sat down at the table to read what the encyclopedia had to say about Labrador and I stood awkwardly in the middle of the room looking up as if I were in an invisible elevator. Finally I looked down at my watch.

I had slept in. I had dropped Hannah off last night at the city dock and she had walked away. Now I had to get out and I might as well start off by finding Mathews in what daylight there was going to be.

"I can make a freight flight and maybe see this guy out near Angoon. You gonna be okay?"

Todd looked at me through his thick lenses with his wobbly stare. "Yes, I will be fine. Cecil, the people at Social Services heard about your being in the bar and getting arrested. They said they want to talk to you. They want me to stay somewhere else for a while."

"Don't sweat that thing. I can work it out. You won't be gone long," I said without much force in my voice. He looked down at the encyclopedia he was reading.

"No. I won't be gone that long. I hope not, anyway. Do you

think I should take my own television down to the office when I go? Or do you think they will allow me to return to my place of residence and pick up my effects?"

"You're not going to jail, for Christ's sake. You're just going to see the social worker. You don't even know for sure if they're going to put you anywhere. I tell you, don't sweat this. I'll talk to them or something. It will be fine."

He continued to stare down at the table. On the street some kids were rolling a metal drum down the pavement and a dog was barking.

"It's going to be fine."

He didn't look at me but got up and cleared some dishes off the table. I went to my room and packed a day pack with a change of clothes and some survival gear.

Steven Mathews lived near Angoon, which was fifty stormy air miles from Sitka. Closer, if the float plane could clear the top of Baranof Island. I would get dropped there but I didn't even know if Mathews would be at home. Because the weather was chancy, I could get dropped on the beach and be stuck there for hours and if the chances broke the wrong way I could be there for days. I packed my emergency kit with a lighter and matches and some small chunks of pitchy wood. I packed a book by Richard Nelson about Eskimo hunting. I had lied and told someone I had read it, so I figured I needed to cover my tracks. I packed my Gouker hunting knife. This was the second knife Gary Gouker had made me and it was still creased into its leather sheath. Gary had oiled the harness leather and the knife molded perfectly inside it. It curved in the leather like a starlet under satin sheets.

I packed a tape recorder, a candle, and a yellow water-proof notebook. Then some pens, a box of crackers, a piece of cheese, and a ring of Polish sausage still in the plastic wrapper. I didn't feel like eating anything but I knew that might change if I was standing out on some beach for a couple of days. I put on my rubber boots, packed my romeos, and took my heavy rain gear down from the pegs in the mud room. I jammed all of this into an old canvas Forest Service day pack, then walked out into the living room.

Todd had his clothes packed in the suitcase and he had a shopping bag full of his photo albums. He was wearing a tan dress raincoat that someone had bought for him when he went to his mother's funeral. It was too small by far for him now, but I knew it was useless to try to talk him out of wearing it. I really think he had a strategy of looking crazier when he was mad at me.

I didn't look at him for long. The clock over the stove sounded on the hour. The dog was still barking down the street. My head hurt with the fine sharp pain of a paper cut.

"It will be all right."

I walked out onto the street with the pack over one shoulder. Alfred Tom's house was just up from mine. Alfred Tom and I went back a ways.

The house on Katlian was weathered. The siding had turned from the almost peachlike glow of clear cedar to gray, until now it was almost black under the eaves. The windows were sagging in their frames. The rain had been falling for fifty years on this wood. The porch of the house was next to the sidewalk that ran along the street. Ten years ago the street wasn't paved and it was impossible for cars to speed down it, but now it was smooth and black, and the cars hissed past with their tires churning the water and gravel into little ruts on the new pavement.

I knocked and waited. The radio was loud in the background and I could see William Tom sitting in front of the radio in his recliner. He had his house slippers on and a cup of coffee in his hand. He heard the knock but I suppose it never occurred to him to get up and answer it. I knocked again and suddenly Edith, a tiny, birdlike Tlingit woman, appeared and opened the door. I'm just under six feet but she looked up at me through her thick lenses as if I were a sequoia.

"Hello, Mrs. Tom. I'm Cecil from down the way. Is Alfred around?"

She did not answer, but squinted up at me. Then she cupped her hand around her ear and I heard the two-toned squeal of her hearing aid feeding back directly into her ear. She winced and with the routine gesture of someone sliding their glasses up their nose she pulled her hearing aid out and started knocking it against her hip.

"Who?" she yelled.

"Alfred! . . . Is Alfred around?" Stupidly I made a circling gesture with my fingers trying to illustrate "around."

She jabbed the hearing aid back into her ear, looked up at me with frustration. "Yes, he's here. Come in, come in . . . but who are you?"

She had a soft percussive voice that retreated into the room as she stepped back from me. She walked backwards and I moved forward. The floor was old linoleum and it was buckled but very clean. The oil heater sat prominently in the center of the wall that joined the kitchen. Edith had been canning salmon and the room was damp with warm fish smell and heating oil.

"I'm sorry. I'm Cecil Younger. I live down the street. I knew Alfred over in Juneau."

I didn't want to tell her I knew him in jail, but as soon as I spoke, her expression changed and she winced as if she had bitten her tongue, and I knew I didn't need to let her know where it was I knew him.

"I think he's asleep. Just sit here." She pointed to the couch opposite her husband. I sat down on the edge of the cushion with my hands dangling between my knees, expectantly, as though I were waiting for a date. Mr. Tom was listening intently to the radio, which was featuring a local buy, sell, and trade show. We heard a woman who had a hide-a-bed and a .357 magnum for sale.

There were two painted enamel icons of the Madonna above the diesel stove and a painting of Saint Herman of Alaska above the doorway to the kitchen. A picture calendar from a fishing supply house hung near an open window and the troller on the page fluttered like a flag. The woman on the radio gave her telephone number and the DJ thanked her, going into a local commercial for an outboard supply shop.

"You get your deer yet?" Mr. Tom spoke up as if coming out of a dream.

"No . . . actually I haven't been out yet. I guess I . . ."

"Yeah." He rocked back in the recliner and looked up at the ceiling. "Yeah, it's a little early. Might as well wait. Wait and they will come to you."

He clicked off the radio and continued to stare at the ceiling. He rested his hands on his magnificent belly and rocked back and forth. The silence sat there like a spilled beer neither of us wanted to clean up. I heard the clock tick and the pressure cooker rattling on top of the gas stove.

Finally Alfred came down in his sweat pants and a T-shirt. He had blanket tracks across his face and his eyes were red. He barely looked at me and he motioned to the kitchen.

"Come out here. Get something to drink."

I stood up quickly as if I had just gotten my chance to see the parole board and followed him into the kitchen. Mrs. Tom walked in behind us and handed me a mug of black coffee. Alfred took down another mug and poured some coffee in his. Then he reached over, broke off a piece of cooked salmon and popped it in his mouth. His mother slapped his forearm but he turned away as if he didn't notice. He sat down in the kitchen chair and set the mug on the Formica.

I knew Alfred when he had worked as a contract counselor at the jail. He would come in twice a week to teach a class called Heritage. It was a writing workshop and a group session. It was meant for Indian guys but the state couldn't limit enrollment so it was open to all. He only taught it a couple of months and then his contract was jerked. He refused to read any story where an Indian man died. This caused some kind of stir, a small one at first because nobody in the administration really gives a shit about what goes on in these classes. But a young Tlingit guy had written a heart-wrenching story appropriately full of sorrow and remorse for his crimes. The story ended with the narrator's strongly hinted-at wishes to die. Alfred read the story in group and tossed the pages on the table, saying, "Okay. But this is no story." The inmate complained and the counselors at the jail had a fit. There was lots of talk about "validating inmates' feelings of loss as a process towards growth." One of the white prisoner advocates said, "Surely you don't mean to imply that Native men are immortal." And Alfred answered, "I don't imply anything. I'm saying that ain't no story."

I was in the group and suggested that I wouldn't have to write about white men feeling guilty about the Indians. I felt it was kind of a quid pro quo situation. And he partially agreed, saying guilt was okay, he just didn't want to read about it. It might have blown over but when the controversy worked its way to the superintendent, he suggested to Alfred Tom that he just stick to Indian fairy tales and leave the rehabilitation to the professionals. Alfred could have drawn from the centuries of Tlingit oratory or from his degree in comparative European literature to construct a reply. But he just said, "I'm not telling any more stories about how Indians die." His contract was not renewed.

"What's going on, man?"

"I'm sorry about waking you up," I said, and he waved me off, rubbing his eyes.

"Don't worry about it. I was dreaming about getting up."

"You used to work up at Otter Creek before the shutdown, didn't you?"

He nodded and took a sip from the mug. His mom was back at the canner.

"Yeah, I was up there for a while. It wasn't a bad job but, man, those guys from Las Vegas and Texas. They were always on my case—in high gear all the time. Like they couldn't make their money fast enough. I didn't get it. I wanted to work, you know, but I wanted to make it last."

He smiled and took another sip.

"Was it a dry camp?" I asked.

"It was dry, but that wasn't a problem. I mean, there was booze around, but booze isn't a problem for me. It was attitude. Like nothing else mattered but how many numbers were on your paycheck. It was crazy up there. No women. No family. They had porno movies in the middle of the day. Any time they wanted to do anything fun they ended up shooting birds or breaking bottles or getting into a fight. It was weird. I ended up watching a lot of TV. I said the heck with it, came home."

"Were you there when Louise Root was?"

He smiled broadly and looked down into his cup. He shook his head. "Yeah, she was a good cook. Man, you could eat till you got sick. I think I almost did. I used to help her out some. There was a place where I could go and get grayling. Out of a lake up behind the mine. It was upgrade. I don't care what they say about those tanks, I wouldn't fish downgrade from that place. I used to get her fish and she would cook it up just for me and her. She was okay." He leaned forward and lowered his voice, looking over to see if his mother was listening. "Most guys said she was a tease. You know, she wore bikini kind of things in the kitchen." He gestured, cupping his hands out in front of his chest. "They used to talk about her and about how she knew what she was doing." He leaned back and pulled his hand around the back of his neck. "I worked around her area . . . on some stuff in the kitchen. I never had any problem with her."

He reached over and took a wooden match that was in a box on the counter, whittled it with his pocketknife, then stuck it in his teeth. As he put his pocketknife away I saw that he had an ugly two-inch scar on his palm, like mine.

"I heard she had a problem up there. Can you tell me about it?"

"All I know is one day they were talking about a party and the next day she was gone on the flight out. A company guy got shipped out, but no one ever talked about it, least not to me."

"You go to the party?"

He smiled again. He brushed his black hair back across his forehead. "Cecil, I was the only Tlingit up there. Just for their company stats. I had my picture taken the first day on the job and it showed up in the local paper. It was a good job, I guess, but it wasn't a life. No." He shook his head. "No, I wasn't at the party."

His mom was pulling jars out of the steamer with tongs. She was setting them on a white cloth laid out on a stained cutting board. She tilted her head back to try to keep her glasses from getting steamed up but it wasn't working. Her voice bounced off the wall.

"Money . . . lots of talk about money. There wasn't a church up there. Where are those boys supposed to go to church? There was no school. No doctor. What if he gets sick? Nothing. I tell him. I say over and over, What good is the money if you don't have a church? All these men and the jobs, where do they go? They buy drugs. They buy alcohol. What good is that money?"

Alfred was shaking his head, trying to head her off. "Okay, okay." He lowered his voice again. "She wants me to get a job here and live in the house. She wants me to go to church all the time. Hey, man, what am I going to do?"

"I hear that. Don't think I can't hear that. You didn't talk like that until you went to work with all those white . . ." She stopped and looked at me and fished into the steamer, absentmindedly letting the sentence drop into the mouth of the pot.

There were two large stainless steel bowls next to the cutting board on the counter. They were both mounded high with chunks of salmon. The pieces were a dark red, and the skin was a silver gray. A gray short-haired dog walked into the room, his nails clicking on the floor. Edith hissed at him twice and he lowered his head and backed out of the doorway.

Alfred looked at me. His eyes were clearing and the sleep tracks had faded from his face.

I said, "So what are you doing these days?" and took another sip. I breathed in the coffee aroma. I waited out the pause. When I first met him I always tried to rush his replies. I thought he hadn't heard me or I thought he didn't understand, but like a lot of Native guys he likes the pauses. The ball's in his court and he knows it. He also knows it drives me crazy.

He drew it out until he could see that I was almost going to repeat myself and he spoke. "Aw, I'm fishing with my uncle, out past the cape. He's got a little boat. Not much but, you know, we catch enough to eat and to sell some. . . ."

He nodded to the fish. His mother slapped him on the shoulder and moved around from behind him and took the cup out of his hand and put a glass of juice in it.

"He means he's trying to live like an Indian. He just doesn't say it. He thinks there's something wrong with it."

Alfred rolled his eyes and drank the juice.

"Listen, Alfred, I've got to find Steven Mathews. Can you tell me anything?"

He shook his head and took a long drink of his juice. "He bought a place out on the edge of Angoon. He made a big splash. He started coming to all the meetings and he started getting up and talking. Nobody knew who he was. He was talking about 'community,' about taking control of 'our' lands. Nobody knew who this guy was."

He let the pause speak.

"He even had what he called a potlatch. I don't know, he found a beached whale and he got all dewy-eyed about it. He got some of his buddies to fly up from the Lower 48 and he gave a bunch of stuff away. It was funny, really, because the old people just looked at each other and went, you know, 'What the heck?' But they went anyway. They didn't know what this guy was doing but he was giving some pretty good stuff out. There were these actresses beating drums and wearing buckskin shirts. The people from the village went and cleaned him out. It would have been a silly party, just a goof, but he came out wearing a shirt with a killer whale sewn on it."

He stopped and looked over at his mother pulling the glass jars out of the steaming pot. He sucked on the matchstick and shook his head. "That was no good. Killer whale's the clan crest of a lot of the people there. My uncle saw that and he smashed the radio he was going to take and spit on the pieces. Mathews shouldn't be wearing the killer whale. Mathews said that because he had a special affinity for the whales, he considered himself in the killer whale clan. This guy just didn't get it. He won't last long. One of my aunties got a boom box out of it but everybody made her break it and dump it on his beach."

Alfred was smiling at me as he continued. "Mathews claims to talk to the whales and the trees. But no one in Angoon ever heard of him."

"Do you know anything about him and Louise Root?"

Again the pause.

"Let me think about it." And he stopped. "I'm not saying I know anything or not. . . . It's early, man. Come back later on, maybe. I might remember something. Who knows?"

Even if Alfred Tom did know something, he most likely wouldn't say a word. And if he didn't, he wouldn't want me to know that either.

We both stood up and Mrs. Tom looked up at us, mystified perhaps as to why I wouldn't be staying to eat. I thanked her for the coffee. Alfred put on his slip-ons that were made from a pair of cut-down rubber boots and we went out to the porch. Across the street an old white man and a Tlingit kid were wiring some crab pots, and a truck rumbled by dragging its tailgate chain. On the porch a five-horse engine was fixed to the railing and there was a garbage can of water underneath it. Alfred reached under the porch and threw aside some bag buoys and a couple of empty plastic cans and pulled out an old army poncho wrapped with parachute cord. He handed it to me and our eyes met again.

"You gonna talk to that Steven Mathews guy? He knew her pretty good." He stood close to me and was not smiling. "You might think about being careful. Take this. It could rain." He smiled broadly, knowing that it was certainly going to rain.

I looked at him and this time I forced the pause.

He shrugged. He pulled his hair over his forehead and lifted up his T-shirt to scratch his stomach. "When white people argue about the land, it's always about money. Their corporate guys are slick. Hell, *our* corporate guys are slick, but in the end they don't care what happens to the workers or to the land as long as they see the money coming in. There isn't anything money can't fix, but everything stays broke."

He shivered and turned to go into the house and he spoke over his shoulder. "You find that dog, man? That's detective work. Let the mine stuff go."

The old man mending crab pots said something to the kid

and the boy leaned down and handed him a pair of pliers. The gray dog slunk down the street toward the ravens and the gulls who were still fighting over the garbage spilled on the sidewalk.

"I can't find the dog," I said, and Alfred smiled in a way that irritated me because I figured he knew already that the dog was dead.

SEVEN

THE STREET WAS quiet except for the hum of the generators in the freezing units, which I had long since stopped hearing. A light rain was starting to fall. Like the sound of the diesel generators, I had discounted it as any kind of weather at all. In Southeastern the rain becomes second nature, like your clothes. You get up and step outside and it's raining. That's it.

There were crows swarming around the overturned garbage can. They were taking short hops over a diaper and an empty orange juice can to get to the wet coffee filter that was spilled out with an orange peel: bright orange on the wet pavement. When I waded through them, the largest crow took the orange peel, hopped three times, and lumbered into an awkward flight around the corner and away.

As I eased down the ramp, Paul was standing out on the front strut of his airplane putting furniture wax on the outside of the windshield and toweling it off with a handful of paper towels so that the rain would bead up nicely in the propwash. Paul had come up from Utah and apparently he had some land there. Once a year he would fly down to camp on dry land. He loved the Beaver so much that he would rig it with wheels and fly it all the way to the grassy strip that sat above the orchard at his Utah place. He told me he would just set up a tent not more than a dozen yards away from its wings and camp. He would sit around the fire at night and sing like a cowboy to his horse. After about a week he would load all of his empties into the back section of the plane and fly the trip north.

He wore a flannel shirt with the sleeves rolled up. His waist was very narrow and he had the arms of a bodybuilder. He swung around as I made it down to the edge of the dock under the wing.

"Good morning, sunshine!" he said with the square-jawed good humor of a camp counselor. Paul hated me because he thought either that I had snitched him off to his girlfriend or that I was having sex with her, neither of which was strictly true. So I knew the "Good morning, sunshine" shit was his attempt at irony.

I had a high school friend who died in a plane crash when he was working on a trail crew for the Forest Service. I sat next to his bed down at the Seattle Burn Center and he told me about flying into the narrow pass when the clouds closed in and how the pilot tried to steer a compass course to the other side. He talked about the engine easing back slightly as the pilot considered banking and heading out and about the weird feathered ticking the prop seemed to make as they cut through the fog and then the treetops, bombing the floats, and the one loud crunch as the undercarriage of the plane was torn away and the mossy rocks at the top of the pass spun up in his face. The rest he didn't remember, except the quiet of the engine being off and the rumble of flames.

I got in the front seat of the DeHavilland Beaver and pulled on my shoulder and lap belts. Paul swung around the front of the plane on the struts under the prop. He climbed into the seat next to me and started pumping the levers to prime the huge radial engine with fuel.

Paul loved flying the Beaver the way most guys who fly them do. The Beaver is the flying tractor of the north. Almost all of the small communities are served by the old-style Canadian aircraft. They are loud, slow, and powered by a gigantic gas-sucking radial piston engine. The cockpit is spare and has an industrial feel with heavy metal levers on an ironlike dash. This plane has more in common with a piece of mining equipment than it does with modern aircraft.

It rattled awake and the blast of the engine swept the beads of rain flat against the windshield and then they dissolved. Paul took a roll of towels and used it as he would a sponge and wiped the inside of the windshield so he could see out. Then he threw it behind his seat and nodded to me.

"You heard the speech. Keep your belt on."

So much for the preflight. I guessed champagne and honeyed nuts were out of the question. We pulled into the channel as he sighted a likely slot past the trollers and skiffs coming into the dock. He nodded again at me, glancing at my seat belt, then gave the engine throttle. We jolted down the chop of the waves and the air blared with the rattle and the fire of the pistons turning the prop. As the suction of the floats eased away from the water, he pulled back and we were flying on the bumpy air.

We curved the coastline, staying below the seven-hundred-foot ceiling of the clouds. As we moved inland, the ceiling rose and he began to navigate towards inland passes to take us through the passes of northern Baranof to Admiralty. I looked out the side window, trying to take deep, even breaths and running down everything I remembered reading about Mathews.

Steven Mathews had grown up in Connecticut. He claimed Native American heritage but was vague about the specifics. Apparently he went to private schools. He had gone to Dartmouth before he quit to go on the road and into the merchant marines. He was on the periphery of the Beat poets and claimed to have gotten drunk with Kerouac, Ginsberg, and Snyder at most of the bars in North Beach. He was a compartmentalized kind of person who had had several incarnations—as scholar, activist, and populist storyteller. He had run a small ranch in eastern Washington and tried to form a research institute for the development of "the ecological aesthetic for the twenty-first century." He had a following but he no longer wrote poetry. He wrote continually longer and longer technical position papers on the "democratic environmental left."

I liked his old poetry, but I guess I was in the minority, because the East Coast reviewers hated it. He had one poem about a yellow cat in his lover's garden being nose to nose with a snowshoe hare. I remember reading it once on a sunny afternoon, floating in a raft down the Tanana River from Fairbanks to Nenana. The poem had made so much sense, I read it once and drank a beer, then read it again and it was like remembering a vivid dream I had the night before. It was goofy and maybe a little bit loose, like a bad band playing a great song with lots of energy. It was just the thing for a float trip.

Now Mathews wrote pieces that joined science, spirituality, and poetics, but mostly they were political. He had that same cloying tone of an energetic politician who wants to help you make up your mind. My sister, the hotshot lawyer, had sent me copies of his new essays and I had put them on the stack of mail next to the phone. I liked to watch them sit for weeks and soften in the moisture like leaves on a compost pile.

We were starting into a 1,200 foot pass and the ceiling was staying fairly stable at 2,200. Occasionally the tops of the peaks came out of the cottony moisture and looked like jagged islands cropping up. I looked down and saw the coastline slide by beneath and the muskeg, dotted with stunted trees and ponds. I watched it give way to the steep forest and then the alpine. We hit an air pocket and fell a hundred feet. I gripped the sides of my leg. Paul sat up and put both hands on the yoke. He looked at my fists on my thighs and smiled. He leaned over to me and yelled above the engine noise, "We'll poke in here. It might get a little bumpy, but there's plenty of room to stop and back out." And he laughed that irritating laugh of someone in absolute charge of a scary situation.

Hannah was excited about Mathews moving to southeastern Alaska. She had sent me the stories about his buying out the rights to an old cabin and moving in. She had sent me a clipping from a Seattle paper. The headline read, ENVIRONMENTAL GURU HEADS FOR HERMITAGE IN ALASKA'S WILDERNESS. In the picture he stood flat-footed and straight, smiling into the camera lens with a kind of cock-eyed grin. The text had him quoting himself from his most recent book, which was called *Here and Now: The Ethics of the New Poverty*. Heady stuff about living off the bottom of the food chain. I didn't want to read it. There was something about the way he was standing in the picture that made me doubly not care what he was thinking.

Hannah was crazy about him. For a time I had the feeling that she might shave her head and follow him around. There was something about a man "confronting his power and shaping it into the nurturing foundation of creative play" that attracted her, but I had no fucking idea why.

The plane moved into the pass, and the ground seemed to come up fast enough underneath us that I was sucking my breath in and holding even more tightly to my thighs. Wisps of clouds were looped up the side of the pass looking like cotton strewn over a rug. The peaks were not visible but the shadows behind the clouds were dark and jagged. Paul smiled and gave me a thumbs-up sign like an insurance man does when he looks around your new patio. This is not confidence, this is a sales job. There was another air pocket and our wings pumped a little and flexed along the center of the plane. The engine changed pitch slightly and I decided to close my eyes. I would be there if we crashed. I didn't have to see everything leading up to it.

Mathews had liquidated his ranch in eastern Washington and moved to an old hunting cabin outside the village of Angoon. Alfred's family had come from Angoon. It was a village that held its heritage close. The people still told stories about the day the U.S. gunship leveled the town after a party of Tlingits sought reparation for the death of one of their own. The elders of Angoon were skeptical of development and placed a high value on their cultural identity— that was perhaps what had attracted Mathews to the village. But they had never sought his help.

My skin was sticky with fear as we skimmed over the

northern ridge of the pass. There was good visibility above us, but unfortunately the ground was not above us. Clouds and thin fog dotted our view of the ground. On the side window of the Beaver was a plexiglass air scoop and I turned it to breathe in a full hit of numbingly cold air as we crossed fog laden Chatham Strait. I took one deep breath and felt the oxygen hitting the blood vessels in my eyes and felt my stomach fill with cold, which was better than the iron filings that I thought were going to come spraying out before I touched the ground again. Paul tapped my knee.

"Cheated death again," he yelled above the drone. He pointed to the canal off Admiralty and the islands that spotted the entrance of the cove. He cut power and I felt my body lighten in my seat as we dropped down through the one clear section of air between the beach and the clouds.

By the time we landed in the cove I was pissed at the pilot, I was pissed at the weather, and I was pissed at the state of industrial America for making small-craft aviation a viable way to travel. I was also sick to my stomach.

Paul guided the plane slowly toward the beach and turned into the wind. He jumped out and unclipped a canoe paddle from the side of one of the floats and paddled the plane in slowly. Just as we backed into the rocky shore, he opened my door and stepped behind it.

"This is a freight run. I'm going to hop over to Angoon, Tenakee, then maybe back to Sitka. I've got to meet a company fare. I'll swing by in a couple of hours. If you need a pickup, just wave your arms on the beach. Better hop off the end of the float now. We've got a bad tide to be standing here talking."

I grabbed my pack and walked the float to the end, rolled up my rubber boots, then stepped into about six inches of water and up the steep beach. Paul waved and hurriedly shut my door, climbed in, and started the engine. He didn't want to bang the aluminum floats against the rocks.

Up under the canopy of the woods near the fringe of the rocks was a heavy bench made of beachcombed timbers. Sitting there was a man smoking a pipe and wearing a flannel shirt, straddling the bench with a double-bitted axe sunk in the wood between his legs. He had on leather gloves and was holding a twelve-inch flat file. As I came up the beach he was tapping the file on the legs of his canvas pants. He stared at me from under the brim of a ball cap. I wasn't expected and I wasn't sure what kind of reception this would be.

The plane blared and filled the anchorage with the explosive sound of its takeoff. The man watched the plane bounce on the surface of the water and then hop once in the air and fly. As the wings took hold and the floats came off the water, the engine eased back and soon it was quiet again.

He turned back to me and stared for half a second and then took off his right glove, tucked it under his arm, and held out his hand.

"Welcome. I'm afraid you've missed lunch but I've got some tea inside if you like. I'm Steven Mathews."

"I'm Cecil Younger. From Sitka."

"Was I expecting you, Mr. Younger? I'm not certain but I think I remember your name from somewhere."

I looked down at my boots and then over to the front door of the old cabin. "I don't know. It depends on who you talk to. My father was the Judge. My sister's an attorney—" He kept looking at me quizzically. "But probably you heard it from some rumors about a shooting."

He smiled. "Of course. The detective. Cecil Younger." He continued to smile at me in a disarming way. "I love rumors, Mr. Younger, don't you? I listen to every one that comes by me. I don't listen for—I don't know what you'd call it. I don't listen for historical accuracy, but I listen for what is being revealed about the teller. Rumors are like abstract art or graffiti—they give you the mood of a place. They give you an emotional background. I like what I've heard about you, Mr. Younger."

We walked up to the cabin. The smoke from his pipe swirled in the shadows cast by the trees. There was a pile of cut rounds surrounded by woodstove-sized pieces of wood. A deer hung in the woodshed and a teapot bubbled on the woodstove. He handed me a mug of tea. I was disoriented by the flight, cut loose from my preconceptions of what he was going to be like. I was kind of floating.

I sat on the doorstep and looked down at the hard flattened ground in front of the cabin. Mathews sat down beside me and sipped his own tea.

"I've got a pretty good idea about why you came. But can I say just one thing?"

I looked up at him and his eyes were shiny and somehow happy and serious at the same time.

"What you don't need, give up."

This was worse than being in debt to a cop. To have a witness start playing mind games with you before the first question was out of your mouth was not what they recommended in those private dick academies advertised in the back of the *Police Gazette*.

"Mr. Mathews, do you know Louise Root?"

He backed away from me and gave me an appraising look. He put his work glove on his right hand and rubbed his left as if it were injured.

"First, you can call me Steven, unless you are working for Global, and then you can call me long distance through a lawyer." His ancient eyes were not glittering or gay. "Are you bringing me a message from them, Mr. Younger?"

Since it took him the record time of a handshake and a cup of tea to start messing with my head, I decided to try to outrun him on this issue.

"I started out working for Louise Root. Then it was suggested that I stay out of it by the state of Alaska. Then I was bought, lock, stock, and barrel, by Global. I'm really not sure what I'm going to do, Mr. Mathews."

"Don't you have an obligation to the clients who pay you?"

"You mean like ethics? I don't know. If they had hired me to work on the criminal case, and I was defending them in court, I would protect them. I have no problem with that. But they are vague with me, so I guess I can be vague with them."

"While accepting their money?"

"It's their money that everyone in this whole state is spending. I'd have to go back to blankets and guns if I didn't use their money."

"We are collectively guilty and, so, collectively absolved? Is that it?"

"I've got their money and my own reasons. You don't have to help me even though I know you can."

"Who did you talk to at Global?"

"They came to me. Someone named Altman and a quiet guy in fancy loafers named Potts."

"Altman? Must be serious. If they brought Altman in, that

means it's gone beyond the regional level, and the people in Texas are making the decisions. He's got Potts on a mighty short leash. What did they tell you?"

"Not much."

"What did Louise tell you?"

"She didn't. She's dead, you know."

Steven Mathews set down his tea cup. His hand was trembling. He looked down at the cup. He took deep, even breaths.

"Are you sure? My God."

"Her throat was cut and she was dumped in the slough down in Ketchikan."

"She was my student at the Early Winters Institute in Washington. Do the police know who killed her?" He was intense. The pipe smoked like a steam engine.

"Not that I'm aware. Do you?"

"You have a flare for the dramatic, Mr. Younger." Mathews's voice was quavering and had a slightly irritated tone. He kept rubbing his left hand. He had the air of a man who didn't like surprises unless they were his. He also was a man who didn't like to acknowledge any lack of information.

"No. No, I don't know who killed her. The Global people are thugs, but murder . . . I mean, outright murder? It seems a little messy for them. Why murder someone when you have enough money to buy anything you want? Murder seems a little . . . final for a growing business."

"When was the last time you saw Louise Root?"

"She was here for just a few days . . . it could have been a week ago. In fact, she flew in with that same pilot you arrived with. She came up from Ketchikan." His voice trailed off. Then he looked at me squarely.

"Lou was damaged. She had a great burden of suffering and anger in her heart, but she . . . wouldn't have gotten mixed up in anything . . . vengeful. Would she?"

I was feeling bad about myself because this guy was asking more questions than I was.

"Tell me about her. Anything."

He looked at me and I could tell he was sizing up whether he could trust me or not. He was like most people when it came to murder. Even if it was stupid to do so, he was going to talk.

"Louise was—God—a remarkably bright person. I met her maybe seven years ago. She studied at the institute and she traveled. She was not one of my best students. But she was . . . ardent, you know? She was always taking me on for being too involved with the elite. She claimed that philosophy would never save the planet. That if anything was going to matter it had to come from working people. That's why she continued to work the logging and mining camps. It was sweet really. She didn't preach but she tried to live an ethical life and hoped that those who were interested would use her as a resource for change."

"Were you and she lovers?"

"Lovers? No, I don't think that would be accurate. I'm sure she was smitten with me." He lifted his gloved hands out flat in a kind of who-wouldn't-be? gesture. "But she never had the . . . courage to declare herself. It stayed high-minded, much to her frustration."

"Was she angry at you?"

"She was angry at everyone after the incident up at the mine."

"What did she tell you about that?" I asked.

"It was her birthday. There was some pretty rowdy drinking. Lou had been friendly with all of the men. She had a philosophy about it. She wanted these guys to know that feminists were funny and loose and could talk about sex. She thought of it as a subversive thing, almost as if she could win them to her point of view if she spoke their language. But apparently she was sending the wrong message. Or, excuse me, the men replaced her message with their own. Anyway, it ended badly. She was raped. The law couldn't do much for her. By the time they investigated, the perpetrators had their stories in place. And there was no physical evidence. The company didn't do anything. Rather, they did everything they could to make sure it didn't hit the press."

"Did Louise Root have anything to do with the mine closing down?"

"You mean did she cause it or anything like that? No. Global had that well enough in hand. The dikes were built on the cheap. It's really pretty common. Environmental protection is very expensive: the liners in the test areas and the substructure for the tailing pits, the warning devices, and all of the spill response capability. It's the cost of doing business these days. The stockholders say to spend the money. As long as you can manipulate the prices of your other holdings to cover it, everything's okay. The front office budgets for all the costs. But the on-the-ground guys resent the new rules. They really feel that the new regs are bullshit. Nothing's ever going to happen, right? Even if it does, this stuff won't really hurt. I mean, it's natural. So they cut back and it shows as pure profit. They bring the project in under cost. The head office knows what's going on but turns a blind eye. The on-site manager skims a little, the workers get a couple of weeks on the books when they're on vacation, and it's done. The regulatory agencies are too lazy or too scared to do anything more than fly over in airplanes and take an occasional public-relations walk-around tour.

"Anyway, apparently they got caught at Otter Creek with some substandard structures and they closed for an upgrade. It's all pretty hushed up but no one cares as long as they fix it."

"What did Louise have to do with the closure?"

"Nothing, as far as I know. She liked to walk around the site between lunch prep and dinner and she started to tell me what she'd seen of the construction operation but then the birthday party happened and that ended that. That's the reason Altman keeps Potts so close. They can't have him out running around."

"What do you mean?"

He looked at me in a curious way. "Potts. He's the one. He's the man who raped her. I thought you knew that. From what I've heard they either keep him on the slope or right by Altman's side."

The wind whipped around slightly and Mathews tapped his pipe against the corner of the cabin and then he dug his index finger into the mouth of the bowl and stirred the charred tobacco out.

"Louise and I talked about it when she was here. Potts covered it up and made sure it never embarrassed the company. I don't know much more than that. Louise and I never really talked about the specifics of that night. We only spoke about anger and healing."

I thought about Hannah wanting a gun, and I thought of Potts on the North Slope. "Are you sure it was Potts?"

"Rape is a hard thing for two men to sit here on the steps and discuss." Mathews's voice had the tired, patient quality of a man who has learned from years of experience how to communicate with his lessers. "I'm sure you know that and I won't try and rope you into any collective guilt or anything. She was hurt and, yes, angry. She told me that this man Potts had violated her. She loved her life and her cause. When that happened, it was an attack on everything she believed. She had always been funny and, I don't know, skeptical about men. But she was mostly straight, you know. She liked men, she liked the work they did, and she liked to work beside them. She liked their humor and their physicalness. She was at home in those camps. After what happened she soured."

"You said she was *mostly* straight?"

He shrugged his shoulders and lit his pipe. "I didn't pry," he muttered.

We sat on the steps and let the conversation die. A male merganser with an emerald green head and white wings was preening himself in the water twenty feet from shore. The wind blew through and the wood smoke whipped around us like dust. The trees bent and sighed. I knew I needed to get out of there and to Juneau so I could catch Hannah who, I figured, was most likely in Deadhorse by now, chasing after Altman and Potts.

All I could do then was wait for the plane. I spent several hours with Mathews doing chores. I split the wood that lay next to the chopping block. I stacked kindling by the small woodstove inside the tiny plywood cabin. Then I stacked larger pieces in the woodshed. Mathews hauled water from the beach trail that led to the estuary. He had a yoke and would hook the pails on each end and balance it across his shoulders. He made three trips and filled a small cistern outside the window near where a small sink looked out to the bay. He was still wearing his flannel shirt when he returned from the third trip, and after he emptied the pails he stripped it off and sat on the stump in his damp cotton T-shirt. I stood next to the shed and finished straightening the pile of wood. It was good work; the wood smelled sharply sweet where the strains of pitch had been severed and exposed to the air. The bulk of the woodpile was reassuring, even if it wasn't mine.

He looked over at me and then took the axe up again, put it between his legs, and started sharpening it with the flat file, in the way someone does who must be doing something useful when talking to a stranger.

"I remember Lou in the garden in the Methow Valley. It was a dazzlingly clear afternoon and she was digging. I could see her through the fence, a twelve-foot deer fence surrounding the vegetable garden. We had flowers around the edge of the vegetable patch and she was on her knees hoeing and moving the bucket next to her knees. She was wearing shorts, you know, and a thin shirt." He looked up at me and then down immediately, embarrassed. "Not that. Not that," and he smiled back down at his work. "She was just so perfect . . . I said her name. I don't know why. I just said it involuntarily and she turned and stood up. And the sun caught her just right, her hair across her neck and chest. She had a very—I don't know—lovely mouth. Standing there with damp black dirt on her knees, she smiled. Just standing there with a basket full of weeds and flowering peas."

He winced as he took a long stroke and he brought his glove up bloody. The axe had cut through the leather and the blood dripped down on his pant legs. "Damn, I keep doing this." He took off the glove and cupped his hand with the other. I offered to look at it for him but he waved me away with a gesture. But even the blood and the momentary pain didn't take him out of the memory of the garden. "She stood there and I just smiled like a dope. She went back to work. It was just that moment. She had some power. I'm not expressing myself well. But she had something that humbled me. I changed my ideas about wealth."

Just as his voice began to drift away I heard the plane swing low over the short ridge behind the cabin and make its approach for the landing. I shook his hand and headed for the beach. I was distracted, maybe because of the sudden shift I was making in my opinions about Mathews or maybe because I knew I had to get back on that airplane and head over the pass again.

It wasn't the same pilot. He had a light shiny shirt and snakeskin boots that I looked at almost rudely while I walked along the floats. His snakeskin boots were soggy and so were his pant legs. There have always been a lot of guys from the resource industries—oil and mining—and a lot of them wore cowboy boots, but not many made out of snakeskin, and I had never seen a pair get wet like that.

"Hard on the boots." I looked up at him and he had mirrored aviator glasses on so I could see myself squinting up at him. His hair was thinning and slicked to one side in the camouflaging curl of a balding Lothario. He was wearing a gold chain with a very large nugget dangling in the chest hairs.

"Heck yeah, darn it. When I swapped planes with that other fella . . . he . . . he . . . didn't tell me I was going to have to do a beach landing. I'm used to going from dock to dock, you know."

"Yeah, scheduling," I said. "More docks—that's what this country needs, a port in every storm and a dock in every bay."

I didn't know what the fuck I was talking about but I find this is a common thing for me before I get on a plane with a strange bush pilot. I figure if I'm friendly and try to make him laugh, he'll be less likely to kill us in a fiery crash.

The pilot looked over at Mathews, who'd followed me, and said, "The folks at the dock in Angoon said you had a bunch of freight in. Looked like copies of books or something. Got your picture on the outside of the box. I'm going to hop over there. I could give you a lift if you want."

Mathews was staring at the pilot looking puzzled but when I turned to him he patted his pockets down and tried to look in control. "Yes, I suppose that would be okay," he said and teetered out towards the float.

"Then, on the other hand." He stepped back off the float and onto the beach, looking up with a worried expression at the pilot.

"I think I'll save it for later. Thanks anyway."

"Suit yourself." The pilot waved and pushed the tail section off the shingle.

I climbed up through the front door and strapped myself into the front passenger's seat. The yoke was pulled back almost to my lap. The waxed cord whipping around the handles was bumping into my stomach. The pedals were near my feet. I never touch any of this stuff, knowing with a kind of certainty my mother taught me that if I touched things not meant for me they will most likely explode. I crammed myself into the seat, adjusting my headphones. The pilot got in and pulled himself up into the seat. On the side of his blue shirt I saw a long smear of bright blood. He slammed the door and pumped the controls. Then I smelled it, almost like the inside of a dirty refrigerator, but somehow heavier—salty.

The engine sputtered several times and caught, and the plane began lumbering away from the beach. I looked across the panel of the Beaver and on the airspeed indicator I saw smears—red—and fingerprints. I turned to look back to see Mathews but the plane taxied away from the beach and built speed quickly. Too quickly. The pilot wasn't testing the engine or getting into any kind of lineup. He was powering into the air. I pointed to the controls and yelled above the blare.

"You been transporting hunters? Looks like they got a little blood around."

He turned, first uncomprehending, then smiled. "Heck yeah, somebody got themselves a moose. I reckon it's not in season. They threw it in here in a hurry. I tried my darnedest to clean it up. You won't say anything about it? I could get in Dutch with the boss."

I spread my hands and yelled, "I don't give a shit. Not my moose, or my plane, for that matter."

I didn't know where anyone would have gotten a moose this time of year but I was not about to criticize this guy for a game violation while he was hurtling us toward the far end of a rocky beach at a ground speed of sixty miles per hour.

We were pounding down the water. He was leaning forward over the yoke as if his eyes were outdistancing his thoughts. Urgent. He was bouncing hard, and I saw that we were threading our way past some barely submerged rocks. His hands were gripped tight around the yoke. Mine were gripped tight to my thighs in professional courtesy.

"Boy, you must know this anchorage pretty good."

He didn't look at me. He was trying to horse the plane into the air. We didn't have the airspeed and we were rocking hard and bouncing onto the small waves. The inside of the plane sounded with each thump like the inside of a metal drum. I heard the fastening on the cargo net in the rear give way and the air seemed dense with the dirty refrigerator smell.

I put my hand on my seat belt buckle and turned around. I saw a blond head and shoulders lying on the floor of the plane. Blood was shimmering in an irritated pool away from the gash on his neck. It was Paul, the pilot who had dropped me off. His eyes were open and unblinking. His tongue was bitten in half.

We were two hundred feet from the shore and the floats were about to leave the water. I looked to my right. The water blurred by in a slur of gray-green. I opened the door and jumped.

I remember pushing off from the doorway and breaking past the currents of air. I was lying flat, stretching out awkwardly, holding my pack, reaching for distance like a swimmer's racing start. My shin hit a float strut and I spun, turning my head away from the direction the plane was going. When I hit the water, I had a flash of what a serious mistake I had made, because I had obviously landed on frozen concrete. I curled in a ball and rolled. Dazzling cerulean forms like tropical fish swam past my eyes while my body was turning into slushy broken meat that softened as I began to slow and then to sink.

EIGHT

I'VE ALWAYS BEEN afraid of dying, maybe more than most people. Even when I was a little kid I would make my mother check on me in the middle of the night just to make sure I wasn't dead yet. If she forgot, I would pad into her room to remind her. I was considering doing it now as cold seized every inch of my body, like glass grit being blown onto my skin. Floating, sinking. Somewhere a whine in the water. Slur and pauses of waves hitting my head. I clutched my pack and lay on my side. There was a wobbling gray sky, the green water, and I was nowhere on earth. My memory reeled.

Riverton, Wyoming. I was picked up by a crew of Lakota Indians off the oil rigs. The men had long braids down their backs and one of the women had a blue-and-red tattoo of a running horse. I heard the whine coming closer and some squall of commotion as my head hit something very hard. They told me they were smuggling weapons onto the Pine Ridge Reservation and I believed them. We danced in the redneck bars and when someone offered to fight we laughed our way out into the parking lots and drove away.

I was flying out of the water, a great thing both heavy and light, a long way from the earth. I woke up with my butt hanging out of a broken lawn chair somewhere on the banks of a slow-moving river. I had a searing headache but the sparkle off the water was like the sparkle off the gray water that day long ago when I jumped out of an airplane and died.

A magpie sat in a low branch of a cottonwood tree that bowed out over the river, watching, and the woman with the tattoo came out and handed me a Bloody Mary and some eggs wrapped in a tortilla. Her jewelry clicked lightly like water over small rocks. Her lips were red and warm. As she bent over to kiss me she held her wet hair away from her face. Then she went back into the kitchen to eat breakfast with her brothers and her husband, who were looking over maps of the Dakotas with all the back roads and the police stations marked in red. I had broken a tooth and I smelled dead fish lying on the bottom of an aluminum skiff. I saw her husband, the man from Pine Ridge, driving the boat and the sky was the same slate gray as it had been on the day I had died. But I was too late because I was always too late.

"You aren't dead. Just dreaming."

The stove was roaring like a jet engine. A young man was sitting, without his shirt on, next to the bed I was lying in. He had dark skin and straight black hair. The room smelled like boiled cabbage, gun oil, and orange tea. Sweat was beading down his chest. He was wearing a bandanna around his forehead and he was mopping his face with another.

"You must be crazy, huh?" He handed me a cup of tea. I struggled to sit up and held it in my hand, breathing in the steam of orange and cinnamon. I smiled at him, lay back down, and went to sleep.

Alfred Tom woke me. He said it was time to eat and he put a cheese sandwich in my hand. I opened my eyes and looked around. The cabin was small, maybe twelve feet by sixteen. The walls were plywood and the windows were small panes looking out to the bay. There were shells on the writing table and glasses filled with smooth stones. One eagle feather rested on the sill, a loon feather on the edge of the writing pad. The room was filled with the drowsy light of the kerosene lamp and my clothes hung from a drying rack above the stove.

"Are you feeling better?"

I looked up at him. He was sitting on a straight-backed chair mopping his forehead. My clothes were swinging in the heat that rippled above the stove. The loon feather on the writing pad rocked back and forth on the table. I think coming back to life begins in the dream that precedes it. Realizing I wasn't on the bank of a slow-moving river, I looked at him and for the first time I fully recognized him. I took a bite of the sandwich.

"Yeah, I'm warm. Thanks," I said as I tried to rub my eyes but my hand fell to my side.

"My cousin found you. He looked in your pack. He saw you were from Sitka and he called me. You're lucky. He was just fooling around, jigging for bait. Then he sees you floating in the water." He stood up and leaned over towards the door. "Okay I open this up?" he asked. "I'm about roasted." I nodded my head. He moved toward the door and opened it a crack. I zipped the sleeping bag down.

He sat again and spoke to me slowly. "You've been talking. Did you really see somebody dead? Are you sure?"

I thought about it. Paul was out there somewhere with his throat cut and the blood spreading onto a green blanket. Doggy was standing by and there were tourists on the boardwalk above Creek Street in Ketchikan. I hate it when people ask me if I'm sure.

"Yeah, I'm sure."

The light swung from the nail on the beam and the shadows in the cabin swayed drunkenly. I held my hand to my forehead, looking straight up at the ceiling.

"Mathews changed his mind and stayed on the beach. He must have seen something. Paul's dead. Can you call the police?"

Alfred Tom leaned down over me and looked closely at my eyes, trying to figure out if I was in this world or not. "The police already called you. That Doggy guy. Said you're supposed to go to Juneau from here. He will talk to you when you get there."

"Is he going to do something about the plane?"

Alfred Tom spread his hands in a helpless gesture. "I don't know. I told them what you were talking about in your sleep but it wasn't much."

"Did Doggy say anything about the plane?"

"No. Listen, Cecil, you can take it easy. Maybe it was a dream or something. Maybe you were wrong."

"I'm not. Mathews was there. The pilot said he had gotten some freight in. It was supposed to be . . . a short hop."

I lay back down and my head felt like it was spinning back into itself again. I leaned up on one elbow.

"Is Mathews back at his cabin?"

"No, but that doesn't mean much. He comes and goes a

lot. That's what my cousin says. He went over there and everything was okay. He said it didn't look like Mathews had packed for a trip."

"Didn't Doggy tell you anything?"

Alfred Tom moved over by the stove and closed down the back damper. He opened a package of cheese and cut off a slice, then wrapped it back up and put it in the cooler beside the door.

"Yeah he did. He said they got the guy who killed Louise."

I looked up at the beams and the swinging shadows. I thought of her lying on the dock with her throat cut and I began to lose my confidence that all of the plane ride wasn't a dream.

Alfred came over to the bed. "They have a detailed confession. He said to be sure I told you that. He said he had to talk to you, to fill you in."

"Who was it?"

Alfred looked out the window and he had a sour expression on his face as if the cheese had gone bad in midbite.

"Phil Dominic."

"No fucking way!"

He spread his hands again in that apologetic gesture as if it were simply too ridiculous to explain.

"That's what the man said."

When I had been with the Public Defender Agency in Juneau, it had acted virtually as in-house counsel for the Dominic family. The Dominic men had been in trouble most of their lives, drinking and fighting. But none of the Dominics were killers. Phil had come home from Vietnam and had fallen off the dock one night while he was drinking. He nearly drowned and, in the few minutes that his brain was deprived of oxygen, he became a visionary who could not be bothered with the mechanics of the real world. I could believe Phil Dominic was the legendary Kooshtaka—the Otter Man of the Tlingit legends—as he stood in the shadows on the streets of Juneau with burning eyes and matted hair. But I could not even imagine that he had killed Louise Root.

Alfred stood looking out the window staring. Then he spoke: "Doggy also asked where Hannah was." He turned back to me in the bed, and sat down on the stool. He lifted the sleeping bag and looked down at the bandage on my leg.

"He seemed real interested in that," Alfred said, as if talking to the bandage. "He wanted to know how she got Jake's handgun and if you had helped arrange that."

I felt my memory untangle itself and I took another bite of the sandwich. I didn't know anything about the gun. Jake had bought one for bear protection when he thought he was going to stock his freezer with steelhead and salmon. But I wasn't even sure if he still owned it.

Alfred picked up a newspaper off the desk, the *Juneau Empire*. "It's been in the paper already." And he flopped it in my lap.

The picture showed Phil Dominic in a belly band of chains with his wrists cuffed to his waist. He was in a prison jumpsuit, a state trooper leading him by the arm through the open courtroom door. Phil's eyes glared past the shoulder of his attorney and straight into the camera with the intensity of a wolf caught in a flashlight beam. His lawyer was Sy Brown.

I put down the paper and flexed my fingers into fists. "Could you radio Sy Brown and have him meet me at the plane? I have money for the flight. You wanna come?"

Alfred looked out the window, still chewing his cheese. "No, I don't think so. I've got stuff to do."

His cousin, who had been staying in his boat shop while I was in his cabin, ran me over to the float dock in Angoon the next morning. Alfred was taking the ferry back to Sitka that night.

My pack had dried out and I left it on the dock as I walked around and asked a few people if they had seen Steven Mathews. No one had, and no one seemed to care.

The sky was overcast and the harbor was calm as slate as I waited for the plane. A couple of kids played on their bikes and near the dock two trollers plowed into the chop out to Chatham Strait heading for the old cannery. A bufflehead paddled near the float, an awkward little black-and-white duck. He pushed ahead as the drone of the plane from Juneau blared into the harbor. A raven hopped up on the bull rail holding a potato skin in his beak. He did not move as the floats of the plane bumped against the dock and the pilot jumped out, threw a loop from the floats around the cleat, and slowed the plane to a stop. I asked the pilot if there was any news from Sitka about Paul and he shook his head, saying only, "Yeah, I heard he left town for a while."

I got in, strapped down, and closed my eyes for most of the smooth ride to Juneau.

Sy Brown was one of the best defense attorneys in the state and better now that he was sober. He didn't like me because he thought I was bad-mouthing him to my sister, whom he desperately wanted to have as a law partner. He wanted to get me to go to law school too, and was always giving me lectures on how to improve myself. I told him being a lawyer seemed to me like having homework every night of the year.

When I saw him at the float plane dock he was wearing a canvas duster–type raincoat, a broad-brimmed hat, and some odd-looking silver jewelry. He was nervously flattening his moustache against his upper lip as the plane cut power and glided into the dock. I waited until the pilot tied the plane to the dock and opened the door.

"I like the coat, Sy. Are we going to rob a stagecoach or something?"

"Yeah. Funny stuff, Younger. You look like a street person. Christ, you could at least order from a catalogue."

"Don't sweat it, Sy. I hear you got a new murder case."

He fussed with his silver bracelet and looked past my shoulder to the water in the channel. "Yeah, new case. Man, bad facts, though. This guy not only confesses, he does everything but go on *Good Morning America* with details about the murder. Jeez, I just don't see why I can't get something triable once in a while."

"Cheer up. Have you talked to Doggy?"

"Yeah. I talked to Doggy. He told me you're yammering about some missing pilot named Paul and a missing plane, but there is no plane missing, and Paul left for vacation down in Utah. He left this afternoon. The company gave him the time off as a bonus. He was getting burned out and was thinking about quitting. They gave him the trip south to keep him happy. Doggy said you had seen a plane with a body in it. You haven't been on some kind of tequila-and-blotter-acid excursion, have you?"

"I wish. I never told Doggy anything."

"Hey, I just got off the phone with him. He said you've got an appointment to talk."

"I bet Paul is burned out. And once he's down south I'll bet he has a change of heart and decides to stay there for a while. A long while."

"Why's that?"

"Because he's still a little miffed about having his fucking throat slashed."

"Get a grip, Younger."

"Did you really call Doggy?"

He took the deep breath of an exasperated parent. "I called him. He wasn't interested in talking to me. Well . . . that's not true. He asked me a heck of a lot of questions about you and your old girlfriend—Hannah?—She was a good-looking gal, if I remember. You really messed up when she dumped you, man. Anyway, he asked me all the old who-what-where shit. I thought he was writing a book, for Christ's sake, but at the end of it he just said the Sitka police would probably look into your complaints if you had any. And he said for you to get hold of him, that you could reach him or leave a message at the trooper detachment in town."

"Leave a message? He said I could leave a message? You sure?"

"Hey, get used to it. He doesn't love you like he once did."

"Just what kind of message am I supposed to leave him? 'Cecil Younger called and said that someone is slashing throats and you are apparently trying to cover it up. Please get back to him.'"

"Take it easy. I think maybe you're making too much of what you saw. I know what you think you saw, but maybe it was something else. You know, you've been under some stress and the mind can play funny tricks. It might even be something to do with being off alcohol. It could be biochemical. I had a lot of weird shit happen to me when I stopped drinking."

"You always have a lot of weird shit happening to you, Sy. This was not physiology. This was a guy dead in the back of a plane with his breathing impaired very much the way Louise Root's was."

"Yeah, well, big deal. You going to work on my case or what?"

"I'm probably a witness in this investigation, Sy. It could be messy if I go to work for you."

He led me by the arm up the ramp. "Exactly. That's why you're not going to charge me much money."

"What kind of work do you need on this case? Do your suits have to be picked up at the cleaners?"

"Jeez, you're touchy. I only did that once with you."

"What do you want?"

"Right after they pull the girl's body out of the slough it makes the news. Phil Dominic is down there visiting his aunt. I guess he's been drinking a while. He starts crying in a bar and telling everybody within earshot about this girl he threw in the water. They search his house and find some bloody clothes. Phil Dominic carries a sharp folding knife in a sheath on his belt. The sheath is there but the knife is gone. The aunt IDs the net and the machine parts the girl was tied with as stuff that had been lying around her yard. Then Doggy gets a pretty detailed statement from Phil. I haven't listened to the tapes, but the cops are calling it a complete confession. You know how that goes. My bet is he wasn't sober enough to know what the hell he was saying but I'm sure there's some bad shit on those interview tapes. I'm going to listen to them today but I want you to talk to him.

Try to bring me back some good news and I don't want to know the whole fucking truth. Just see if there is a factual defense that is even plausible: some alibi, or even some diminished-capacity angle. See if I should have him shrunk."

The rain splattered down as we walked up the ramp. There were a couple of guys standing under the shelter by the bus stop sharing a bottle of wine. Another was squatting near the hydrant smoking a cigarette. Sunday in the capital city was quiet.

Sy stopped me at the top of the ramp and turned me towards him. "You and I know Phil Dominic. If he killed this girl, there is something more to it than what the cops have. The facts, so far, stink. But I want to help him. Talk to me later." Then he turned and went up the hill to his office, his duster fluttering behind him.

The tangle of the mountain was backing Juneau into the water. The stores were mostly closed and if you listened hard you heard the streams running down the hillside. I could see the snow in the basin almost straight up from where we were standing. The alder trees were yellow up the avalanche chutes. The last of the salmonberries had long since rotted on the vines, and a couple of the men at the bus stop were wearing two sweatshirts and a sweater because they didn't have coats. At night black bears would ease out of the brambles and quietly snuffle the dumpsters behind the capitol building where some legislative aides dumped the remains of their takeout salmon fettucini.

Sy had given me some money for cab fare. I still had my pack with some cash, but I used a little of Sy's on coffee in the bohemian coffee shop. Teenage girls with asymmetrical haircuts and black urban-guerrilla outfits smoked cigarettes and talked about "film." Their boyfriends flicked their own hair back off their shoulders and assented to almost everything that was said. I read the posters and flagged a cab.

The jail gets prettier the more minimum-security prisoners there are. There were still some sweet williams in the concrete flower bed inside the first security fence. The other plants had been matted down by the rain, but somehow the sweet williams were standing. As I passed through the first gate there was an older white guy, in prison blues, on his knees, tucking the dirt up around the stem of a plant. He was patting it gently into place. Twenty feet away a guard in a shiny blue jacket was holding a bolt-action rifle with a scope. He was leaning against the pillar of the main door talking with a woman holding a brown file folder. I excused myself and eased behind them through the door. A guard shifted on his feet to let me go around. His leather utility belt creaked like an old saddle.

I had a little bit of a squabble getting in to see Brown's guy. It had been a while since I had been in jail, either as a resident or a visitor, so most of the guys on the shift didn't recognize me. They referred to procedures that had to be maintained, but no one was really sure what the procedures were for me and nobody was in a hurry to find out. I used to think this was sloppiness or bad management but now I'm sure it's intentional. They change the drill often enough to make it pointless to argue. Once they settle on a system they have to defend it.

Finally I was led to the interview room and the guard shut

the door with a heavy click. Since this was a legal matter, I would get to sit in the same room with the prisoner. It's called a contact visit. I wouldn't get hassled coming in or going out. But the prisoners are strip-searched after every contact visit.

I settled into the metal chair and waited. There was a count going on. Guards moved past the interview room and I could see them through the bulletproof glass. Iron doors slid on tracks, closing one by one, and the rhythmic drone of the voices came through the radio. "One four four clear. One four five . . . clear. Inside three . . . clear."

I always have to pee each time I get locked up. I was thinking about picking up the phone to ask to use the can but I knew that was not in the count procedure. So I sat. The sore on my leg ached and I absently started picking the scab, clearing my mind of anything. And waiting . . . waiting for the doors to open. This was the meditation of jail.

The doors stopped clattering shut and the handheld radios stopped squawking. The count was over. It was quiet in the hall and since my guy was in maximum segregation, I knew they had cleared the main hallway down the center in order to bring him to the interview room. He arrived a few moments later.

Phil stood in the window flanked by three guards. He was dressed in the red jumpsuit worn by men held in segregation. He was in leg irons, belly band, and manacles. One of the guards spoke into his radio and the door clicked. He pushed against it. The first guard walked in and asked me to stand. He looked in the tiny interview room and took in the details, making sure everything was bolted down. That over, he nodded to the others and they brought the prisoner in and uncuffed him from his belly band and chained him to the bar on the wall opposite my seat at the table. His eyes were cloudy. His hair was wet and he smelled faintly like soap. My guy smiled up at me and nodded. "I just got out of the shower and they told me you were here."

I remembered Phil but I didn't have all the paper on him. He looked thirty-five or so. He was a white man who had grown up in an extended family that included Filipinos, Indians, and blacks. He had long black hair. I knew he used his time in jail to wash his hair and he used to joke that it was the only time he really needed to clean up. He had a tattoo of a guitar on his right hand and a dagger on his left. His head bobbed slightly as he looked at me as if there were some rhythm running in his body. "Hey, Cecil."

I have my own protocol when interviewing murder clients. I tell them I don't want to know what happened. They should listen to the police interviews. They should read the reports before they tell anyone—anyone—what happened. I just want to know if there is anything I should look for.

Was there any witness who could say Phil was somewhere else when the killing happened? Was there any physical evidence he knew about that the police didn't have that might show someone else had done the killing? Anything but what had happened.

"Hey, Phil, what's going on?"

He peered up at me and smiled sadly. He looked up at the ceiling and was quiet.

I asked him again. "What's happening, Phil? They say you confessed to killing Louise Root. What'd you do that for?"

He looked at me and shook his head no.

I tried again. "Are there any witnesses who could testify that they saw you do this?"

He stretched his arms out in front of him as far as the cuffs would let him and shook his head. "I don't know. The fish were running. Maybe a gull," he said softly.

I waited. The hall outside was busy again with prisoners going up to the craft shop and down to the dorms. Talking and laughing echoed down the hard corridors.

I tried to smile casually as if we were talking about the weather or putting down a bet on a football game. "Do you understand what is going on? Do you know that you are in big trouble?"

He nodded his head and looked past me into the cream-colored wall. "I'm pretty sure there is no other physical evidence. I mean, there might be somebody out there, I just don't know. I was sitting in the bar and it was sunny outside. I don't know. I don't like it when I'm in the bar and it's sunny outside."

"You were down in Ketchikan?"

He nodded. "I was visiting my auntie. I was putting up wood for her at her house out in Ward Cove. She dropped me off downtown and I was supposed to meet my cousin after work. I saw a guy. He was walking with the girl. They were just coming out of the hotel. He looked good, you know. He looked like he had a good job. I don't know, maybe some yuppie thing. He was with this pretty girl. He looked like an asshole. That's all I can tell you. He was white, and he looked like an asshole. You know what I mean? It's just how he looked. He got into his taxicab and the girl was arguing with him maybe. The guy turned around and I could see him say something and the pretty girl stopped talking. I watched this from the bar, and I started to feel bad. I started to feel bad and then I just got pissed off. I don't know, he was making me mad. Him and his girl. How could he just talk and drive with this pretty woman, then make her feel bad? How could I be in this fucking bar with no more money and a fucking bartender who was going to stiff me for this drink and not run a tab that he knew I was good for? Fucking guy. I just kept thinking about that guy. His clean sweater and his taxicab. That could be me, I thought. But that made me even madder because, fuck, I know it can't be me. I mean, they'd find out. It wouldn't take long. I've had jobs and it never takes long. They always find out. I'm not like that guy. All the times I've tried, they always figure out I'm not like them. It's not that I'm a drunk. Most yuppies are drunks. I'm just . . . different. Hell, the animals know it: dogs, crows, the females know it faster than males. Females smell it. Like, what would I even say to that guy? His wife? I'd open my mouth and they'd know—they'd know. This makes me mad.

"The barkeep did just like I thought and eighty-sixed me and wouldn't run any kind of fucking tab. I think I got to get money. I go out the door and I see the guy stopped, looking at the flat tire on the taxicab. I mean, fuck, it's just a matter of time and they'd know. They're not going to talk to me. Even if I did go out and change that tire for them. They're going to look at me, just like that fucking kid that works for the bartender."

I held up my hand to stop him. "Listen, you don't have to tell me any more. You have to live with what you tell me now."

He looked at me again as if I had just appeared from a cloud and he seemed quizzical. "Yeah? I thought you wanted to know the truth?"

"There will be time enough for the truth. Just tell me a few things. What did she look like . . . the woman?"

He squinted up at me in surprise and pity as if I were just wandering in. "She looked just like her picture."

"Picture? You knew her from a picture?"

"Sure. The police showed it to me."

"When did they show it to you?"

"When they first came in."

"Did you ever talk to her?"

"I go out and I offer to change the tire on the cab. Maybe I'll get some money, but the cabby yells at me and the man and the girl walk away. She doesn't talk to me. I follow them. I'm mad at him. I don't know why really but he says he'll buy me a drink. The girl is crying and the guy goes into the liquor store and gets a fifth. He gives it to me. I don't remember too much after that. Just crazy shit, Cecil." Phil started to sob and the chains rattled as his chest heaved.

"Are you sure you killed her?"

"Fuck, Cecil, I was drunk. I mean, they say they got evidence. They say they got my shoes, and some blood on my clothes. I remember having my knife out. Now it's gone."

"Where'd they get your shoes and stuff?"

"They took them when I got arrested down in Ketchikan. They got them from my auntie's house."

"Somehow we were down by the creek under the docks. The salmon were running, there were dead fish all over the rocks. The fish were silver and the rocks were black. Everything was slick. I remember blood everywhere and the birds were talking. They were just screaming, man. Get out! Get out! Get out! I could hear them talking to me. The fish were dying. Blood in the water, on the rocks. I think I fell down on the rocks. My head hurt. Then this girl she wasn't moving. Everything else was moving, everything, man—the birds, the fish, the water, everything was moving except this girl. It scared me bad. I hid her up under the dock. I went home and got some stuff. I took her wallet. I don't know why. I lost it somewhere. I threw my knife in the water out by the mill. I came back. I put her in the creek at the deepest spot.

"Where was the guy?"

"I don't know. Cecil, really I don't. I just remember he made me mad. I hated him. But . . . I don't know if he was even under the dock. I don't remember under the dock too much. Blood and a hissing sound. Blood and the girl crying. And . . . my knife."

He was twisting his wrists in his restraints and tugging gently against the chains. His head bobbed down to his chest and the wings of raven black hair gently swayed against his face.

"You got any money here on the books, Phil?"

He looked halfway up but not straight into my eyes. "No. I mean, not much. Not enough for a lawyer. Enough for a month's rent or something. I had some money from the oil spill but that's gone now."

"Listen, I'll put some money on your books. I'll talk to Sy and I think we may work on some bail or something. Don't talk to anybody, okay?"

He looked up at me and shook his head. "What you think is going to happen, Cecil?" He was staring at me now and his eyes were wet, the tears tracking down. "You know I've fucked up a lot but nothing like this. What you think is going to happen?"

"I'll try and find out."

I lifted the phone on my side of the table and called the officer in the control station. I was ready to leave.

The electric bolts swung open with a sudden click that

made both of us jump. The guards gently unhooked Phil from the wall and stood him up. He tinkled softly as he tried to lift his manacles away from the chains to his belly band. Then he turned back into the room. "When you going to be back?"

"I don't know, Phil. I'm sorry, I just don't." I waved absentmindedly, already thinking about how badly I wanted out of that iron door. I could hear the belly-band chains clink lightly as he disappeared down the hallway.

My door opened finally, and I got through security and turned in my visitor's badge. I made it out past the two gates and through the corridor of galvanized fencing and razor wire. I waited for the bus that would take me back to town. The wind was cold but the sun was out. I knew they were doing the strip-search on my guy. Making him squat and cough to see if I had smuggled any drugs or weapons in to him. But he had asked for nothing, and I had given him nothing. It was hard for me to believe that he had killed Louise Root but my belief was useless to him. I wanted to talk to George Doggy.

I stamped my feet to keep warm. A heron flew overhead making its way to the slough, its head and throat tucked in and its large wings working the air with audible strokes. Off in the neighborhood I could hear rap music thumping behind a closed window. The wind was changing, and I could make out the faint smell of the mud flat. If Phil were going to lie to me he would have come up with something better. He would have spun something about self-defense or he would have blamed it directly on the mysterious other man. No, his story was so bad it had the definite heft of truth. If Phil Dominic were innocent I was going to open myself up to the possibility of a conspiracy and it felt like I was inviting some paranoid disassociative disorder. In my experience it was stupid to invest in conspiracy theories. Most people who espouse them are trying to sell you something. Usually it's political. And most of the time the facts that hold the theories together broaden out to encompass the known universe and the conspiracy becomes as distinct as background radiation. It's the cops. It's the Trilateral Commission. It's the hippies, the Republicans. It's everyone except me.

I was still pissed off about Phil having to squat and cough for the guys when I didn't even bring him an aspirin for his headache. Even for a guy with a high tolerance for ambiguity, I was beginning to get sick of being in this alone.

A kid from the Department of Corrections drove up to the bus stop and rolled down his window. He handed me a note. I was following this weird calliope music of facts around and I was hoping for one clue or maybe one piece of information I could get to hold still for one moment. I unfolded the note and it said, *Call your mother.*

NINE

MY MOTHER WAS the first person to tell me the earth was round. She said it had been discovered by women waiting for their husbands to return from sea. They would stand on the balconies of their houses, waiting and watching the horizon. When the ships first appeared, the flags would seem like tiny disturbances above the shimmer of the distant line. Then the masts became apparent. Then the hulls. And they would watch all afternoon as the ships came closer and closer, rising up over the hump of the earth until they could make out the striped shirts of the sailors in the rigging. They would strain to see if their husbands were standing on the deck. They would watch and say their Christian names under their breath as each face came into focus, as the long boats were lowered, as the lines came out from the bow, the anchor let go, and the chain rattled. The women would come down from their perches to go to the harbor to learn if they were widows.

My mother loved stories, but they all had that flavor. The elements were romance, longing, and death. She smoked cigarettes and sat in the window seat in our house that overlooked the bay out the road in Juneau. I watched too. Her voice would surround me like a quilt as the smoke drifted toward the open window. The horizon was too short to see the ships emerge into view, but there were skiffs zipping by, heaving into the short chop.

Of course, by the time I was a teenager I had blown off all of her stories as romantic nonsense. I recognized that she was drinking there on the window seat and I, being no fool, knew that what she was revealing was a projection of her own unhappiness. She had been laying a trip on me and calling it truth. I vowed that I would be committed to a higher form of information than that. The earth was round, and that was that. The widows' watch was simply a portrait of her own weakness. I was hip to her and during my adolescence I carried that dangerous secret around like a butterfly knife tucked in my boot.

I looked up at the walls of the house and walked around the backyard. The fiddlehead ferns had been thick in the flower beds and the grass on the furthest borders was tall enough to conceal a small child. I stumbled on an old horseshoe from a game we hadn't played in years. When I picked it up, its track was scoured in a damp yellow print into the dead roots of the grass. I flipped it toward where I thought the pit had been and heard a faint clank of metal striking metal. Then I walked around to the front of the house. I let myself in and went upstairs to the master bedroom where I heard the radio playing some subdued version of a Duke Ellington tune.

She was in her housedress, sitting by the bed, her hands folded in her lap, staring down at the quilt as if she were reading the texture of its surface. There was a cigarette burning in the ashtray, a book open on the bedside table, and a glass of water next to a bottle of pills under the lamp.

She looked up and said, "You are going to cooperate with George, Cecil. He was a good friend of your father's, you know."

"I know. But . . . George is not being too forthcoming with me, Ma. I don't know what's right in this."

She looked over at me past the smoke sucking out the window. "I don't know what the right thing is either, Cecil, but my guess is George is closer to it than you could be."

I let that drop and walked over to my father's closet. I fingered the thick wool jacket that still hung there. How long ago had he died? It was the first time I had been home since the funeral. The Judge had died in Las Vegas, but the funeral in Juneau had been written up in the Anchorage, Fairbanks, and even Seattle papers. There had been a strong complement of mourners, sycophants, and distant relatives. We had been overrun with casseroles that my mom froze, but, I suspect, never defrosted. In the following months she had gone on a Caribbean cruise with her sister and had set up the charitable committees that had been established with the trusts the Judge had left behind. But she was running out of distractions and she was back at the window seat looking at photo albums and reading proposals from the real estate firms that wanted the house.

For her it was only a few days ago.

"What should I do about his clothes, Cecil?" she said.

"Box them up. Give them to Uncle Jack, or give them to the sisters out the road. Or, if you want . . ."

"What I *want*," she snapped. "What I want . . . I don't want to do anything with these clothes." She looked up at me angrily. "They are all here. They hang in there like they want to come out, but I don't want them to come out. I don't want to touch them."

"I'll take care of them."

"No you won't! Just leave them."

She clenched her tiny hands into fists. She closed her eyes. "You just leave them. They'll be all right."

I remembered the big band music they used to play on our birthdays. The loopy trombone of Jack Teagarden and the fine curlicues of Benny Goodman. She would swing out away from the table and dance a brief step towards the cabinet where the supply of birthday candles was kept. He would sit on the porch and wait. She would ask my sister to turn off the lights and she would carry the cake out to the table where I would look up as if for the first time. Her face would glow, floating above the icing, the music, the smell of the wax hitting the chocolate, and that brief sour smell after the candles were blown out. And in the moment before the lights went on, she always whispered, "Don't tell your wish. Don't tell your wish." Year after year.

Now she sat by the bed, the house surrounding her like a storm cloud, the rain ticking on the windows, and the wind wheezing through the spruce trees. She wasn't ready for winter. She wasn't going to get ready.

My father had been dead for almost two years and although I didn't know for sure, I was betting that his briefcase and toolbox were still in the same inconvenient spot behind the door of the pantry, his coat on the peg above the stove. When I rounded the turn to the long driveway that had been the entrance to the Prohibition hunting lodge that later became our family home, I hadn't really been thinking about my father or the fact that he hadn't walked this drive in many months, but as the house came into view I had the sensation that the whole place had been wilted, however slightly, by grief. The lawn overran the borders and several shingles flopped out at odd angles near the gables overlooking the bay.

"Do you think we deserve everything we want?" my mother asked and her eyes were sparkling.

"Are you really asking? Or are you turning into a creepy old lady, like some Bette Davis character?"

She smiled up at me. "I knew I could count on you. You want something to eat?"

We walked down the narrow stairs to the landing and around the back corridor to the large old kitchen. The wooden cabinets were painted red and the cutting block in the middle of the room was worn and uneven from the years it had been used in cutting up the halibut and the deer the guests of the lodge used to bring in and hand over to the Chinese kitchen boys to clean. Mother walked around taking pans out of the lower shelves and clattering around the ancient gas stove. Soon the sizzle of olive oil rose up from a pan and I stood at the cutting block chopping onions.

George Doggy arrived as if by some prearranged cue. He sat himself in the corner with a drink in his hand, watching me, cool and disinterested, but watching me.

"You quit drinking, didn't you?" He spoke up over the mouth of his highball glass. "After she left—"

"Christ," I said. "I'm giving it a try."

"You'd probably better go easy on the cussing if you really want to get Hannah back, don't you think?"

"Oh, fuck. How about one vice at a time?"

My mother wiped down the butcher block, and said in a breezy, irritating voice, "It most likely wouldn't hurt you."

"What, most likely, wouldn't hurt me?"

"I don't know—taking hold of yourself. You're a pretty decent guy when you're not acting like a little shit."

"Nice mouth. You eat with that mouth? You're not supposed to talk like that. You're supposed to coo and say things like, 'I'm sure it will all work out,' and shit like that."

She snickered. "It's you that's in love with a good Christian woman. Not me. Dump those onions in." She tapped the frying pan with a wooden spoon.

The onions hit the oil and softened as the sweet steam rose up around our heads and mixed with the wood-oil smell from the cabinets. I stood over the frying pan, shaking my hands. My eyes stung with memories of my childhood. My mother, who had seen me go off into these dreamy states before, pulled me back. She placed her hand between my shoulders and rubbed up and down, kneading the muscles along the spinal column.

"It's okay."

"Fuck it." My eyes were brimming with tears but I stayed next to the onions for cover. "I want to drink all the time. When I'm sober, I think I'm crazy, and when I'm just on the edge of a drunk, I feel sane."

Now Doggy was standing next to me too. "But you can't stay on that edge. Is that it?"

My mother began chopping venison backstrap and talked down into the cutting action of the knife.

Doggy reached into the pan, plucked out a piece of onion, and popped it into his mouth. "The Judge could keep that edge, if I get what you mean. He drank just enough, and very rarely to the kind of extreme that caused him or . . . us . . . any problem. I don't know, Cecil, it was a point of honor with him and it was kind of expected too. It was part of him."

"Yeah, I guess I'm just not as good a drunk as that," I said down into the steam.

My mother nudged me with her hip and said, "The Judge may have been a lot of things, but he wasn't a *sad* drunk."

Doggy took the bowl from my mother and dumped the venison in the pan. She went to the walk-in cooler and got a bottle of milk that her friend down the road had supplied her. She pulled open the flour drawer and held up the scoop. She looked up to me, then over to Doggy.

"I can't stand sad drunks, Cecil. Arrogant drunks, stupid drunks, even mean drunks are better. Because a sad one will be all of those things in turn."

I stood by the cutting block limply observing the onion and the venison bubbling in the gigantic pan. I stared and tried again to drift off into the dream state of my childhood. Again she yanked me back.

"Oh, Christ, don't sulk! You know, you might not be a sad drunk. You just might be a sad person. If you got a little happier, maybe you could drink."

Doggy put a hand on my shoulder and said, "Take a load off your mind, Cecil. Take a load off yourself. You could get happy and then . . . maybe you could have a drink." Doggy patted my shoulder with his heavy paw as if I were a Little Leaguer who had just struck out.

"Take it easy. This isn't going to last much longer."

"What do you mean?"

My mom bit her lower lip. "George is in a bind. You should feel good about being able to help him out."

"Feel good! I recently jumped out of a moving airplane and I was doing a hell of a lot better than the passenger in the baggage compartment who had his throat cut. Mom, this is more than just a little fucking bind."

159

She nodded her head absentmindedly and I could tell she was holding herself back from murmuring, "Yes, dear," but she did whisper out between clenched teeth, "Language . . . language."

Doggy leaned back and wiped the fog off the inside of the kitchen window. He stared at the overgrown garden. "The plane and the pilot who took you out to Steven Mathews's cabin are gone. I got a tip from the flight service that something was wrong. The company—a subsidiary of Global, by the way—said the aircraft has been decommissioned just this afternoon. It flew out south of Sitka but now it's supposed to be in a hangar in Craig. I've got some guys trying to get in to see it. They're getting stalled. They need a warrant and the magistrate is tied up in hearings."

"Doggy. You talk. You never tell me a goddamn thing."

"Come on, relax."

"Don't tell me to relax! You've been jerking me around from jump street. You know the whole story and you keep playing games. I'm not playing anymore."

Doggy looked at me carefully. He was wearing a crisp gray suit and his usual cop shoes.

"Cecil, I don't know what's going on. The governor's office started off wanting plausible deniability but they gave up too much.

"A few months ago the Otter Creek mine had to shut down. The tanks that held the cyanide solution for the gold process leaked. Global had so much trouble with the permits and with the Department of Environmental Conservation they wanted to keep it quiet. They couldn't just flush the tanks into the bay because of all the stink about the outfall going into the fresh water. So the company brought some of their empty tankers from Valdez down to draw off the solution and haul it to the processing center in Long Beach, California."

"Now wait a minute, Doggy. Oil tankers hauling hazardous waste? Can they do that?"

"Louise Root knew about it and told Mathews. They were squeezing the company for money for his foundation and now the company is scared that it's all out of control. They want all the information back. That's the stuff Hannah has. The papers in Louise Root's pack. All of that is firsthand stuff. It would print up nicely in the newspapers and it would hurt the company pretty bad. They want all the information that came through Root to Mathews tracked down and destroyed."

Doggy's eyes were tired. "Cecil, those boys have big problems. They include Hannah, and you, if you know where those papers are. Or what's in them. All they want is to take care of all their problems, and move on with business as usual."

"What do you care? You've got Phil Dominic in jail. You can try him and get a conviction."

Doggy stirred the ice in his drink. "Cecil, I'm sure I can get a conviction on Phil. But I'm telling you there's more. And that's all I can tell you right now."

"What do you want?"

"Don't go home for a while. Help me find Hannah. She needs protection too. She would be okay in the Sitka jail until I can get most of this sorted out."

"I'll protect her."

He smiled in a patronizing way and shook his head.

"Hannah was seen in Fairbanks heading north in a truck. I believe she flew up there today on the two o'clock. She was headed north towards Prudhoe. I know Hannah has some important pieces of evidence from Louise Root's pack and I know she has borrowed a gun. I just need to know what she is going to do."

His eyes held that flat affect of a cop who was working a body for clues. He was serious. "This is no time to try and redeem yourself, Cecil. This is real and it's dangerous for you, and for Hannah. I can do something about it, and I know you can't."

Doggy was tired. It wasn't around the eyes or in his face as much as it was in his posture. He looked like a man who had kept too many secrets for too long. He looked like he needed a shave.

I said, "What about the pilot, the one who flew off with Paul's body?"

"Right now I don't know much about him. But he must have some protection. I don't know how he gets around. He may have circled back and taken care of Mathews, who must have seen you jump out of the plane. But really, Cecil, I don't know. After he flew out of the cove that day . . ." He held his hands up and shrugged his shoulders. Then he sat down and went on.

"I don't know how it got this way. I'd like to blame it all on the politicians. But . . . I was there. I was with them all along."

He let out a sigh that seemed final. "You did the right thing not being a cop."

"I don't think I had much choice," I said.

He wasn't listening but had his head cocked to one side. I could hear the wind blustering against the window and rain coming in under the eaves. Doggy lifted his cup. His voice dipped into it, coming out with a slight echo.

"I had a choice. I remember the first time I told a woman

her son was dead. I could have got out then. I've done it a hundred times since. Her son was drunk, stole a car, and smashed into a retaining wall. There was nothing much to see. But when I told her, it was like she just popped. She cried. I never saw anyone cry like that. I stood there. I didn't know how to feel. I didn't know what to say. I mean, her kid had been drinking. If I had caught him I would have arrested him. Maybe he would have been alive, I don't know. But he was drunk. Then he was dead. I told her he had died, and I let her think it was all his fault."

I pushed his stool back against the wall of my father's house. Doggy leaned on the kitchen counter.

He said, "People think crime is like a puzzle and they always want me to put the pieces back together. But hell, Cecil. It's not a puzzle, it's an explosion. All I can do is pick up the pieces. I can never put them back together."

"The Commissioner and these Global guys, are they asking you to pick up the pieces before anyone else can get to them? Is that why you're in this?"

"I should have known when they wanted to do the meetings off the record. I didn't mind running backgrounds on their political opponents. Helping out here and there. It's part of the game that everybody plays. But when they stopped asking me to meetings, when they started to talk about 'proactive planning strategy,' I should have bailed out. I didn't need this."

"You could still bail."

"It wouldn't change anything. Not for you, and not for me. I'm in." He examined his knuckles. His hands shook slightly.

"How come you fucked up your life so bad?" he said suddenly.

"I don't know. Maybe I don't think it's so awfully fucked up."

He looked down again. "I know you probably don't want to hear this from me, but your father was a good man."

"Yeah, I know. Listen, are you all right? You're spooking me."

"I got you into something deep. I shouldn't have. This stuff . . . this 'plausible deniability' is chickenshit. But . . ." He took another breath to clear his head. And he looked at my mother. He stood up. "No one will tell me where the pilot is. No one. Nothing from my official channels and nothing from my sources. It's quiet as a rock. He flew out of the cove north of Angoon and from there . . . it's a blank. Now you've got to tell me where Hannah is. Please, Cecil, no one is telling me anything."

I looked at him closely and shook my head no.

He tossed his napkin down on his plate and walked from the house. I knew there would be a patrol car parked out past the driveway. The door shut. My mom looked at her plate.

She whispered to me, "I'm sorry, Cecil. He wanted me to help."

She reached over and turned on the radio. There was a staticky dance tune and then the news was on, with people arguing about why the herring were gathering near the shore and acting like they were going to spawn in the fall. The storm was still holding off the coast and it was making some people a little crazy.

TEN

MY MOTHER GAVE me a ride down the dark road to the
Juneau airport. I ate a sweet roll in the car and drank one
cup of coffee from her thermos. At six in the morning it was
forty-four degrees in the temperate rain forest of southeastern Alaska and seventeen below in Deadhorse, which
was experiencing a cold snap, compounding everyone's
feeling that the earth was out of kilter somehow. I boarded
the plane and dozed through the uniform world of carpeted
aisles and honeyed nuts as we jetted across rain forest, the
subarctic mudflat of Anchorage, then to the boreal forest
and near-desert of Fairbanks, and lastly down onto the
Arctic plain.

The stewardess opened the rear door of the plane once
the stairs had rolled across the runway to let us out. She
opened the door and then stepped back. The warm air
boiled out through the opening, and I walked out into the
afternoon twilight of the arctic.

I don't know what I'd been thinking. I had been to the
north slope of the Brooks range before but every time I am

amazed. I had flown twelve hundred miles north and although I had packed some warm clothes and was expecting the world to look different, nothing else in my life ever prepares me for it.

Looking away from the buildings, the earth is long and flat. Standing on the tarmac I had that sense of vertigo: my center of balance tipping out across the snow towards the sea ice. The cold air was needling my skin, and as I took a deep breath the hairs of my nose frosted.

I always expect to be standing on the edge of an abstractly quiet plain but there is the metallic grinding and coughing of machines, and yet the silence presses in with the smell of salt on the wind that blows off the Beaufort Sea. The sky and the sea and the ground are so similar that the horizon is ephemeral, like a dream you can't remember.

The footing was hard on the frozen dirt and there was a light dusting of snow as I walked across the parking lot to the Global airport office. The wind whipped up in short swirling devils around my ankles and then up to my waist. I opened the door of the first office I came to and the warm moist air rushed in on me inevitably followed by the smell of food and the tinge of coffee in the air. Quiet and warm, the air tastes like the air in any Ramada Inn or roadside resort in America. Beige carpets and windows looking out onto the Arctic industrial zone. Men in flannel shirts sitting with folded arms staring at the TVs. No one looked up or nodded and I walked back outside.

The light was thin like a smear of milk. Diesel fumes filled my nose and the sounds of trucks rumbled in the air. The extraction of fuel for the world. I thought of Altman and his broken-record lecture: All wealth comes from the ground.

All motion made by machines is trapped under the surface. It takes strong men to pump it to the surface, then get it to flow eight hundred miles to an ice-free port. The movement of cars and the production of inexpensive toys in China. The grandeur of our machines and the designs that they require.

The guy from the company spotted me right off. I walked out into the parking lot, into the exhaust of the idling pickups. He jumped out of one of the blue trucks with his glove off and his hand extended. He had white hair thinning on top and a soft white face. He was wearing loafers and a flannel shirt under an expensive nylon parka with a wolverine ruff.

"Cecil. Over here."

We had never met, but he was reaching for my bag and taking me by the arm as if I were a visiting relative.

"Hey, glad you made it in. There were some problems with the weather earlier on and a bunch of the guys didn't make it out for the shift change but it looks like it's going to go okay the rest of the day." He jutted his hand into mine as he opened the passenger side door of the crew cab. "Ed Walters from Global. Altman from the Anchorage office told me you were coming in and to give you whatever you need."

"Altman is just the picture of efficiency, isn't he?"

Ed looked back at me a little startled. He knew that I wasn't expecting to be met. My comeback was not computing. Public-relations types have a hard time processing irony right off the bat. Give the good ones enough time and they can work it into their act, but it takes even the good ones more than a handshake and a pickup at the airport.

Walters said, "Well, let's get you over to the crew house

and get you settled in and then we can grab something. You had lunch?"

Aside from pumping oil, the real business on the slope is eating. As much and as often as possible.

"No, I just ate breakfast two hours ago."

"Well, we can get something then. They start serving in a half hour and we can sit down and talk about where you want to go and I can see if we can round up who you need."

"Charlie Potts around? I'll need to talk to him."

"You bet. . . . Like I said, let's go get something to eat and sort of lay out a plan. Are you going to try and make it out on the evening flight?"

"I don't know yet. I guess it depends on how much I get done, and what Potts has to say."

I was not going to mention Hannah's name and wait to see if it turned up on anyone else's lips. Ed looked straight into his steering wheel. "Well, the weather has been iffy. You can stay as long as you like, of course, but you never know when it might close in and you could be here longer than you want," and he turned to look straight at me.

When a crime has been committed most suspects babble on and on trying to explain themselves and they almost always sound guilty as hell. Corporations always cooperate. Their representatives say they want to help you in any way they can, they'll bend over backwards to further your investigation, but they want to go through their attorneys. And all investigations involving corporations start with meeting your chauffeur. I was going to have to shake Ed if I wanted to see anything of use to either me or Doggy. That would have been easier if we were almost anywhere else in the world but on the edge of the Beaufort Sea in the northern Disneyland of

Corporate North America. It wasn't the best place to go by foot. In fact you wouldn't call more attention to yourself if you set your clothes on fire. More people walk in L.A. than on the slope.

We drove into the main part of Deadhorse, which is where the smaller supply companies have their shops and offices. It's mostly a collection of iron sheds and insulated trailers piled together on small leased lots. Machine parts and pressurized tanks. It looks like any supply spot in the oil patch, anywhere in the world. We drove out the bumpy road along the long flat plain to the security checkin. We were technically on state land, but the company security looked our IDs over and they gave the truck the once-over for contraband and weapons.

Prudhoe Bay. A whining jet and the smell of diesel. Tire tracks frozen for months in the mud. The long horizon and the sun low in the hazy air. The strange combination of gas and sea smell. Long rows of trucks always left running. Exhaust. The bumpy gravel roads, cracked windshields. The smallest car is a King Cab pickup.

In the distance, the gas flares blow a bubble of light. The flames top the towers, others plume in long rows like birthday candles. A cap of natural gas sits on top of the oil in the ground and sometimes the gas surges up through the wells and the flares burn it off. The larger flares send one large flame that twists and curls like a flag on a windy day. Their light blusters across the flat ground casting weird, uneven shadows.

The drill rigs are marvels of halogen lights, piping, gauges, steel tanks, all wound around themselves, hunched over the beating heart of the iron being twisted into the ground. There are pump stations and gas plants and supply depots and corporate headquarters, all on the icy gravel road system across the tundra. Just like the one Ed and I were bumping along.

The truck stopped at the headquarters complex. When he opened the door, Ed ducked his head away from the steam pouring out through the doorjamb and we walked through the double doors into the boot room. We took off our outside shoes and put on some rubber slippers the company provided so there would be no oil tracked into the living environment. We pushed on through the inner doors and stepped into the headquarters. There was piped-in music and the hush of soft shoes on carpeting. There were women walking past with file folders and guys in blue canvas jumpsuits lounging on leather couches watching a TV. From the kitchen nearby came the faint clatter of dishes and the hissing of water being run.

"Hold on," Ed said and stopped so abruptly that I bumped into his back. "I'll make sure we got you signed in and then we'll grab something to eat." And he disappeared behind the security booth in back of us, where a couple of guys in uniform stood watch. One was talking into a hand-held radio. I shuffled around for a while making patterns in the shag of the carpet with the toe of my slip-on and then went to the lounge next to the kitchen.

It was meant to look like the living room in the Cart-wrights' Ponderosa . . . but industrial strength. It boasted a huge fireplace that had what looked like a woodstove but was really a forced-air oil heater. The furniture was leather and canvas and the tables rough-hewn pine. Four guys ate hot fudge sundaes and talked about playing golf when they arrived home the next week. They were wearing brown jumpsuits and one had an insulated vest on even though it must have been seventy degrees Fahrenheit inside.

I strolled on into the kitchen and past the steam table where the day cooks were setting out dinner. There were crab legs and prime rib, hot potato salad and hush puppies, creamed corn, steamed cabbage and cheese, red snapper in butter sauce and rice, carrot salad and green salad, doughnuts and pies. Soft ice cream machines and tubs of chocolate sauce. All the food glimmered behind the sneeze guard. It was surreal, like the first time I skinned a deer and saw how the fat shimmered against the meat, and I had reached out and touched it, feeling it with my fingertips, knowing what it was but not believing it was real.

"Hey, are we in luck or what?" Ed came up from behind. "We can eat and Charlie Potts is up here right now. The guys at the center flagged him down and he said he can come to the meeting room just after we get something to eat."

"I guess I'm okay. I don't really need anything to eat right now."

Ed glanced over at the steam table and then ran a hand down the front of his shirt and looked at the crab legs as he spoke.

"I . . . hope you don't mind but I'd really like to grab a little something. Like I say, he won't be ready for a bit."

He was picking up a tray and I told him it was okay, I'd just take a look outside and then come on in and grab a cup of coffee—was that all right?

Ed was stumped. I'm not sure he knew what to do with someone who refused a meal. He was torn between his two desires but he would succumb to the most urgent one.

"Go on, take a look around. Just pay attention to the

safety signs and the security areas. Oh, and here, let me give you your badge before I forget."

I walked back through the kitchen as Ed moved toward the line. I stepped out on the loading dock for the kitchen and saw something move away into the sharp line where the darkness had fallen just beyond the garbage area.

The Arctic foxes ease silently out of shadow and snow drawn by the promise of food. The men are told not to feed them but they do. Foxes dart around the back doors of the kitchens across to the waste bins where some of the most calorie-rich waste imaginable is stored, waiting to be incinerated. Beef bones and the rinds of cantaloupes, hot chocolate scum and egg-yolk-encrusted fried potatoes, the hearts of lettuce heads, and hundred of pounds of coffee grounds. I spotted one. The fox's coat was turning white and its eyes were set close. They were dark as onyx and designed to suck up whatever light the arctic winter had. The fox scanned the lot. It scanned the sealed dumpster and its nose worried the air, searching for the source of that nagging warm smell of animal fat. The fox saw the bull cook and politely waited until he had set down the roasting pan in the corner surrounded by shadow.

The cook looked around out into the darkness and paused, listening to the thump of the machines and the slurry of the wind across the snow. He stepped back inside and the fox moved into the light briefly and then into shadow where the pan was full of fat from the prime rib and bread soaked in juices. It was strictly forbidden by the company to feed the foxes because the biologists knew that in the long run the animals would become dependent on the handouts and would not be able to make it in their world. But this bull cook and this fox were not creatures of the long run and they knew that it was in their natures to break the rules.

I turned back and walked through the kitchen. I grabbed a cup out of the stainless steel rack on the other side of the assembly-line dishwasher. The bull cook came back in and our eyes did not meet. I went to where Ed was sitting and reading the information that is laid out at every table detailing the dangers of heart disease in high-fat diets. He was shaking his head.

"Man oh man. Did you see this? Of course, I don't eat that much red meat. But I guess this stuff can sure build up in your system. You sure you don't want something? We got vegetables, fish, ice cream, anything you want."

I shook my head. He pitched another forkful of crab meat and prime rib into his mouth, dabbed his lips, and looked up past me with a hazy stare of confusion that was building to panic. I heard a scuffling sound.

One of the security guys was wrestling with a man who looked like he was dressed in golf clothes. He had on a peach-colored cardigan sweater, burgundy slacks, and white shoes. The guard was floundering around, trying to grab enough of the sweater material to force him to the floor. But the golfer pulled away from him, yelling loud enough that the boys by the TV looked up at him drowsily from their high-caloric stupor.

"You dog fuckers! You act like you got all the muscle in the world. This man wants to know about Charlie Potts. I'll tell him about Charlie Potts. If we're going to do this, then let's do it."

Ed murmured, "Jesus Christ. S'cuse me a second, will ya?"

He moved past me just as the security guard grabbed the man by the wrists and got him turned around, and the three of them went toward the door of the security booth. I was behind them, trying to move in closer, when he wrestled free for a moment and I saw his face clearly and he tried to speak but the steel core door swung in front of me and I heard them disappear behind it into the hiss of radio noises and doors swinging shut over the scene.

A few minutes passed. Ed came out and turned me toward the kitchen and clapped his hand on my back. "Just a little mishap. Nothing to worry about."

We looked back to Ed's plate where a cook was freshening his coffee and pouring me some next to a plate of fruit and vegetables that someone must have figured I needed.

"You have to understand, Mr. Younger, this whole area is a secure zone, and alcohol free. But sometimes," Ed sucked on his gums, "sometimes we get guys that can't stay away from the stuff and they can cause some problems. Around here . . . well . . . we are concerned about our people and about morale."

"Where is he now?"

Ed made a gesture with his hand, swerving it like a plane taking off.

"He's been sent to the health center. Most likely he'll be eighty-sixed from the slope until he goes through the alcohol program down in the Lower 48. Don't worry, he'll be back. He'll just lose out on the hire lists for a while and it will take him a bit of time."

We were standing by the door of the security corridor and Ed picked up a chocolate chip cookie from a basket by the security phone. I was shuffling from foot to foot.

"Well . . ." I finally exhaled, trying to be as casual as I could. "What do you think about my talking to Mr. Potts?"

"Hey, good idea. Let me ask Jerry." And he tapped on the glass.

"Hey, Jerry, is Charlie Potts still out in the conference room?"

Officer Jerry was in full rent-a-cop uniform and his expression was both pained and stony-faced, as if he were being given a lecture in front of the whole school. He did not look from one side to the other, nor did he refer to a sign-out sheet or clipboard. Or anything.

"No, I'm sorry, Mr. Walters. Mr. Potts said that he couldn't wait but he would try and meet up with you and Mr. Younger later, if you would just give him a call." He slid a yellow sticky note under the glass shield.

"Well, shoot." Ed emoted just enough with that "aw shucks" tone in his voice. "Well, I'm sure we can catch him after we look around at the facility. I bet we'll have time before your plane goes."

This tour was turning into a babysitting job. Altman had apparently not told Ed that I had met Potts at my house. So Ed was not worried about my seeing him by chance and recognizing him. But I could tell I wasn't going to get anything more interesting than the standard gee-whiz-ain't-the-twentieth-century-something! tour.

I asked Ed if I could find a desk and use a phone to make some calls back to my office in Sitka. Ed looked a little worried. But the tone in my voice suggested that it would be more trouble than it was worth to jack me around any more than necessary. He led me to a phone in a cubicle near the copy center. There was one door, a glass partition, and a window to the outside world. He sat me down and told me the codes to dial out for a credit-card call. He closed the door and sat down in the outer office, talking to one of the beefy white men who was walking by with a roll of blueprints. I dialed the main number for Global in Anchorage and obtained Ed's number on the slope. Then I called Ed's office which I assumed was just down the hall, hoping that whoever answered would not be familiar with top headquarters personnel as to recognize voices.

"Hello. Ed Walters' office."

"Yeah, this is Altman. Get Ed on the phone."

"I'm sorry, Mr. Altman, but Mr. Walters is with someone right now. Can I give him a message?" There was no recognition in the receptionist's voice.

"Yeah. You can tell him to talk to me right away. This is urgent. He needs to know about this. He has my number."

"I'll tell him right away."

I hung up. I held the phone to my ear and swiveled in the chair to look out the window at the gas flares across the tundra and watch Ed in the dark reflection. The bubble of gas light floated above the tundra like an industrial island. The darkness was easing in and the flares twisted, illuminating the vapor that poured from the vents. I focused on the reflection in the window. I could see behind me: a woman with an intense expression was talking to Ed. He shook his head several times, glanced at his watch, and looked back toward me. I was nodding and cradling the phone to my ear, all the while listening to the incessant mechanical voice asking me to hang up and place my call. The woman walked away, patting a message slip against her hip, but Ed stayed. I watched the light from the flares dance on the snow like the swirling play of leaves and waited a beat to dial Ed's number again.

"Yes, Mr. Walter's office."

"This is Altman. This shouldn't be coming down on you but I haven't heard from Walters and if I don't, it is going to have some serious consequences for me. And then for him. Tell him I don't care if he's got a full line failure and a total shutdown. He is to call me in the next five minutes."

Then I hung up. I must have sounded angry and odd enough that she wasn't going to take any chances. I watched as a convoy of security trucks drove up to the gate of the distant pump station and saw the little men of the floating city walk the fence perimeter with their flashlights bobbing. There in the reflection she had her mouth next to Ed's ear and he was nodding gravely. Again he glanced at his watch and frowned. He nodded and pointed at the back of my head and spoke rapidly to her. She gazed vaguely at me and nodded as he lectured. He walked away and she watched me like a spaniel on point. I waited a minute and then hung up the receiver, spun in my chair, and marched toward her.

"I just had an urgent call from Mr. Altman and something is up. I need to talk to Mr. Walters."

She only had enough time to say, "He's—"and I was out the door, waving impatiently, calling over my shoulder: "I'll just go down to his office and take my call there. Thanks."

I turned the corner, pressed the heavy bar that swung the door to the outside, and stepped out onto the Arctic.

The cold wind enfolded me as if I had jumped into an icy bath. I wasn't dressed for the weather. I ran around to the main entrance. In the boot room hung dozens of parkas on pegs and I took the largest one that did not have a name stenciled across the back. I slipped on my own romeos and found a white hard hat that said Department of Environmental Conservation above the brim.

Back outside I headed out across the road to a drill rig. I was not going anywhere in particular. I just had to get off Ed's tour and try to find Charlie Potts somewhere in this cushy little gulag—and maybe Hannah.

The drill rig was enclosed in a cloud of industrial noise: generators and compressors, hydraulic lifts and the metallic thrumming of trucks with portable shops built into them being backed into position. The actual drill core was exposed and men in coveralls were working on the heavy pipe coupling, wrapping chains around the shaft and lifting sections of pipe off a truck and onto a larger rack, positioning them near the hole.

Everything was antiseptic and tidy. There was no real sign of the Arctic tundra inside the rig. The floors were built up and some sections were poured concrete, others were plywood over the joists. Near the hole I could only see the narrow circle of earth with the thick rod of the pipe stem rammed down into it. The only sign of oil was the thin bleeding around the edge of the sleeve where the drilling mud bubbled up. It was like a surgical procedure; the only blood was at the tip of the knife. Everything else was cleaned up and sucked away. I felt a hand on my shoulder.

"We're going to move these rigs in here. Sorry, but can you back out of the way?"

"Yeah, no problem. Hey, have you seen Potts around? I've got some paperwork for him. He actually has some money coming."

The guy had earplugs in so he yelled back at me as if I were hard of hearing.

"Lucky bastard. I can't believe it. First the babes and now money. How can I get some of what he's got?"

"Babes?"

"Yeah, there was a woman around here looking for him just a while ago. She was fine. I think they went on down to his trailer." He smiled and looked down at the pipe above the wellhead and pumped his pelvis in a comic grind.

I said, "I was supposed to meet him at his place. Is anybody going that way?"

He glanced back over his shoulder at a kid standing next to the rig and jerked his thumb in his direction. "Yeah. Hank has to go back to the shop and get some of those fucking absorbent pads." He looked up at my hard hat. "Oh, sorry. I mean, we have them just in case, you know, we get an oil-pan leak on a generator and have to clean it up."

"Hey, don't worry about it. I just got to get this check to Potts."

"The kid will drop you. But hey, I wouldn't go knockin' if that trailer's rockin'." And again he made with the pelvic pump.

I waved and walked toward Hank, shouting, "Well, hell, he shouldn't be having any more fun than the rest of us. I'll just see if he needs any help."

In the truck Hank was listening to his headphones thump out wailing heavy-metal guitar riffs. We took off with a start. As we drove the mile and a half to the lease-lot trailer, several Global security trucks went past in both directions, bubble lights flashing. I assumed Ed was looking for me, but not in this truck with Hank.

He pulled up behind an iron shed where there were drums full of an unknown liquid and a turquoise trailer house with a plywood shed built onto the entrance. The structure looked like a discarded refrigerator lying on its side in the snow. There was one light on. I thanked Hank and he nodded a deaf acknowledgment in time to a riff as I swung the truck door shut.

The snow was dry. My romeos with my numb feet inside squeaked as I walked to the door. I took one mitten off and knocked. There was no answer and for some reason I stood to the side of the doorjamb and reached around for the next knock. I put my hand on the knob.

Once I stood in front of Bernini's *Ecstasy of Saint Theresa.* It is a monumental piece of polished marble that depicts an angel thrusting an arrow into the heart of the sainted nun. The stone is polished purely white, almost translucent at the edges. It rises into folds and feathers, an illusion of flight that ignores the bulk of quarried stone. But what captures you is the nun's face, which is grateful and ecstatic. Her head bent slightly back, she accepts the blessing of the angel's arrow. The inside of the trailer was almost as unexpected, and for the first few seconds my reaction was almost ecstatic until I realized I was witnessing something different.

The pipes had burst and arches of ice folded down from the ceiling, puddling onto the floor. The ice was crystalline and white, flowing into twisting patterns that traced the contour of the weakened linoleum. The chairs were turned over and the table was broken. On the edge nearest the door was a thin etching of red that whirled into the patterns and followed the flow—red that was liquid and bright, almost dancing into the pattern like a pinwheel. I stepped onto the ice and it cracked and the shattering instantly broke a web across the floor.

I followed the red as it moved into puddles and sheets. Red, as it pooled unfrozen on top of the ice . . . as it dripped from the man in tasseled shoes and lightweight parka who was lying propped in the back of the closet.

He had been shot in the head with a very large round. His skull was smashed and the skin of his face was distorted like a rubber mask stretched out of shape. His mouth was open in a snarling howl and there was nothing beautiful or grateful in his expression. His eyes were open and his teeth broken. The water from the ceiling continued to drip and ice caked around his shoulders and arms. One of his arms was bent back around his head and the other lay on the floor palm open. There was nothing that suggested angelic flight.

I didn't touch him. I squatted and looked closely above him and beneath him as far as I could and then back behind me to remember where I had walked and what I had disturbed.

Above him there were a few shirts pulled aside on their hangers. Snap-button western shirts and a pair of western dress pants. A golf cap that had RAM'S HILL across the front was on the floor. There was also a new-looking short-brimmed ivory western hat. It was sitting with the natural crease bent back against the inside of the band. The body was resting on a pile of suitcases and below it, near his slippers, were hundred-dollar bills. They were scattered in a semicircle at his feet like an offering and I counted thirteen of them. They lay partially on top of the ice with their ends curled up tightly as if straining to touch both ends together. They had been stripped off a roll.

The bed frame had been broken and the sheets had been pulled off and were wadded up in the closet. By the bed was an overstuffed chair and at the base of it was a pool of what looked to be vomit. The painting on the wall was crooked. It was a western print of an Indian hunter riding into a herd of buffalo.

There were empty file folders strewn everywhere like banana leaves. Some had file stickers and some were creased back. But one was laid out neatly on the table. The label across the top was hand-written in pencil and read "Steven Mathews—Accounts." The folder was empty but stuck to the outside, in a smear of red, was a canceled check from Potts Service Company made out to Steven Mathews in the amount of five thousand dollars.

By the time I made it back to the airstrip I was seriously shivering, for although my parka was keeping my upper body warm, my thin shoes and pants were not nearly heavy enough. Security trucks were turning the night red. I hunched down behind the door of an open generator shack and watched for the security trucks that were churning up the frozen gravel between the Global Patrol office and the main road system.

I didn't know where Hannah was but I hoped she was either headed south down the haul road or would be flying out tonight.

I tried to make out what was going on at the Global office but all that was apparent was slamming doors and lots of foot traffic. The airport was quiet except for a corporate jet resting on the runway and the ground crew pulling the fuel truck around for the commercial flight due within a half hour.

The picture of Charlie Potts back in the trailer haunted me, and the flickering of the gas flares made it all the worse in my hidden corner away from the light. Across the way at the truck depot drivers were backing in their rigs and I noticed one standing by his rig. The colder I got, the more I wanted to be him.

It was a beautiful truck, an almost China blue Kenworth. It looked like he had washed it that night, which would be a crazy thing for anyone to do on this end of the haul road, but he looked like a guy who would do it. He had on clean blue coveralls and soft leather gloves, gray cowboy boots, and a black ball cap without a logo on it. I tried to imagine the story my mother would tell about him. She would know he had a big metal lunch box and a one-gallon stainless steel thermos, a set of expensive tools in the back of the sleeper, with a lightly oiled rag that rested on top of the tray of wrenches. She would know he had once spanked his three-year-old boy for taking them out and playing with them on the washroom floor.

This guy was waiting for the loader to give him a number for the dock. He would take on the waste fuel and sludge and head down the haul road to Fairbanks. His truck would run perfectly for him the whole trip down. I knew he would listen for every fire in the cylinders. Listen for the whisper of the carbon building up on the valves. He would listen, but it wouldn't happen because he loved this machine.

I hid behind a dumpster, waiting for the last call on the flight to Anchorage so I could slip on quickly without having to talk to the security guys who were standing around looking for me. The trucker got his load, turned his rig around the corner away from the airport, and was gone. A trace of diesel and a flurry of light snow, then nothing.

The commercial flight landed. On the runway five people huddled and made their way toward the corporate jet. The two in front looked like the crew and the two on the end looked like security with their utility belts and holsters. They were holding a woman by the elbows. She appeared to be sobbing, her shoulders hunched and bobbing, her head bowed. As soon as she was aboard, the door was sealed.

There was just no stealthy way to do this. My poor old canvas day pack sat like a rotted plum where someone had plopped it on the stainless steel luggage chute. Two guards stood next to it. They were calling for boarding on the commercial flight and I was going to have to be on it. I walked out from the shelter of the doorway and nonchalantly took my first three steps when Ed came around the corner and saw me before I could use my secret powers of invisibility. He started toward me and then looked at the ground, stopped, and turned around, walking away fast. I trotted up behind him and took his arm.

"What can you tell me about what's going on?" I blurted over the whining jets.

He stared at me fixedly and I knew that he wanted to talk. He badly wanted to take a bath on me, but knew he wouldn't get very clean.

"The proper authorities have been notified, Mr. Younger. And I assure you that we want to cooperate with any official investigation that will progress from here. But for now, I've been directed to work through our in-house counsel down in Anchorage. I'm sure you understand."

"Of course."

Corporations always cooperate and they let their lawyers be the assholes. Poor people have to be assholes themselves so they usually spend more time in jail. But the game was over for Ed. His career potential was dimming as we spoke and I guess he knew it. I didn't know what to think.

I still thought Global was too slick and media wise to have a guy's head blown up. It was too messy. There was an edge to it that wasn't corporate and wasn't professional. The person who did this wasn't looking for a merit increase. This person took a personal interest in his or her work and liked it.

I walked across the parking lot and the snow creaked like the floorboards of a haunted house. The whine of the jet was an anxious whistle ballooning out into the Arctic night. Ed was walking toward his truck and the security guards stepped back very deliberately as I passed through the metal detector.

ELEVEN

THE GUY WHO met me at the Anchorage airport was not holding a sign with my name on it. He simply took me by the arm, saying he had been sent to pick me up. He seemed as large as two vending machines stacked on one another. There was no sense in arguing.

He led me to a burgundy American sedan that had darkened windows and sat me in the backseat with another representative of the Welcome Wagon. We didn't talk about the weather on the way into town. We didn't even talk sports. They just shifted in their seats like their holsters were getting uncomfortable.

I enjoy Anchorage. The whole place is like the strip development around a major airport. You can rent a room or buy gas on any corner. It was a great place to ride out the several boom-bust cycles the state had undergone. Gold, wars, earthquakes, oil, environmental disasters, everything was good for Anchorage. Except peace and stability. If things got too stable people would forget why they had to live there. Right now things were fat and the big build-out was over. Investors were interested in building a few buildings that didn't have wheels under the skirting.

The parks were in place and early in the morning moose still browsed the aspen leaves and sometimes worked their way through the midtown traffic to the reach slopes of the mountains. The car glided by a red log cabin that was rotting on its stone foundation next to the mobile massage parlor that was next to the new Vietnamese restaurant with the fountain on wheels in the parking lot. I wanted to stop for a spring roll but my request fell on deaf ears.

We stopped at the elegant hotel and office tower downtown. I knew we were downtown because we were across the street from the abandoned underground fuel-storage site. My escorts turned me over to another buffalo in an Italian suit and we stood in the elevator watching the numbers and trying to think of something clever to say.

I was led into a private dining room. Its decor was meant to evoke a captain's stateroom on a sailing vessel. There were copper plates and brass rimming the oak bar, and polished wooden beams like the keelson of a ship. Everything was substantial or meant to look so: the hemp rope whipping around the corner posts, the silverware and the heavy tiles on the floor, the soapstone bear, the Inuit spirit masks sitting on the window sills. Out the windows, Anchorage lay against the shadows of the Chugach Mountains like the little houses and hotels on a Monopoly board. I was distracted by airplanes circling the airfield like bugs, snow-fields in the distance, the larch yellowing on the edges of the valleys. The air seemed clear as gin, waiting for the long shadows and the beginning of winter.

I recognized him from his pictures in the paper. His

friends called him "the Commissioner" even though he no longer worked for the state. He had been the commissioner of commerce under one of the early governors. Before that he had worked for the justice department and for the Forest Service. He knew resources. In the last ten years he had worked so successfully as a lobbyist for the energy industry that the press referred to him as the third senator from the state of Alaska. He was said to have been a policy advisor to two presidents. And he made policy for the state.

The Commissioner had a green suit, and gray close-cropped hair. The muscles of his jaw were set tight. He stood up or actually half-pulled himself from his chair and motioned me to a leather captain's chair opposite. He was older than I was and had the look of a former college athlete who had aged gracefully into the low-impact sports. He sat down in the saddle-leather seat and looked out toward Cook Inlet. He was silent.

I looked down onto the street and saw a man in front of a church. He was dressed in two sets of baggy clothes and unlaced boots. I had seen him on other trips and knew he was working the corners for change and working the pay phones by sticking paper up the coin return and blocking it for half a day, and then pulling it out with a wire clothes hanger. By evening he would be looking for the homeless shelter or, if that was full, a warm vent on the street where he could pause between running his trap line of the downtown phones and dumpsters.

The Commissioner snapped out of his contemplation of the view and turned in his chair to speak to me.

"I took the liberty of ordering us some steak tartare and bourbon . . . neat. I hope that will be all right."

I nodded assent, and then quickly said, "Water will be fine."

He smiled. I'd been sized up like this before. It makes me feel like I should present my papers and show my teeth.

"I understand that you used to be an investigator for the public defender."

"Yes."

"Did you get disillusioned working for the poor, the oppressed, and the downtrodden?"

"No, I got fired."

He held my stare and his smile didn't break, which made me add, "Which you already knew."

Here he smiled. "You know, I used to be a public defender back in Denver. I worked my ass off for years. It was fun to feel the blood pump and to fight the government. It was especially nice since at the end of the day, when I had flexed my muscles against the system, it wasn't my ass they were leading away to jail."

I nodded and looked out the window. A large ship drifted over the shallow channel of Cook Inlet. There was a froth in the water and I looked carefully to see if it might be beluga whales. There were gulls over the surface disturbed by the wake, but no whales.

A man in a gray suit brought us our drinks in heavy cut-crystal glasses resting on a pewter tray rimmed with hemp. He set silver coasters on the walnut table, placed the drinks without a sound, and disappeared.

"Some of my idealism still remains, Mr. Younger. For, you see, I think the environmental movement is a class war. Almost everyone believes that money comes out of a mailbox. All you need is the right address and you can get a check. Money is coming dangerously close to becoming an abstraction in this country, Mr. Younger. Money is no more than a note on a huge debt. When that debt gets large enough the government owns us all and they can decide who gets mailboxes and who does not." He gestured toward the window where a large Air Force jet was making its approach out past the airport and the sun had disappeared over the distant peaks.

"But Alaska . . . has the real wealth." And he paused for the dramatic effect as we both watched the jet lower its landing gear. "Real wealth comes from the ground. The people who want to control the earth, the ones who say they are speaking as advocates for it, really want to protect their wealth, their investment, if you will, in this abstraction that the government calls money."

The steak tartare came. It was raw hamburger, egg, and spices and looked about as appetizing as an exit wound. He picked up his fork, and staring into the meat, he continued.

"Liberals like to talk about giving this 'money' to the poor, but they never really sacrifice their positions of power, do they? All of their images are that of aristocracy. They want their minions well fed and silent. The real revolution in this country is happening in the resource-producing states where the working man can get rich and make a life for himself that's based on substantive wealth: oil, gold, and gas. You've been to the oil patch. These are the free Americans."

He looked up at me with a small smear of raw egg yolk clinging to the side of his mouth. He saw me looking and he smiled, then daubed his heavy napkin against his chin.

"Mr. Younger, after the *Exxon Valdez* mess, we were never going to be caught so unaware. The environmental left has gone on the offensive. We needed to take precautions. The oil companies hired some legal operatives, men in your line of work, more or less. They had them do the usual: surveillance, trash searches looking for correspondence, infiltration of our opponents' offices. The usual nonsense that I'm sure you're familiar with. Well, the man who came to see you in Sitka and gave you the money—Mr. Altman—he shopped around and hired a man who was, you could say, independent. A serious mistake, this recruiting, and I'm afraid it is becoming a bigger problem than the one we started out with."

"I can appreciate that."

He set down his fork. "You've been around lawyers and the legal profession long enough to know there are many different kinds of hypocrites. Charlie Potts started off as a regular workingman. A good man. He probably could have worked his way up to anything that he wanted. But he wanted a shortcut. Hell, shortcuts are fine. I mean, some are just about efficiency and nobody has anything against that, but after a point it goes from efficiency to exploitation, and then to extortion. Potts wanted to stop working and to just collect the money based on what he wouldn't do. That is not acceptable."

He tapped his fork against the bottom of his plate, scoured out some more of the meat, and put it into his mouth. He noticed my untouched dinner and raised his eyebrows somewhat beseechingly. I nodded and he took my plate and added my dinner to his. I leaned back slightly and drank from my water glass.

"Potts was blackmailing Global?"

He smiled with a full mouth. Then awkwardly gulped. "Now, you know I can't talk about things I don't really know about. I've only heard vague rumors that come up this way. I don't really have that much to do with the slope anymore. But Potts was involved in that situation at the mine and I think before that he had some more information about plans and operations that he may have shared with that female cook."

He signaled to the waiter in the corner and made a gesture over his plate.

"All I was saying was, there is good money to be made by people who want to work from the ground up." He looked at me again and stopped chewing. "It might be something you would want to consider. We need a good Alaskan boy."

"Where is Hannah Elder?"

He leaned back and shook his head. "There are some people around here, Altman among them, who are worried about what this girl might say. As long as she doesn't have any documentation, I'm not all that concerned about what she says. About rape, or anything else. Life has always been rough out in these camps. There is no way around it. That girl—the cook—she knew that when she went out. She knew what she was doing and she had her own agenda of seduction. The mess that happened between her and Potts, that was nothing compared to what we have now. That rape allegation is just a minor public-relations matter. Something can be worked out."

He took a long and practiced sip on his drink. I raised my glass to my lips but the water seemed almost dusty.

He turned and looked out the window again and spoke toward the expanse of Cook Inlet. "I was thinking more of Mr. Steven Mathews. To my mind, he is the worst kind of hypocrite: a wealthy aristocrat who doesn't really want to get his hands dirty except for little showy projects. And poetry, for God's sake. Poetry's always been the distraction of the privileged, no matter how they beat their breasts about their friends in the 'working class.' And yet he wants to tell everybody in the world how to live. He believes in poverty. How many of his friends in the working class want to buy into that? The new poverty."

He set his fork aside and took a large swallow of the bourbon. I could smell it reach across the table to me.

"The girl had told Mathews all about the mine project, had given him some very critical paperwork. I don't know if it's authentic, you understand. Most likely she fabricated it. We thought you had it for a time and then we thought that Hannah Elder had it. Steven Mathews, as it turned out, had only a small piece of what we are looking for. But he still used them to his best advantage, the son of a bitch. The aesthetics of the new poverty . . . he was starting to gouge us for real money. We had to funnel the cash through Potts. It's the hypocrisy that bothers me most. It's not the money. The money doesn't matter that much, even the large amounts we had to siphon off for Potts and Mathews because . . ."

He leaned forward and placed his large hands out flat on the cream-colored cloth. They were the color of a scraped melon rind. He whispered and his breath was sweet and bitter with alcohol.

"Mathews doesn't hate wealth. He hates the disparity between rich and poor. Well"—he leaned so far forward that we were almost touching in an unwanted intimacy— "we can make up that difference for him, for you, and everyone in this whole primitive state. We can make them rich. You want a one-class society? Why not a rich one?" He leaned back. "What—five hundred thousand people in Alaska? We can do that. We can make them all rich. This is not some political baloney, Younger. We can do it," and he nodded to the waiter standing obediently in the corner to freshen his drink.

"Is there enough oil to do that?" I found myself asking, as the new drinks appeared.

"It can be done, yes, certainly. Oil, gas, water, hell—even sunlight. There will always be something, and there will always be a hand on the spigot. We can do it. But what we can't do is give up our position near that spigot, for without it"—he gestured around the room as if he were a huckster at a carnival and all this was his illusion—"without it, there is nothing."

He set his napkin down and pushed his plate away. "Which brings me back to Mr. Altman's big mistake and the problem I would like you to help me with." He furrowed his brow in a calculated gesture. "I think Altman underestimated you and that was part of his mistake. We should have come to you first."

He turned and gestured with his chin and a man standing in the doorway came forward and handed him a file folder. He started to look at it, then set it in his lap. He looked at me as if he were trying to use X-ray vision. Then he spoke.

"Two things. First, where is Mr. Steven Mathews?"

"I don't know. Last I knew he was standing on his beach and I was about to fly off with a cowboy and a dead body. I don't know where he is but my guess is there is someone on your payroll who does."

He dismissed this line of talk with a vague gesture, like shooing away a fly buzzing his nose. He set the folder onto the table. He opened it and a color photograph flopped out. It was an enlarged driver's license photo of the pilot in the snakeskin cowboy boots.

"Frankly, Altman's got us involved with someone he shouldn't have. We were told he was reliable but our information"—he shrugged—"was . . . incomplete."

"What, you didn't check his references? Who else has he killed for?"

He looked at me sternly, reproachfully. "His name is Eli Pick, and I don't know for a fact that he has hurt anyone. I don't know that with any certainty. Altman hired him to bring us Louise Root and . . . take care of the Mathews situation." He seemed to hold his breath slightly as if weighing the next. "Now he is 'off the screen' so to speak."

"Meaning he's not slashing the right throats?"

He rapped the heavy spoon on the tablecloth. "I don't know that he's cut any throats. I just know he was in the general vicinity and he is now not responding to our requests. He was supposed to be surveilling Hannah Elder. Instead we heard he was accused of disposing of some pilot. *He* claimed Mathews had killed the pilot."

"Why didn't you turn him over to the law then?"

"We didn't know what we were dealing with. We needed Eli Pick, and we needed the plane before we brought in the law. But Pick is gone. He flew to a remote part of the islands where we didn't have the . . . right people to handle the situation."

"You believe Mathews killed that pilot in the back of Pick's plane?"

"Right now, on the record, there is no pilot. There is just your raving to some Indian man in Angoon that was reported over an open channel of the radio waves. I'm like you, Mr. Younger. I'm a skeptic. I don't believe anything until the end of the day and everything is back in the barn and put away. Right now there is no dead pilot. All I know is there are more problems turning up, and Mathews and Pick are missing."

He took a drink from his glass and rattled the ice. "You see, it really comes from a silly misunderstanding. There . . . there was a meeting in Juneau. The highest state and corporate officials were at the meeting and the problem of Steven Mathews and his financial inducements came up. Someone, in what I'm sure was a joking manner, said—just, you know, talking more or less to himself—he said, 'Just take care of the bastard and put an end to it.' Well, someone may have taken the joke quite literally." He spread his hands in a helpless gesture, making it clear that whatever throat slashings had happened were only the result of a misunderstanding by a naive underling.

"Where is Hannah Elder?" I asked.

"She is not your concern. He is."

He gave me a computer printout describing Eli Pick. It had age, weight, and description, but nothing else.

"Global brought Mr. Pick in from Las Vegas. He is a pilot, qualified for helicopters and fixed wing. All the rest of his background is either faked or untraceable. None of his numbers—Social Security, driver's license, even date of birth—none of them match anything in any computer bank in the world."

"So?"

"We want you to bring him in."

"What?"

"We know you don't carry a gun. We know you aren't violent. We're not asking you to do anything illegal or even vaguely unethical. Just locate him and keep him in one place long enough so we can speak to him and perhaps have him transported down to Global's national office."

The way he said "national office" made me think of a long tunnel of light with New Age music playing.

"What makes you think I would do anything like that? I've seen a few too many corpses in the last several days."

"You've got shit for a reputation, Mr. Younger, but I think you can handle this simple errand."

I was searching for that perfect comeback that I knew I would think of days later; that concise phrase that would turn his arrogance to curdled milk and reflect the fifty thousand dollars my parents spent on my education. But the words jumped out unedited: "You can blow me."

He made a face as if he wanted to spit. Finally he laughed, and eased back in his chair. He smiled at me patiently like a mean gym coach watching a fat kid throw up from running too fast.

"I guess you need it to be put in terms of your own self-interest. Is that it? Okay, Cecil, you'll do it for Hannah Elder. Mr. Potts has died of gunshot wounds. Ms. Elder was on the slope looking for him. She had a gun. It's a sad thing when someone you love commits a terrible and unexpected crime. You've seen it before, haven't you, Cecil? Well Mr. Potts may have committed suicide or he may have been murdered. Global's security investigation will determine what goes to the coroner . . . and the D.A.'s office."

My stomach tightened and my brain felt like raw spiced meat. He leaned back in his chair and drummed the tablecloth with the tips of his fingers. He was watching me and smiling as he kept on.

"Of course, a lot will depend on the result of your assignment to locate Mr. Pick."

I reached across the table and started to grab him. Two hands the size of baseball mitts took me by the shoulder and eased me down. The man who had driven me from the airport and had been standing in the corner of the room smoothed the shoulders of my coat and signaled the waiter that I might like a drink.

"Just relax, pal. Have a drink. No one needs this kind of trouble."

The Commissioner chuckled as if my emotion were an unexpected entertainment. He pushed a glass of bourbon toward me and lightly tapped the rim of the glass.

"You're not the violent type, that's why we like you, Cecil. Find Mr. Pick. Make him stationary. Then Ms. Elder will not have to worry about . . . legal questions."

"Why not just have him arrested? Get your boy George Doggy to fetch him."

"George is a good man, a damn good cop. But we can't have Mr. Pick in the system. Lawyers and defense investigators would be too complex. Find Pick and this will all clear up."

He stood up and shook my hand, making it clear that I was to go. He lowered his voice for a friendly goodbye. "Then we can get back to work. Get our hands a little dirty but feel good after a hard day. What do you say? Thanks for coming by."

The storm was moving slowly onto shore. The airports in Southeastern can shut down for days during storms, white sheets of rain and sometimes breakers spitting across the runway. On the last few flights the big jets would rattle and dip in the air currents, swerving past the mountains to try their approaches as the pilots decided on the safety of the landings.

What the Commissioner had said worried me. I needed to get from Anchorage down the coast to Sitka. Doggy was in Sitka and there were thugs who wanted to work out on me in Anchorage. But even if I was earning miles toward my frequent-flyer award, I still didn't want to get on that plane.

The storm was miles to the south so our takeoff from Anchorage was smooth. I waited until we had climbed through ten thousand feet, and the flight attendant had fed and watered us, and then I pushed my seat back and slept. I dreamed about mountains speeding beneath me, the ice and stone, the scrubby plants clinging to the rock ledges in the alpine. I saw Saint Theresa and Hannah flying beneath the plane, their white robes fluttering like curtains. Hannah had a nosebleed and was turning her face toward me when her skin turned gray as the shadow of a wing passed over. I woke up with a start.

Eli Pick was in the seat beside me.

"Good morning, sunshine," he said in a nasal western twang, and I remembered Paul saying the same thing to me the day he died. "I know how you feel, partner. Sometimes I think the only sleep I ever get is on these damn planes."

His head was right next to mine, so that his face filled my sight. He was not as scary as I had come to remember him. He was pudgy and older than the image I had carried around from the day I jumped out of the plane. Sitting here he looked small. His skin was tightly drawn over his skull. He had thinning hair and a bad haircut so his ears looked big. His mouth was stuffed with teeth, and his lips stretched around them in a goofy kind of grin. He looked more like a guy who marries people in Las Vegas than he did a professional hit man.

His breath was warm in my face and he spoke affably. "Hey, you awake there, bud? You must have had some night. Hell, I know I have." And he leaned back in his seat.

Hannah drifted off below the cloud cover.

He looked at me with concern. "I just want to say I'm sorry about that deal on the float plane, Cecil. Heck, son, you didn't give a guy a chance to explain."

"Yeah, I would have liked to hang around for that explanation. I could tell Paul liked it."

He lowered his voice and ducked his head in as if he were letting me in on a great deal.

"Now come on, Cecil, I know it looks bad. But heck, things get so complicated." He let out a sigh, leaned back a little, and tugged on my elbow, then went on, "Holy cow, you folks spend a lot of time in the air around here. I don't think I've flown so much since I was in the service."

I nodded. He looked at me a little peevishly.

"Now don't get sulky," he said. "I'm going to tell you about it. See, I've been flying around so much, I didn't remember all the pilots I'd flown with. Well, this Paul he remembered me. He remembered me from a time I flew into Ketchikan with a guy. That was bad enough, but then he started putting me together with this Mathews fella and that girl. . . ."

"Well, it gets complicated, Cecil. I bet you understand. One thing just kind of leads to another."

"The boys in Anchorage want you back." I spoke to the back of the seat in front of me. "They say you're out of control and killing people. You're an embarrassment to them."

He leaned forward again so that I could smell the peppermint Life Saver on his breath. "Now don't you believe them, Cecil. I know I can talk to you. We're in the same line of work. Those boys in Anchorage are a bunch of pussies. I work for Altman. He hired me to take care of some things for him and I'm doing it. All that stuff about me being some kind of renegade and killing people to embarrass them is a load of BS. I call those boys every day and tell 'em what I'm up to. They got no problem with my game plan. It's the bigwigs that get excited. Nothing makes them pee their pants like ending up in the newspapers. I told 'em, jeepers creepers, if you're going to make an omelet you got to break some eggs. But they want to tell everybody it's my fault so their little white hinders are covered if this thing makes the papers."

He reached over and patted me on the shoulder.

"No," he said, "it's your old girlfriend who's causing most of this trouble. I tell ya, she's one pissed-off little gal. I don't think I've ever seen anything like it."

"Hannah? What are you talking about?"

"She's some woman. Good with a pistol. Boy, that birthday party really pissed her off. Course, I guess she's mad about the boys banging her girlfriend and I can understand that to a point. But she's about to fall apart, you know? I think she may be getting a little wacky. Too bad, too. She looks pretty darn good. I wouldn't mind getting to know her better myself. I bet she's kind of kinky, huh?"

He shook his head and smiled at me sheepishly.

"Where is she now?" I said.

"Beats me." He wiggled his brow like a ventriloquist's dummy. "The company people had her, but let her go. I'm guessing she's on her way to see you." And he elbowed me in the ribs. "You hero."

He settled in his seat and chuckled. The plane shifted and we started to hit air pockets of the low-pressure storm. The seats creaked, and once the cabin lights flickered. I listened to the groan of the engines increasing thrust. Pick looked away and turned back to me. He wasn't grinning.

"You tell Professor Mathews he better pay what he owes and get out of Dodge. He's jerked me around long enough. He can't hide so he's got to deliver. You see him, you tell him. Okay?"

He leaned over me and looked out the window as we broke through the gray-black clouds surrounding Juneau. The glittering lights of the tract houses by the glacier danced up through the rain. The plane lurched and ducked in the gusts. I clutched my knees. He leaned back and his stare drew my attention like a knife tip under the chin. His voice was low and flat.

"And Cecil. Don't fuck with me. This is business. This is something you don't understand."

We were rolling to the gate. He stood up and waved gaily at the flight attendant, who was scowling at him. He patted me on the shoulder again, ignoring her gesture to sit down.

"This is my stop. No need to get up. Hell, you should just take it easy. Spend some of that green Global money. Maybe stay on this plane, go to Mexico, getcha some of that fine Spanish pussy. Good luck and . . . hey, be careful."

He said this last in a hot whisper into my ear. Then he winked, reached up, and took his leather bag out of the overhead compartment and was the first one out the door when the flight attendant cracked the seal.

TWELVE

THE PLANE WAS delayed in Juneau and then circled Sitka because of rocks on the runway. I had been in three other airports but I didn't remember which ones. It was early morning by the time I passed the Pioneer Home for senior citizens and the old post office, and walked down toward the harbor on Katlian Street. I walked past the bar and the gun shop, the Chinese restaurant, and when I could hear the fish-processing plant, I saw my house and stopped. Hannah stood out in front.

Loyalty is the cup that holds my desire. That was what I told the guy I wanted tattooed on my ass. He stood over me holding the needle gun and smiled through his tufted gray beard. "You know, I can't do this if you've been drinking. I got a license. You come back later. I'll give you whatever you want."

That was years ago, and I never got a tattoo. It was that stick of the needle, the pain of putting something on permanently, that kept me away.

Hannah was hanging a plant from the hook that was the signpost in front of my door. She was wearing blue sweatpants and a lavender shirt with a finely drawn rockfish across the front. Her hair hung down her back and I watched her stretch up and lift the basket and then ease down. She brushed her palm across her head and moved the hair back away from her eyes. The gulls came up from the outfall by the fish plant and whirled over my house, making mewing two-toned calls. She looked up at the gulls and at my house, rocked back on her heels, and took a deep breath.

The compressors were blaring at the end of the block and a fuel truck was grinding its gears as the driver yelled, trying to ease around a stalled pickup on the narrow waterfront street. But still the gulls cut through like a fiddle tune. The sun was coming out: the air filled, the shadows darkened, and Hannah was standing in front of my house.

I picked up my bag. I didn't need the case. I didn't need any more bodies. The Judge was gone and maybe I could beg my way back into a real job, if I could just get untangled from this mess.

She turned and saw me. It wasn't a smile and it wasn't surprise, it was a focused attention that bore down on me.

"Cecil . . . Todd let me in. I brought him back here. I didn't think you'd mind."

"No, of course not."

She eased back into the doorway, not timid, scanning me closely.

"I'm in some trouble. I couldn't think of anything else. I came here." Hannah's voice had a quaver to it and she would not hold my gaze.

Todd came out of the door and handed each of us a cup of coffee. He shifted from foot to foot and started to clear his throat.

He spoke loudly as if he were worried that I had gone deaf

on my travels. "Hello, Cecil. Do you need any help with anything? Did you bring anything back with you? Anything in a crate or anything? Anything you need help with?"

I moved past Hannah and stood next to Todd.

"Buddy, I told you we can't get just any old dog from the pound. We need to think about this sort of thing. We need to consult the literature."

I vaguely remembered being in an airport with a gift shop where I had purchased an illustrated book of breeds. I took it out of my pack and slapped it to his chest. "Look this over while I get settled in and talk to Hannah."

He smiled at me and immediately opened the book. He slid his finger up the bridge of his nose and adjusted his glasses. He was looking at the book as if it were a menu and he hadn't eaten in weeks, and he walked back into the house.

There was a break in the weather and a rain squall was beginning to blow through. Hannah stood under the eaves of the house. She motioned with her chin and we moved inside.

Hannah was standing next to the stove upstairs by the time I lumbered up to the landing. She had her hands spread out in back of her and she bounced on the balls of her feet. On the end of the sofa that faced the seaward window Toddy was reading his book of dog breeds.

He looked intently at me and asked, "What do you think of the Newfoundland? It is supposed to be loyal and will pull helpless swimmers from the sea."

"Slobbery and dumb."

"How about a Staffordshire terrier? They are fierce and loyal."

"Mean and dumb."

He looked up at me and his glasses were steamed so he rolled his head in a squinty scanning motion. "Cecil, just what kind of dog do you think is smart?"

I was about to say something smart-assed and mean. Then I looked at him holding the book that was already wilting from his thumb flipping the pages and I stopped.

"Nelson was a smart dog." And I took his glasses off his head, wiped them with a dish towel, and put them back. He looked at me with a sad and beatific smile that made me almost hungry.

"Yes, he was, wasn't he?"

Hannah was smiling at Todd and she did not look at me. I watched her. A strand of her hair escaped her hair band and was touching her neck. I cleared my throat like a sixth grader getting ready to ask her to dance.

"Maybe we should go someplace. I think we've got some stuff to talk about."

She didn't look up but walked over to the stairway and took her coat. Then she went back to Todd and touched him on the shoulder. "We'll be back in a little bit." Todd looked up, his eyes rolling behind the thick lenses, and he smiled the half grin of a dreamer, then went back to his book.

Down on the street our footsteps sounded on the pavement as we walked toward the old post office. Hannah's shoulders were hunched and she walked two feet away from me with her hands jammed in her pockets. We both watched our feet.

"What do we have to talk about?" she asked her shoes.

"I was in Deadhorse. I saw Charlie Potts," I said.

Her shoulders relaxed. She stopped walking. She looked at me for the first time. "I didn't hurt him, Cecil. I found him that way."

We walked on. Next to the waterfront bar it was quiet with just the whispery sound of the kid sweeping out the back.

"I believe you."

"Why?"

"Because I want to."

We paused by the open door to another bar. Soft music and the clatter of glasses being set down in the aluminum sink. "We need to get out of town. It's either that or they take you into custody."

She ballooned out her cheeks and turned against the plate glass of the bar. Her breath fogged the window and she drew a heart on the fog with the tip of her finger. Her lips turned down into a sad grimace and she sputtered her words out.

"I wanted to do something to help her. She had come to me because she wanted to talk about what had happened to her up at the mine. She had been hurt so badly. She had hurt . . ." Hannah wiped the heart off the glass pane with the sleeve of her shirt and rested her head against the cold window.

"I didn't do anything to help her. I gave her some of the usual pap about patience and healing, about telling the truth. But it didn't do any good. When I saw her pulled from the bay down in Ketchikan, I knew it wasn't your fault, Cecil. I felt like it was mine."

Her cheek smeared across the glass, as her head laid flat against the pane.

"I got the pack and I read the papers and I couldn't do anything. When I realized that Potts was the man who had done that to her I swore I would make him admit it. I was going to get someone to accept responsibility. But when I walked into his trailer and saw him with his head blown off—oh Christ, Cecil, it scared me."

I pulled her away from the window and put both arms around her. Her shoulders trembled and her head pressed against my chin. I watched us in the reflection off the glass, blurred and rippled in the old pane.

She looked up at me, inches away. She was gulping the air for her words.

"I just wanted to help her. I wanted justice. I bent down, I touched his face. Some of his blood got on my finger. There was water dripping and his blood was freezing. I didn't want that. I didn't want that. When Alfred and I went up there we were just going to talk to him. We . . ."

"Alfred Tom?"

She nodded. "Alfred met me in Fairbanks. He had borrowed a truck and we drove the haul road. He loved her, that's what he said. He wanted to help me."

"What about after? How did you get back here?"

"After all that blood, I kind of lost it. I ran out of his trailer and just walked around. I was cold. I don't know, I walked for hours. Then there was a commotion and lots of security cars driving around. Somebody picked me up and took me to the plane. They flew me to Anchorage. They didn't say much, just an ugly guy who asked a lot of questions."

"Did he have fancy cowboy boots?"

She looked at me and nodded vaguely, like it was just dawning on her that I knew anything about this.

"Yes, he did. And he asked about you. And if I knew where Steven Mathews was."

"Do you?"

She rubbed the back of her neck and stretched. She turned toward me. "No, Cecil. I don't. When I met Alfred up in Fairbanks, he seemed to have talked to Mathews. I think he had talked to him just that day. But he didn't say where Mathews was."

"What about Alfred Tom? What happened to him?"

"We split up early. He dropped me at one of the pump stations and left me on my own. I had to ask around about how to find Potts. I think Alfred Tom must have found out about Potts and made it out of there. He must have driven back down the haul road."

"Do you know where he is now?"

"His cousin called me and said he was coming in on the noon flight today. If it lands. If not he was going to go by boat to a cabin north of Angoon."

The plane didn't land that day. This time it was fog in Juneau that screwed up the flights. But I knew just where I could find Alfred Tom. Early the next morning I flew up to Steven Mathews's cabin. The worst of the storm was yet to come in so it wasn't as bad a flight as I was expecting. Except for the first stormy part around the coast we flew the water route, staying a couple hundred feet off the deck to Admiralty. I told the pilot to wait because one look would tell and I also needed a witness.

The door to the cabin was open. A marten was wrestling with a can and beans flicked into the air each time the animal flung the can in one direction or another. My foot slipped on a barnacle-encrusted rock and the marten froze, its small nose and doll eyes burning in my direction. I imagined he thought he was still enough to be invisible. I took another step and the choice was clear. The marten was gone.

Reaching the door, I looked in. The mattress was turned upside down and everything that had been on the shelf was on the floor. Flour was tracked across the litter of pencils and silverware and notebooks, flashlight batteries, Band-Aids, chain-saw parts, wooden matches, dried noodles, and flecks of colored paper. Spattered on the floor were marten tracks and mouse droppings, curling around the room in a frantic spiraling pattern. The stove was open and the drying rack was in splinters on the floor.

I looked in all four corners of the room: no blood, no body. Mathews was gone and hadn't been in the cabin for several days.

I looked in a notebook and found lists, tools that were needed or parts to be replaced. I picked up another and found a diary of food eaten each day. The first entry read: black bread and boiled beans, coffee, oranges, and chocolate. There was nothing else in the entire notebook other than lists of food.

I remembered there had been books stacked in every spare part of the cabin. Now there were only a few manuals and a couple of detective novels left. The serious books were gone. I doubted that the mice had dragged *The Anatomy of Melancholy* and *Remembrance of Things Past* out to a burrow under the woodpile.

The table was swept off. There was one clean yellow tablet with the front page torn out, and resting on the tablet was a black plastic pen with the cap off. Next to the pen was a stopper from a bottle. There were no human tracks in the flour, and there were no traces of flour tracked down toward the beach or the woods, but next to the pen was a wooden match that had been whittled into a toothpick. I looked out the door and Alfred Tom was in the woodshed. He had pulled his cousin's boat up on the beach.

"Nobody here," he said and gestured, spreading his arms wide.

"Yeah, I guess," I said cleverly.

"How's the weather look? Do you have money for flying? Maybe we better stop by the mine before we go home. I'll show you."

The pilot stood at the tail of the plane, the water was glassy calm, and he had the floats gingerly resting on the small cobble beach. He was smoking a cigarette and skipping rocks out on the surface. I watched a rock skip six times and each skip made a commingling echo of rings that joined and faded on the water. A male scoter sputtered on the surface of the water. An eagle pushed off from the tree overhanging the bay.

Steven Mathews was not dead. But he was gone. People were looking for him. The first intruders were not friendly. The next were. Now the animals were reclaiming the cabin site from the man who spoke for nature.

I closed the door and bent the hasp back around so that it hooked shut and then I walked once around the cabin. The area was matted down so hard that no tracks could be seen. I picked up the can of beans and set it on the chopping block. Some flame of light flickered in the edge of my eye and I turned to see the marten on top of a stump ten feet from me, frozen again and staring with the wisdom of patience, knowing that one of us was slowly becoming invisible.

Alfred looked past me and started walking to the plane. He spoke to me over his shoulder. "I'll tell you a story, Cecil. Can't do it here. Leave this for the marten."

"Hey!" I yelled at his back, "wait up," and I ran after him, leaving the food, the cabin, and the evidence to their new owners.

We flew just above the water and then a hole appeared in the pass over Baranof Island. The snow spumed off top ridges and curled down into the valley. Dark clouds lay further to the west. I closed my eyes. I leaned back into my seat and gripped the anchors of my seat belt while I tried to think of any prayers I might have picked up in my travels. I knew it was useless because I suspect God doesn't waste much of his attention on opportunistic converts.

I jumped out of the plane as it swung into the dock and went out ahead of Alfred Tom to get my first look at the shoreline development of the Otter Creek mine. Natural gas tanks lined an area as big as a football field and there were smaller steel tanks laid like huge rolls of half dollars. The bulkhead on the beach was held together with logs wrapped in thick wire cables and the waves rushed against shot rock piled against the bottom.

The pilot agreed to wait. Alfred and I walked up the ramp to the plane shed where there was one guy sitting listening to his tape player, drinking coffee, and reading a hunting magazine. The mine was still shut down and he was in the shutdown crew to maintain the machinery while the work to redo the tanks was going on. Alfred knew him, and waved as he poked his head in the shed.

"Hey, what's up, man?" Alfred Tom yelled out to him.

"Well, there's Mr. Tom," the kid said as he lowered the

magazine with the painting of the trophy buck cresting the hill. "You going to come back on the shutdown? I thought you had enough of this place."

Alfred smiled his I'm-just-a-regular-guy-who-doesn't-know-anything smile and spread his hands out wide.

"Man can't get enough of a good thing. I'm just looking around for some tools I left. Okay if I look around?"

"Well . . . what ya lose? Maybe I seen it."

"I brought my own gauges and some welding tips. I think they may be up at the toolshed. We'll just run up and get them."

The kid stood up and I could tell he was feeling uncomfortable. He started to reach for the radio and he kept looking at the clipboards.

"Well you know, Al," he was almost stammering, "it's kind of different now. You're supposed to sign in and stuff. Only card holders can come on site." Then he looked at me with a mixture of uncertainty and fear as if I were suddenly radioactive.

"I don't have you on the list." His eyes met mine for the first time.

"The name is Altman. I'm there. Look on the Houston office list."

His eyes frantically scanned the clipboards. I was betting that Altman wasn't a hands-on kind of manager and this kid had never laid eyes on him.

"Yeah! Oh, yeah, it's here. Listen, I'm sorry. This isn't really what I'm supposed to do, but with the mine shut down I'm here. I'm not really sure why. I'm a welder too. You know, like Alfred. Hey, you wouldn't happen to have any ID, would you?"

I groaned and rolled my eyes and started patting my hip

pocket to begin my own listen-you-dumb-shit-can't-you-see-I'm-really-important-and-besides-I-lost-my-wallet routine. Alfred Tom waved me on through, saying we were just going to be a minute. Altman's name must have been on top of the list because this kid was babbling as if I had caught him in the bathroom with dirty pictures. I kept walking past him and he called out to me, "It's okay, Mr. Altman. Of course you know all the safety regs and the tank area is a level A and there is no access today."

Alfred Tom and I were well down the dock by then. We were headed for the tool storage area that lay behind the tanks. We were side by side and I leaned closer to Alfred.

There was no one around the tank area. It was closed off because of hazardous materials. Up on the hill a generator sounded and I looked up the steep slope to the containment dike area and the upper bunkhouse and the cookhouse. The alders were bare in the avalanche chutes that cut up a thousand feet to the solid rock where snow etched the outlines of the stone.

"All right, what is the deal here?" I said.

"Okay, they mine gold, right? It's not like a hole in the ground with Gabby Hayes and some burro. They tear down the mountain and put it into these tanks with cyanide solution. They process the stone into a slurry of minerals and the gold settles out. Then they take the tailings and put them up behind the dikes and fill the valley."

"That's the secret?"

He looked at me with pity. "That's no secret. Everybody knows that. Do you know about the big stink when they were getting all the permits for the mine? Well, they had a hassle about the outfall into the salt water. The mine discharges into the bay and they got a permit to have the inner bay called a mixing zone. That pissed a lot of people off so the government watched it carefully. They monitored everything that came out of the pipe. They watched so close that the company was real careful about its outflow. But . . ."

We heard a clatter of falling rock and looked up quickly to see a bear crossing the avalanche chute a couple of hundred feet above us. The bear was moving easily over uneven steep ground. She paused a moment and watched down the hill as the stones bounced, then scampered in an odd lumbering gait straight up the hill and into a thicket of alder.

Alfred Tom turned back to me, not commenting on the bear.

"They weren't so careful about the cathodic protection they put in the floor of the tanks."

"Cathodic protection?"

"The metal on the floor of the tank. With all the chemicals in the tank and salt water in the atmosphere, metal will conduct electricity. Without the right kind of protective measures the floor of the tanks will just rot out. They didn't design enough protection into the tanks. Cyanide solution started seeping into the ground."

We ducked under a yellow barrier tape near one of the tanks. We stayed up high on an embankment and rounded the corner that was away from the water and near the hillside. Down off the embankment was a depression that had been scoured out with a backhoe and was now lined with white plastic and covered with a black netting. Under the netting and pooled in the tarp was a beautiful blue liquid that was maybe a cross between unfinished turquoise stone and a clear winter sky.

"Cyanide . . ." Alfred said the word slowly. "It worked

okay for the gold process. No one really knew that there was a problem until it started showing up in the groundwater-monitoring wells. The engineers almost shit nickels worrying about what would happen if someone found out that it was getting into the surface water. They fucked around and talked and talked until it started pooling out on the surface."

I looked down at the netting. There was a goldeneye duck caught and motionless. I looked around and talked more softly. "But the company copped to this. They closed the mine and started repair work. Nothing to kill anybody over."

Alfred squatted on his haunches. "They never told anyone that the stuff was getting in the water. They kept it quiet about draining down the tanks. The regulatory agencies knew but they didn't want to go public because they had approved the design of the tanks. The tanks were finally drained down on Christmas Day. The company knew no one from the regulatory agency would come out and look. The inspectors wanted to keep it quiet anyway—their asses were on the line too."

He looked up the hill where the bear had disappeared. "I was never really sure until all this started but I thought there was a bigger problem. When they decommissioned the tanks they made a deal to bring the Global tankers down to draw off the tank level and take it to the processing plant in Long Beach. But the stuff never made it there."

"Why?" I asked.

"Think about it, Cecil, there are lots of ways of transporting hazardous waste. All expensive. They should have used special shipping procedures. But the tankers were already in the neighborhood. They pulled up and took on the cyanide for the drawdown of the tanks and they sailed off into the sunset. Everything all clean and tidy."

"But—"

"The tankers couldn't load cyanide into their tanks on top of the oily ballast. So they pumped the ballast out here—" And he swung his arm around and pointed to a pumphouse on the other side of the swale that had a six-inch pipe leading from the dock. "They pumped it back into the ground," he said.

We walked to the shed and Alfred peered in. The pump was off and the pipe made a right angle into the earth. The sleeve around the wellhead was thick with shiny black tar.

"They pumped the ballast oil into the monitoring well and used it as an injection well. They had to dispose of the ballast oil because it is more expensive and harder to get rid of than diluted cyanide. This was a good place to hide the ballast because no one was looking for it here. The cyanide they had to get rid of another way."

I shook my head, still looking down at the wellhead. "What do they gain?"

"They were supposed to treat it but they used to just dump the ballast into the ocean. After *Exxon Valdez* they couldn't risk having that oil show up on a cute little creature somewhere so they had to get the stuff to treatment facilities. Oily ballast is a hazardous waste and it's a pain in the ass to treat and transport. Real expensive. This way they inject the ballast and take on the dilute cyanide on top of the remaining ballast."

"What did they do with the cyanide?"

"Dumped it and then offloaded very diluted ballast in their treatment center. It was the cheapest solution of all. It's a shell game with waste. They move it around and gradually dump most of it, then treat a few gallons and say they're in compliance. Louise Root knew this."

I squinted at him and nodded. He went on. "She got the ships' manifests showing loading and unloading quantities." I thought back to the papers I had seen in her pack. "She got them from Charlie Potts. They were actually kind of friendly, before the birthday party.

"She also had pictures, notes, work orders, descriptions of the well refits. She had them by the nuts and that is what was in those papers. I guess she gave most of them to Mathews but not all, and not the originals. He was working a deal for himself. But after what they did to her up here, she wanted her own justice."

"Were Mathews and Louise Root in it together?"

Alfred shrugged his shoulders. "They started off together, but I think things changed after the party."

I looked back and saw our pilot talking to the kid from the dock house. The wind was picking up hard from the southwest, clouds as black as anvils rolling in. In the mouth of the bay the seas were starting to rise. We were forty miles south of Sitka on Baranof Island and I wanted to get home before the wind picked up any more.

I asked him, "Are the tanks really dangerous inside?"

"They shouldn't be. Before I left I saw guys in regular work clothes going in and out. They got it cleaned up pretty good. They have welders in there patching the floor and some grunts digging out some of the worst contaminated soil. I don't know why they're off-limits now."

"Think we can take a look?"

He shrugged again and stood up. We walked to the back side of the biggest tank. The others were open, with tape across the openings, but the largest tank had a lock on the port. He turned to me. "I suppose you want to see this one?"

I smiled. "No sense looking where they aren't hiding anything."

He jogged over to the toolshed and came back with some bolt cutters and two headlamps. He cut the lock, hoping to make our entry look more official. We stepped in and shut the port quickly.

At first the tank was unimaginably dark, like having no eyes. When we turned on the headlamps the dome of the enclosed space appeared huge. The metal was shiny and smooth and in the center of the cavern were some holes and piles of dirt. As we walked, the thin metal of the floor buckled under our steps. Inside one hole were some shovels and a roll of white absorbent blanket material. They had been trying to find and mop up the streams of contaminated soil under the tank. Not so much to purify the soil but it was unstable where it had been disturbed by liquid and they needed a stronger foundation for the tank this time.

There were extension cords running to the outer port where the work generator had been. A power grinder with a carbide tip sat on the jagged edge of the metal floor. I scanned the hole more closely. Blankets of absorbent material were piled in and there were blotted stains of the blue-green liquid mixed with dirt. But on one pile there was a smear of red.

Alfred was down in the hole before I realized what he was doing. He had his knife out and was bent over a roll that looked like an old carpet. He was stooped, working the roll as if he were gutting it. I could not see past him and moved carefully down into the hole, watching my footing to avoid the damp soil. I moved around his shoulder just as he shook out the roll. I saw the flannel shirt, black and stiff with blood.

Alfred suddenly turned off his headlamp and sat back in the dirt, breathing hard and retching into his hands, which were cupped around his mouth and his eyes.

One of my most comforting beliefs is that everything I know is a transitory illusion. My future is a fictional dream and my past is a remembered one. The moment is fleeting and ambiguous. But finding the pilot's body in the bottom of that tank cut into that belief with a ferocity. It widened my eyes and made the moment broaden out until there was nothing else.

His throat was cut so deeply that his head seemed to wobble free of his neck and his tongue was a stump of jagged meat. There was nothing ambiguous in his eyes, still open and questioning, as if he were asking where I had been and what had taken so long.

THIRTEEN

WE ROLLED THROUGH the dark clouds, but I wasn't thinking of my own death anymore. Doggy would know what to do, I kept thinking, embarrassed to be running to him. Again. But Doggy had what I needed. He could sell this evidence to someone in charge. Doggy had the connections and the wink. He could sell it and protect us . . . if he could sort out who really was in charge. My stomach swirled somewhere in my chest as we rounded the cape near the edge of the coastal mountains, lurching in the air pockets, awkward halting flight, like a feather being blown down a chimney.

Finally the floats touched the water and we ran on-step under the bridge, throttled down, and eased up to my place. I had the plane pull up to the haul-out ramp under my house and looked up the stairs into my makeshift boathouse where I kept my boat supplies, broken oars, gas cans, and fouled filters. In the corner, hunched beside a block of Styrofoam, was Hannah.

"Cecil . . . anyone see you guys come in?" she asked.

"Shit . . . anybody who was looking. What's the deal?"

"News?" Alfred Tom asked as he hopped out of the plane and pushed the floats back off. The pilot turned the engine over and headed for his own float.

Hannah stepped out from under the flooring of the house. "Yeah, I've got some news. That ugly guy from the slope— the one with the teeth and the weird boots—came by and wanted to talk to me. He said I'm wanted for questioning about the killing that happened up on the slope. He said that Cecil Younger gave him information that tied me to other killings, including the murder of my lover, Louise Root."

"Alfred," I said, "could you get enough stuff so you could stay out for about a week? And bring it here. Hannah, get some more food, okay? And let Toddy know we are going to be gone and he should stay with the Social Services lady again. But don't tell him where we're going. I'll be back. I've got to see Doggy quick. Be ready to head out as soon as I get back."

Alfred stood down on the bow of my skiff. He looked under the bridge to the open bay and out to the cape. The black clouds were churning like a grease fire. Gusts were blowing the tops off the waves and the long swells were streaked with the white tracks of the wind. He looked at the water for a few seconds and then back up at me.

"Where we going?"

"Around the cape."

"Around the cape? In this thing?"

"Just get your stuff. This skiff will be fine. If we have to, we can haul it up into the woods and no one will see us. And

I'm not getting in another fucking plane. Just get your stuff. I've got to get to Doggy."

I wore my rain gear even though it was only about a ten-minute walk to the house up behind the police academy. As I jogged I imagined Doggy and his grandkids sitting down to a brunch of eggs and juice.

At Doggy's house the professional young cops were flashing pictures like it was a movie premiere. The doors were open to the muskeg out back. Rain dripped in on the oak-wood floor and spread like a stain out into the room. Doggy was laid out over the plates and EMTs were working on an intravenous lead. Poached egg was smeared across his Mariners jacket and orange juice spilled from the pitcher down onto his lap, puddling on the floor. His face was waxy white and some bits of his coat and shirt lay in the blood sprayed on the white tablecloth that he and his wife had bought on their honeymoon in Ireland. He was breathing. His service revolver lay next to his hand. A technician was picking it up gingerly with toast tongs. He had been shot in the lung. Once.

Mrs. Doggy stood with her back to the door, arms hanging limply at her sides. Five other women were in the room—one was on the telephone and the other four stood close by the sobbing Mrs. D. Two of the women wore trooper academy windbreakers and one was wearing sweats and a hair net. None of these wives of cops was crying. The one in the hair net talked to the children in low, calming tones. Another led Doggy's wife away from the breakfast room.

The chief of police ran into the room with his shirt

untucked and a police radio in his hand. He stopped when he saw Doggy. He exhaled loudly and whispered, "No, no, no!"

When his eyes landed on me, he screamed, "What is he doing in here? Get this clown out. Hold him. Question him. But get him the fuck out!"

Two nice young cops started to lead me outside and I doubled back and leaned over Doggy. He was wearing an oxygen mask over his nose and mouth and as I bent close I could hear him murmur through the hiss of the gas, "Go."

The young cops grabbed me again and turned me over to their supervisor, who had forgotten why I was there. He just told me to "stand back . . . Stand back." This was okay with me.

I went out the side door, and walked quickly to a path that ran near the old geologic survey house. There was a root wad from a scrub spruce tree and I stumbled, put my hand down, and caught myself in the sponge-like ground of the muskeg.

On the edge of a deep hole in the bog was a rim of volcanic red mud and as I turned to regain my feet I saw the one clear impression of a smooth leather boot print, with a very pointed toe, sliding down the edge of the muskeg hole, where someone, just minutes before, must have tripped and fallen much as I had done.

I ran back to my house, pumping my legs hard enough so the heat rose under my rain gear. I yelled at Alfred and Hannah and for a numbing moment heard no response, but they were down by the skiff already and I heard their voices come up from under the floor of the house. I threw the last of the gear in the skiff and strapped my knife onto my belt. I held the life jacket but did not put it on, as I tripped down the ramp.

Hannah and I stood in the stern as Alfred shouldered the bow off and we floated free of the ramp. I made sure the stern plugs were in so we would not fill up with water. If we could go on-step into the weather I would take them out, to drain what was going to ship in during the crossing.

The engine caught with the third pull and I headed out the channel under the bridge. The wind was pushing the skiff in odd bucking jerks like a young horse being ridden on a cold morning. Alfred and Hannah sat facing the stern, hoods up. No one else was out on the water, but a larger yellow fiberglass skiff was at the gas dock where a blond woman with a black dog was fueling the tanks.

I throttled up as we passed under the bridge and I saw two men.

One was Eli Pick, still wearing his muddy boots, with nothing on against the rain but his lightweight desert jacket. His hair was wet and stringy against his angular skull. He caught sight of me before I could duck my face into my hood and he smiled and kind of waved, then he lifted his gun from his pocket and realized, probably, that this was not the right time. He set off running for the end of the bridge.

The engine whined and pushed our skiff up onto the top of the water, and we skidded around the point of the first little island and took a heading through the inner islands of the sound to the outer coast. A white sheet of wind advanced across the inner bay and curled us in a pounding roar. The spray hit my face like BBs. The skiff lurched into a wave and the bow ducked under six inches, green water pouring over the gunwale. Hannah leaned over my lap and bailed with a coffee can in one hand and a cut-out bleach bottle in the other.

As we rounded the point of the furthest island we were in the direct line of the weather. More waves lifted the bow of the boat high into the air and I throttled back so as not to bury the bow. I thought of making a quick turn and finding a place to pull the skiff into the lee of one of these islands when Hannah lifted her arm and pointed over my shoulder to the stern. "Look."

Rounding the point from town was the yellow skiff. It was going dangerously fast and I could see a figure standing at the steering station amidships. Someone was holding onto the rails and bouncing on the balls of his feet as the skiff rocketed through the waves.

The yellow boat was better designed for weather—long, with a narrow beam and a high bow. I knew I could not outrun it to the cape. I turned abeam to the weather and a breaking wave dumped into the skiff. We teetered for a second but put the next wave a quarter to our stern. Both Alfred and Hannah bailed furiously.

I made for a tight inlet between two islands. I was hoping we had been lost to their sight when we descended for a short distance into the trough, and perhaps we had, because once around the lee of the islands where we had to lift the shaft in the shallows, we saw the yellow boat fighting the waves out to the west and then later to the north, moving away from our position.

We waited for an hour while the tide rose and the waves began to break in the shallows. Then we had to move out to the west to follow the coast to the outer rocks where we could camp.

As we neared the cape I saw the fins of killer whales knifing through the waves. They cut quickly. One large male had a long notched fin that sliced like the blades of a windmill with each short churning dive. My eyes followed them as we rounded the cape. The vapor of their blows held briefly in the wind and then laid flat into the haze on the surface. I watched them as I made the final turn to the jagged outer coast, leaving the relative protection of Sitka Sound behind.

There are moments when you pause to think that maybe you have made a mistake and should reconsider . . . then there are times when your mistake pulls you under like a shark. I knew we were mistaken on many levels when we cut too close to the shore as we rounded the corner of the cape. For instead of plotting a proper course around the outside of the break, I had taken a short line that took me unexpectedly into the surf.

The waves were a confused jumble of foam flailing up from the green around the pinnacles of black stone. The yellow skiff was there too and looked ridiculous burrowing into the waves. It heaved in several directions at once, wallowing down in its own wake as it moved up a swell, and then burst over the top into a lather of sea foam and plunged out of sight.

I eased back on the throttle. Our boat was poorly suited to this and we would be lucky to be able to turn around and make our way back out. I looked to sea, and black ridges, like foothills, moved along the horizon. I counted three that were uniform and fairly rounded, but the fourth was higher by a third and its leading edge was dark, sharpened, with flecks that were stripped away by the wind in sizzling bits of light.

This was a swell that wanted to break in on itself out in deep water. As it moved, it steepened and the slurry of white water on the shore sank and sucked back out, carrying even the large rocks back with it. The voice of the waves slowed and held the long rattling sound of the big wave that was pulling all of the available water out past the rocks, past the reef where no other waves had broken. The wave began to shear and spill out into a beautiful green curl.

The yellow skiff operator gunned the engine and ran full throttle for the edge of the curl. The boat heaved and I thought I saw two people standing by the controls. The skiff was pounding and rolling in the white water. It ran up the breaking face of the wave and the bow lunged into the thin curling lip of the breaker. The skiff stood vertical and for a moment looked as if it were going to continue on over backwards, but the slightest bit of power from the engine pushed it through and the skiff banged down hard on the rounded slope of the wave.

I couldn't see it any longer. I could hear the engine rev and the fiberglass hull banging on the humps of the smaller rollers as it beat out to the deeper water around the point.

Near the edge of the surf line sea lions barked and curled in frantic dives. The yellow skiff turned back as if it had spotted us and wanted to step back and watch our next move. The whales blew louder out beyond the edge of the surf line and the sea lions swam through the surf, frantically trying to outdistance the whales to the shore.

"Son of a bitch," Alfred said. "How in the hell did the yellow boat manage that?"

"I don't know but maybe we should ask them for a lesson."

For, as we had idled there, admiring the almost perfect symmetry of the wave and the skiffman's prowess, we had drifted into what surfers call the "impact zone." And the wave that had most likely been generated thousands of miles away was beginning its last tumble onto the rocks of North America. Taking us with it.

We caught the wave broadside and the boat rolled like a carnival ride. Fuel tanks and buckets flew through the air and I saw Hannah's eyes wide and frozen in panic. I saw Alfred dive for deep water. The foam tumbled and filled my nose, my mouth. I was caught in the churning motion, my limbs flailing like a rag doll's. I did not fight. I was drifting away underwater where the sound was soothingly muffled. I saw the churning breakers from beneath and for a moment I was distracted by their tranquility until I realized that I was held down by the anchor line wrapped around my foot. My lungs were searing as I struggled for my knife to free myself. I went popping to the surface like an exploding balloon, just in time to take the brunt of another breaking wave that carried a fuel tank down onto my head and eased me into momentary darkness.

When I pulled myself back, I saw Hannah struggling with a line tangled around her chest and one arm. She was failing. I tried to raise up to see if anyone else was floating. Blood spattered onto the foam from the cut in my head. But all I could see before the next wave was the shiny hull of my skiff rolling like the body of a fish in the surf. Hannah lunged for air and I heard her rasping voice even as the next wave hit me and thrust me down against the rocks.

I pushed against the bottom and as the next wave built and the seas sucked out to the reef, I swam toward her, my head throbbing and the water burning in my sinuses and eyes. In four strokes I had her in the crook of my arm and I fumbled for my knife again and carefully pulled against the line with the blade. The next wave hit and we both tumbled against the hull of my skiff. I remember putting the knife in the scabbard somehow, thinking I didn't want to save her from drowning by slicing her throat.

My feet touched rocks. I made an unsteady foothold, dragged Hannah up on the beach, and laid her on the highest part of the sand.

Alfred was gone. I looked out to the water where the waves broke and scattered white water. I could not see him. The yellow skiff was swamped and floated upside down out in the breakers near what looked like a body in a life jacket floating facedown. I waded through the knee-deep white water of the shoreline looking for Alfred. A merganser flew along the tops of the waves, his wing beats stretching his whole body, and squeaked with short exhalations of air. He veered off over the waves to the south into the low clouds. Watching him, for some reason, I felt like part of my life was lost forever.

I turned away from the beach and walked in under the canopy of the trees. I didn't know where Alfred was. I didn't know what to do for Hannah. I was numb. My thumb was dislocated and my head was bleeding. I knew I couldn't speak, for my mind was floating from the tumble, but I wasn't starting to shiver uncontrollably yet.

In the pocket of my coat I had an old silver lighter and an ancient metal match case so rusted I didn't know if I could even open it. I held it in my palm. Fire wasn't an end, it was a process at this point. Almost a distant abstraction. Fire and food. I don't know why I thought of food because my stomach felt as if it were curling into knots. It wasn't hunger I was feeling.

I thought of a girl leaning over the railing on Creek Street wearing a white tank top, her hair blowing around her head like banners in a parade. Maybe I had seen her. She was watching the salmon flop on the water going upstream. I was thinking, the urge, the urge, the urge, and I wanted to get something to eat and I wanted to start a fire.

Down the beach inside the reef was a narrow sandy cove barely ten feet wide. A deep channel cut through the reef, allowing the fat greenish breakers to hit the sand. I was distracted by a flash of red in the water, then a plume of scarlet. I blinked and then saw the sea lion bellowing and dragging itself up out of the surf. It trailed its intestines behind it, the last quarter of its torso gone. Then I heard an explosion of breath as the orca whale lunged up on the sand.

If I had ever seen a fiery angel in my dreams it would have looked like this because the whale burned my eyes like flame but I was not asleep and this wasn't a dream. Where there had been coarse sand and white crushed shell was now a twenty-ton male orca. His black-and-white hide sparkled with water sheeting down his sides. The six-foot dorsal fin draped loosely to one side and flopped slightly as the whale struggled in the sand, beating his small pectoral fins against the beach. Puffs of breath burst from his blow-hole and he flailed the sand with his flukes. Then as the next swell came, his truck-sized body lunged twice, took the injured sea lion in his jaws, and disappeared into the surf.

For a moment there was no sign, just the fading stain of blood and the faint impressions on the sand. I blinked and held my breath. Then, just out past the breakers I saw the dagger of a dorsal fin cut a tight loop through the water and I heard the blow being swallowed by the wind.

FOURTEEN

HANNAH WAS BREATHING but I couldn't gauge her pulse. In the woods I found a downed spruce with the bark still on, the butt end rotted out. I knelt down and reached as far in as I could, breaking some pitch wood out. The pain in my hand was searing, but the dry wood was light and just holding it seemed to make me feel better. The wood was white and slightly rotted. Encrusted on the edges were globs of pitch. I broke some twigs from the trunk of a standing spruce, about a foot in diameter, near the base. They broke easily and I knew they were dry. There were no needles on anything I picked and I sorted out the twigs that wanted to bend from the ones that snapped with a dry crack. I found a dry spot under the spruce and cleared it down to the driest vegetable matter. It would be hard to find dirt on this forest floor, which was a sponge of moss and decomposed wood. But I made a dry platform and built my meager little pyre. Then I went beachcombing for a small piece of cedar. I was beginning to shiver and I knew that I wasn't going to have a lot more rational time left, but I also knew that if I botched this attempt to get a decent fire going I was in serious danger of dying of a combination of hypothermia and shock.

I scrambled past the canopy of spruce and hemlock trees that draped the beach fringe and stumbled out onto the slick logs that were piled by the tide on the high end of the beach. I shimmied along these logs and finally made it to rocks and gravel. I looked into the back eddies where the tide had deposited the lightest of the floating debris that had washed up from the Pacific.

Amidst the bull kelp, twigs, and stumps, I found a Japanese hard hat and a plastic case for holding sake bottles. There was a rusted fuel tank and two plastic buckets with the bottoms broken out. There were light bulbs and oblong plastic fishing floats and plastic bleach bottles, rubber gloves, a broken piece of a fiberglass transom off a runabout. A strange-looking drum with heavy fittings. Several piles of plastic drift-net material twisted up on the beach with kelp and groundline and whiskey bottles intertwined in the web. There were hundreds of flakes of plastic mixed with the gravel, sand, and crushed shell. There were three dead birds: a duck, a gull, and an eagle. Sitting perched high on the tide line, like a ball placed on a golf tee, was a Japanese glass float. It was green and about the size of a softball. I walked over and picked it up and thought about how lucky I was to find it, until I saw the little red plastic fuel can.

I dropped the glass ball, shattering it on the one emergent rock it must have missed when it was tossed on the beach by a storm wave. The jug had GLOBAL on it and must have washed away from the mine site. It had an inch of diesel fuel in the bottom.

Just beyond, in the shadow behind a trumpet-butted hemlock, I found a beautiful piece of red cedar that had obviously sat high above the tide line for the last few winter storms. The piece was a splintered section of four-by-four timber, about three feet long. It had sat sheltered from the worst of the rain and I was betting it was still dry in the center.

I took my plunder back to the fire spot where Hannah was lying, quite still. I was beginning to shake. I scattered some of the fuel onto the pile of twigs and pitch wood, knelt by the pile of sticks, and held the lighter in my shaking hands. I held it with my good hand and steadied it next to the twigs with the bad one. My thumb was still cocked out at an odd angle. Finally I got the lid off. It was an old Zippo that I left in my coat for emergencies and I doubted that it really would work but I forced that from my mind.

I pulled the roller on the lighter down with my thumb; the flint sparked, the fuel sputtered, and I held it as steady as I could to the diesel-soaked twigs. The orange flame was as purely beautiful as candy corn. Black smoke curled up and into my face. The flame caught the twigs and then I heard the first crackle and smelled the first perfume of burning wood and diesel. The fire popped and I held out my hands over the flames.

I pulled Hannah's head up into my lap. Her hair was wet but tied back and she was beginning to shiver slightly. She opened her eyes as if she had just waked up from a sound sleep. Her lip was cut and the tips of her fingers were bleeding. She looked at my fire and seemed confused. Then she looked at my thumb.

"Oh shit, Cecil."

The thumb was an odd sight, bent back and down toward

my wrist. The symmetry of my hand was so disturbed it looked more like a broken gardening tool than a hand. She sat up and moved in closer to me and the fire, and took my hand.

She took my hand in hers and held my thumb tenderly. She smiled and I winced and trembled, sucking my breath in, but did not pull back.

I was shaking when I told her, "I brought us in too close to the beach. I'm sorry."

"You did all right," she whispered. She leaned forward and kissed me. Her lips were icy cold and weirdly funny to the touch. She darted her tongue in my mouth and breathed her warm breath down my throat. Then, in one movement, she bit down on my lip and pulled my thumb out with all of her strength.

It was such a swirl of sensations, the cold kiss and the numbness of blood and breath, that I didn't feel the sudden pop of my thumb being jerked back into its socket. She threw her head back then, smiled, and gave me an affectionate punch lightly on the shoulder.

"How's that?" She shivered and rubbed my hand, then lay back down exhausted. I moved my fingers and my reseated thumb. It was hot and cold with pain, but at least it was my hand again and she was rubbing it briskly in hers.

About twenty yards behind me I heard the sound of someone or something walking on the fallen spruce tips. I swung around the fire and crouched, feeling the fire was some sort of boundary. I waited. I was listening for the deep-coughing lung of a bear, or the metallic clack of a shell being jacked into a breech. Alfred Tom walked into the clearing.

"You made it," he said, smiling. "I found a bunker back

around the point. But not much luck with a fire. If we take what you've got here and move it inside, I think we can get dried out."

He helped me pull more pitch wood from a hollow log and scooped the beginning of the fire onto the cradle shape of some driftwood. We both blew on the embers that licked up briefly into the air. I suppose it was stupid to struggle so much to move the fire, but with the momentum of hypothermia building it was easier to continue a mistake than to make a decision.

I helped Hannah walk, while Alfred carried the fire through the fringe of trees. He moved ahead on a narrow game trail, up over a swale and around the shore to where, next to a small alder, a concrete bunker stood, gray and improbably monumental on this island of curves and short straight lines.

Hundreds of gun emplacements dot the islands off the coast of Alaska. They were built during World War II to defend against the expected Japanese invasion. But the advance ended in the Aleutians and the military pulled out its men and ammunition, leaving the concrete to stand and be covered with a green velvet blanket of moss.

We ducked our heads and went in through a low doorway and up a set of stairs to where a gun had been mounted. There was a circular iron track in the center of the room. An opening of one hundred eighty degrees looked out to the west and the Orient.

Hannah pulled off her shirt and stood in her long underwear, wringing out her synthetic pile jacket and pants. There were piles of plastic tarps in the corner and a soggy-looking mattress. Next to the mattress was a pile of firewood left by previous tenants. Alfred set the fire down where the old fire pit had been, near the center of the room. Hannah was shivering and her head was shaking loosely as if it were a spring-action toy.

We added dry wood and the flames rose again. With each breath that Hannah took, light and heat blossomed out into the room. Her face and the front of her sweater lightened with each breath. I could see the tendrils of her hair sway against her shoulders, a few faint drops of blood and salt water spilling off her chin.

At first the room was foggy with smoke. Alfred and I squatted, and as the fire grew, the heat carried it up to the ceiling and out. Hannah carefully placed larger and larger pieces in a delicate lean-to fashion. Soon smoke and sparks rose in circling loops toward the ceiling as the three of us sat close enough to the flames to singe the outer threads of our clothes.

I looked at Hannah. Her eyes squinted into the smoke and the heat. She had a square jaw that was set tight against the urge to shiver. She pulled her hair forward toward the smoke. Her eyes were bloodshot and puffy and the lines in her face betrayed some tension, yet her stare was intent only on the fire and the heat.

I cleared my throat and looked directly at Alfred Tom. "You want to tell me about the guy on the bridge?"

Alfred shrugged his shoulders and turned his back to the fire. Hannah took a breath and wrapped her arms around her shoulders like a person all alone. She moved closer but remained out of my reach.

"Let's get some kind of camp together." Alfred stood up and reached into the zippered pocket of his coat and pulled out a stainless steel .44. He flipped the cylinder open and spun it around, checking to see that it had five shells, then snapped it in place with the empty chamber under the hammer. He held the grip out to me.

"There are five shots. You think you can get something edible with it?"

I took the gun. Pistols always surprise me with their weight. We didn't need the food just then. But I had no idea how long we were going to be there. Our supplies were out in the surf. Some might be salvageable and some might not. I felt the bulk of the gun and wondered if I really had to hunt.

Hunting is not like shopping; it is tied up in ritual and luck. I wasn't feeling terribly lucky. I couldn't even predict how bad my luck would be. I took the pistol and pointed it down toward the floor and tried my best self-confident tone.

"I'll take a look around."

"Good," he said. "I will scavenge the beach and see what I can find. Maybe some of our food buckets washed up."

I left quickly because I didn't want to project my dread into the room. I could have handed the pistol back, saying I didn't want to shoot anything with it. I didn't much like the gun but I liked the idea of it being in my possession. I took it outside and walked the game trail into the interior of the island.

The ground cover was thick, and each branch that I bent back seemed to amplify my movements. Alder and blueberry, salmonberry and scrubby spruce trees clung to my damp, smoky clothes. I tried to move silently, placing each step, and then I gave up. What with the way I smelled and the noise I had already made, I was never going to run into anything that would stand still long enough for me to steady a shaking hand in its direction. Blundering along into the wind, I came to an old stand of spruce trees that had sheltering canopy several hundred feet up. Very little light penetrated here, so the walking was easy and silent on the padding of moss. The storm was a swirling hiss above me and the surf was a muffled booming beyond the trees. I straddled the trunk of a leaning tree turned toward the shore when the doe stepped behind the ridge line of the northern swale.

She stopped and stared at me and I froze in place as if I were the hunted. I took shallow breaths. Her nose twitched. She raised her head, trying to make out something in the air. She took another step. A yearling stepped out from behind her and walked brazenly into the clearing. The doe took one step, and I took one, trying to hide myself from view. She sensed me but could not be certain. She bolted one step to the west and stopped again, looking to her yearling, who was nibbling the green shoots of a blueberry bush. I crouched inside the crotch of the tree. The doe eased into the clearing and nosed the yearling's flank. Fifty feet away a buck raised its head and curled its lip slightly. He pawed the moss twice and moved out beyond the trees.

The buck had small forked antlers. His hide was a fine brownish gray and silver flared up his throat to the black rims around his eyes and muzzle. Midway down his throat he had a collar patch of pure white. His eyes were wide and dark. His nose was exquisitely sensitive, working the air as he walked toward the doe and fawn. I raised the gun and steadied it against the tree. My hands shook as I pulled back the hammer. The mechanical click caused him to snort and bound back into the trees. I blew through my lips and made a childish little squeaking sound, and the buck peeked around his own spruce, curious. He knew he should run. Knew there was danger. But he was starting his rut, and the doe, and his curiosity, were too much for him.

I tried to steady the front sight on the top rim of his skull. I was going for a head shot or a miss.

I have waited for ecstasy all of my life, the pure joy of being, and I have never felt it. For each and every moment of my happiness has been tinged with sorrow. Like the swallow of water from the mountain stream that has two tastes—one living, and one dead—my life has been a sorry confluence of wonder and pity. I think this is what bugs Hannah and was part of the reason she left. But being a man stuck in the middle has one advantage: I have yet to be overwhelmed by sorrow.

The shot entered just behind the jaw. The buck reared back and pawed the air. A haze of blood stained the tree and bits of bone stuck to the ragged bark. The buck staggered backwards three paces and collapsed. Limp and awkward, he lay on the moss with his legs splayed out as if he had slipped on a mirrored floor. He exhaled in a red foamy bleating through his nose as his lower jaw was missing.

I jumped over the stump and ran to where he lay and without thinking shot him again squarely in the head. He lay still. Amazingly, the doe paused on the edge of the clearing behind a large tree, nosing the air, inhaling, trying to make sense of the scene. The yearling stood behind her, staring.

I stood over the buck and put my shaking hand on his hide. I spoke to him, or maybe I spoke to whoever was his proxy now. I apologized for his suffering. I felt the heat of his body rise up and away like smoke in the abandoned bunker. The doe and the yearling moved out into the bramble of dense thicket. I took the shells out of the cylinder, put them in my pocket, and stuck the pistol in my belt. Then I hefted the buck over my shoulder and made way for the camp.

Hannah broke through the brush near the bunker and stopped short when she saw me. Blood stained my back and the buck flopped limply with each of my steps. At first she appeared surprised, then sad, but finally she spoke with a smile.

"I heard the shots."

She nodded to the buck and then walked to the bunker. There was a low-hanging alder bough. Hannah reached into her pocket and took out a section of nylon parachute cord. She handed it to me. She looked at the deer as if listening to a song: distant and sad.

"Do you need some help with that?" she asked.

"I suppose I do, my hand is sore. I've got a knife. Can you help me lift this up?"

I tied a bowline in the end of the cord and then a boatman's knot about three inches from the bowline. I put a noose over the head and around the throat. I handed Hannah the end and she flipped it over the bough. She pulled on the end as I lifted the buck up off the ground. As the head neared the bough and the hoofs left the ground, I doubled the end through the boatman's knot and used it as a primitive pulley to hoist the dead weight the rest of the way up. Hannah backed away and stood beside me as I knelt by the abdomen. I took my Gouker knife and started an incision two inches above the penis and, once started, I held the blade with the finger leading under the tip to keep the point from puncturing the gut. Up six inches. Stopped. A loop of gut hung down, tannish gray with blue veins etching around the tubing. When I touched it, the peristaltic motion caused the gut to shrink in a snake-like wriggle. I pulled the gut down and all of it flopped out onto the moss. Then I reached up inside the cavity of the body and pulled out the liver and the heart. The warm air that came from the body cavity was strong with the salty hint of the life drifting out of the meat. I reached up to feel the smooth surface of the diaphragm and cut through it, then reached up further and pulled the lungs out. With all of this, there was little blood. Some that had drained down from the neck and some that came from the surface blood vessels gathered in the saddle of the pelvis.

Alfred came over and smiled. "I've got some alder sticks. Would you like to eat some of the backstrap if we can thread some pieces on the sticks? I found some chicken-of-the-woods fungus and some seaweed. Our food buckets from the boat were smashed and there wasn't much left, but I took some gumboot chitons from the tidepools. Do you know the best way to eat them?"

"It will all taste good once we're hungry enough. How's the fire doing?"

Alfred looked up at the top of the bunker. "It's good. I'm getting cold again. Going in. Okay? You need any help?"

Hannah looked back at me and spoke to him. "We'll get it. You better get inside."

Alfred picked up the bucket he had scavenged, ducked his head, and disappeared into the bunker. I turned back to the buck, cut the hide around the first joint of all the legs, then I cut the throat and slit the hide around the neck. I started at the neck and peeled the hide down away from the musculature. The thin layer of fat bubbled away from the hide as I ran the tip of my knife down the seam. Cutting and pulling the hide, the warm smell of the fat came up. The hide was supple and warm in my hand and it gathered on the ground at our feet.

Hannah spread the hide out on a flat hump of the mossy floor, and then hefted the gut, kidneys, and lungs onto the hide and folded it into a package. She wiped her hands on the moss and looked up at me.

"See any bear sign?"

"No, but I didn't get very far. We're a long way from the big islands but some bears come out here. I just haven't heard of them staying very long."

"What do you think we should do with these?" She nodded down to the hide filled with entrails.

"Maybe carry it away from camp a little. See if you can get it up off the ground. We can retrieve the hide later if we need it. I'll hang the deer up after I get the backstrap off."

She took another section of parachute cord and laced it around the primitive package, then dragged it out past the brow of the hill and down away from the area of the bunker. I stepped in back of the buck and ran my thumb down the ridge of the backbone, then ran the blade at a right angle down the full length and carved out the strip of tender meat that runs either side of the spine. The meat was free of fat and I held both strips in my hands. It warmed them. I set it down on top of my coat spread over the moss. Then I climbed onto the upper limbs of the tree, looped the end of cord in my hand, and undid the knot. By pulling on the remaining upper jaw with the cord, I was able to lift the body up into the alder tree. Then I climbed down.

I picked up the backstrap and looked back into the tree. It was early afternoon and almost dark. The sky was a chalky gray shaded in blossoming forms of dense clouds. The deer swung in the tree with the head and the ears cocked back. I could see the silhouette of the legs spread apart and the tongue hanging out weirdly from the throat where the lower jaw had been blasted away.

I retreated inside where Alfred was sitting cross-legged by the fire. He had a clean bucket and handed me a stick in exchange for the backstrap. He put it in the bucket and I handed him my knife. Alfred cut cubes of meat and skewered them on the sharpened sticks. We fixed three sticks with a pound of meat on each and held them over the flame that flared up several feet. The damp concrete bunker was flickering with a bubble of orange light and heat. The light skittered up the mossy walls and illuminated some graffiti of earlier parties. On the north wall there was a crude naked woman with her legs spread and on the south wall was a detailed drawing, scratched with a nail, of a sailboat with its spinnaker out and the wind billowing it forward.

The meat sizzled and the smell filled the dampness. I ate the first piece of cooked meat and burned my tongue but I chewed through it. I drank water from a plastic cup salvaged from the beach. I chewed a piece of the seaweed. Hannah took a small piece of fat and put it in an aluminum hard hat that she had found, added thinly sliced pieces of fungus and placed it on the fire. The fungus steamed and turned rubbery in the bottom of the hat and we reached in and plucked out pieces with our fingertips. We chewed in silence. The fire, the surf, the wind in the trees gave the silence shape. Finally Alfred cleared his throat.

"I liked her, Cecil. You know—Louise."

"Yeah. Nanny told me."

He chewed the venison and stared out at the fire.

"Did you shoot Potts?" I said.

He paused. Hannah was shaking her head no, staring at him, not speaking. Alfred shook his head back and forth, letting the pause fill out into a long silence that we chewed on like the meat.

A harsh yelp broke it. Hannah's hand was over her mouth and her eyes showed white rims. She was looking over my shoulder, reaching for Alfred's arm.

I turned toward the darkness behind me where Steven Mathews stood, slumped in the doorway, carrying the body of a man wearing snakeskin boots. Mathews's head was cut and his anti-exposure suit was soaked and covered with dirt. It looked like he had buried himself in the ground to keep warm.

"I smelled the smoke. The food." His voice was raspy. "I couldn't stay out there anymore," he said, and fell forward onto the cement floor with a sickening wet splat.

FIFTEEN

ELI PICK WAS unquestionably dead. He had a deep gash in his temple. His skin was cold and bony white. He was still wearing his life jacket. I assumed his was the body I had seen floating by the overturned yellow boat. I laid him out in the corner of the bunker away from our sight and covered him with a black plastic tarp that a hunter had left from an old camp. As I pulled the cover over his head I looked at him, trying to get more clues as to who he was. If he was a professional killer, he looked foolish now: pasty white with all of his muscles flaccid, eyes empty. His teeth still pushed the edges of his lips in a self-satisfied grin. Now he looked like a wax figure in a traveling fair.

Mathews was passed out on the floor. Alfred and Hannah stripped off his exposure suit and tried to towel him off as best they could. He was shivering and his fingertips were raw where he must have clawed the rocks getting out of the breakers. Hannah touched him almost unwillingly. By the time they got him in a comfortable position, his eyelids were fluttering. Alfred made bitter tea from roots and fungus he had gathered. Mathews sputtered when he first drank it but soon he was able to talk.

"I didn't . . . think I . . . was going to . . . make it."

"You almost didn't," Hannah said, and she held a fruit jar with some tea to his lips. "I think you're going to."

His eyes focused and the light of recognition flickered in them. He struggled to sit up. He made it to a sitting position, then wavered and fell to his side, struggling to stay away from Alfred.

Alfred stood up and walked into the dark corner and picked up a piece of wood. When he returned and placed the piece of hemlock on the fire, Mathews edged away from him and looked back and forth from Alfred to Hannah.

"They made me do this, you know. It was their greed and their arrogance. I need those records. That's what they want. If I had them it would be over. I could get on with my work. We could all get on with the rest of our lives."

Hannah leaned in closer and spoke across the flames. "Why do you need them?"

He turned away, speaking into the shadows: "I used the information that Louise sent me from the mine, used it as leverage to get funds for my projects."

"Projects." Alfred knocked the fire, sending sparks up to the concrete dome.

"Yes, my work. But when that . . . ugliness happened at the mine, Louise wanted to go public. Right then. She wanted her—I don't know—her pound of flesh. I could appreciate her reasons but I couldn't allow her to do that. I couldn't allow her to sacrifice our goals to something . . . personal. It would slow our momentum."

"It would get you in deep shit for blackmailing the company," I offered.

He didn't even comment. "She went to the company before I could stop her. The next thing I knew they sent Pick with a message," and he gestured to the covered figure in the corner. "I could maintain my status as a 'paid consultant' with the company only if I could insure that Louise would not reveal any of the information she'd gathered. I had to collect all of the documentation and convince her to remain quiet."

"Wasn't there another option?" Hannah spit her words out.

Mathews smiled patiently at her, a teacher humoring a slow student. He lifted himself up on one elbow. "Not everything is as simple as we'd like it to be. When Pick and I arranged to meet Louise in Ketchikan I still thought Louise and I were in the power position. I was confident we could manipulate the company. After all, we had their toxic shell game documented and we had the rape. I had powerful cards to play."

"Cards," Hannah muttered.

His hand shook as he lifted the cup to his lips. The logs on the fire shifted and sent a sizzle of sparks up with the smoke. Alfred's eyes, looking across at Mathews, were cold.

Mathews wiped his face. "You know, Mr. Younger, we live in a culture that abhors death. What happened that afternoon changed everything for me. In many ways the horror was a catalyst. It is only because we do everything in our power to hold death at arm's length that we suffer the corporate mentality. We allow them to cut the trees and poison the earth so that we may have goods and distractions to keep us numb from the reality of nature . . . which includes death."

"God!" Hannah moaned and turned away, exasperated.

"Yes . . . exactly." He smiled as if only he had understood the joke. "God shows his love through systems. He maintains the balance and protects the cycles. Individuals are expendable. Their deaths fertilize the ground for others to come."

"Louise Root was fertilizer then?" Hannah was standing now. She held the pistol with the hammer pulled back.

Everything was shaking, the firelight made the shadows quaver, and Hannah's hand shook on the black handle of the silver gun.

"I am not afraid to die, Ms. Elder. That was the great gift I was given that day. Those who overcome death are closer to the truth, to reality."

Tears were spilling down Hannah's cheeks. "Shut the fuck up, you pompous . . ."

He looked at the bloody tips of his fingers with a nervous disregard for the revolver. "I tried to reason with her. We argued and she . . . cried, poor child. You see, I really did have genuine feeling for her, but she was too involved in her own personal business. She had lost sight of the good in the work we had started."

"The good?" I moved closer to Hannah.

"We were going to use the resources of Global Exploration to restore the balance. We would take their money and put it to work in my institute. Teaching. Creative exchange."

Hannah was breathing hard. Her eyes started to narrow in a fierce resolve. She was beyond rage and she whispered: "This isn't a grant application, you fucking piece of meat. I want to know what happened to her and I don't want a lecture."

He leaned back on his elbow. He watched the fire, then raised his eyes to meet hers and his voice took on a different tone, as if he were speaking to the gun itself.

"Pick talked to her and when she would give him nothing he left. He said the company was done with me. They would turn everything over to the lawyers. I tried to reason with her again. She left the hotel. I followed. She tried to take a cab to the airport but the cab had a flat. She was crying. A drunk came up. Some street man. Trying to come to her defense for some reason. I bought him some whiskey but he wouldn't leave us alone. Louise was walking, almost aimlessly. Then she said she was going to walk to the radio station. She was going to the press. I pleaded with her to talk to me privately just for a moment.

"We found a way to get down to the water. I tried to lose the drunk but he walked behind us and yelled obscenities at me. We walked until I didn't hear him anymore and we ended up under the wharf. It was dark there and private."

The hammer was pulled back on the gun in Hannah's hands. She was shaking violently but her eyes never moved off Mathews. I slid along the floor closer to her. Mathews went on.

"Louise broke down completely, calling me a hypocrite, and a liar. I thought we were alone. I remember slapping her. When I did I lost my footing on the rocks and I fell. I looked up and the drunk was standing over me with a knife. I stood up, slowly, and punched him once and he fell. No great triumph, really. He was unstable on his feet and the rocks were slick. After I punched him Louise held him and wept. I was becoming very angry because she showed more concern for this bum than for my situation. She cried, clasping him, and I told her to get ahold of herself, he had just hit his head, just a scratch really, a few drops of blood. I told her she had more to worry about than some drunk. Then she attacked me, hitting and slapping. I fell again on the rocks. I reached for the knife and lunged to protect myself."

Hannah knelt forward and stuck the muzzle of the revolver in one of his nostrils. Her voice was frantic: "I saw her, you bastard! It was no accident. Don't tell me that or I pull this trigger."

He pulled the gun muzzle down gingerly as if it were hot to the touch. His voice was a whisper but it built in strength as he went on.

"Obviously I have nothing to lose. I am planning to tell you the truth. You need to believe me. At first it was accidental. I hit her and she was nicked. Just a little blood spattered on the rocks. I won't expect you to understand but . . . it was a completely different sensation for me. I had been stuck, caught between the company and this girl. My work was stalled. My writing dead and lifeless. I had been living in my head for such a long time, but now I was making something happen. The blood. I tasted it on my hand and the moment crystallized. I knew I was on the verge of a breakthrough. This was what it was all about, all of my work, all of my creativity—it was all about that moment in one way or another. It was a creative exhilaration I have never known. She lunged at me again. I pulled her hair back and there was this great salty spray of blood. I remember the hissing and the birds. It was as slick as oil, and hot."

Hannah didn't pull the trigger. I took the gun out of her hand. She stood with fists clenched, biting her lip and breathing hard.

Mathews sat up and focused on her. "I hope you aren't

trying to blame me. Are you so much better than I? Who was it that killed Potts?"

"We should ask your friend taking the nap." Hannah nodded to Pick.

"Pick was a toad. A corporate errand boy. He kept pestering me to get the documents. All he wanted was the documents. But I suspect he killed that pilot. That day in the airplane, when you left so suddenly, he wanted to talk to you, Mr. Younger. He thought *you* had the papers.

"It was an accident really. He was flying out to my cove and the pilot—Paul, was that his name?—Paul recognized him from our trip to Ketchikan. And he remembered bringing Louise to my cove some weeks before. Paul was very inquisitive and he had made an amazing number of connections about Mr. Pick's travels. So Pick killed Paul, imitating the way I'd killed Louise."

Mathews watched a spark settle on his coat. "I should be flattered, of course. He was copying my work as so many others have. But what about Mr. Potts? Eli Pick told me that both of you were suspects for his murder." Mathews was smiling.

Alfred stood up next to Hannah and put his hand on her shoulder. "We don't have to talk to you."

"Quite right."

I walked between them with my back to the fire. I put the gun down beside Alfred and leaned close to Mathews, looking at his face: smooth white skin that was bruised and scratched from the barnacles. His eyes showed pure white around the dark brown irises. His hair hung down in strands that shook with his convulsive shivers, but his eyes stayed steady and laughing.

"What are we going to do next?" I asked.

His smile made me cold.

"Next?" he said. "Next there is nothing. I have done what I can, and it's over. I have laid the groundwork."

The gun landed in his lap. Hannah glared at him. "Do us a favor and do it outside. And try and keep the speeches short."

"Small minds have tried to intimidate me all my life. Unlike you I am not afraid to act and die for what I believe in. In this life we can rationalize anything, only death remains implacable. We should celebrate it. We should roll our executions on our tongues like berries. Embrace them like big friends from home."

Something struck me wrong about what Mathews was saying. The theatrics were familiar yet out of context. "You didn't just make that up, did you? I mean someone else said that first. I can't remember who."

Alfred Tom looked into the fire. "Mandelstam . . . Russian poet. He said it." He looked straight at Mathews. "He was talking about Stalin."

Plagiarism embarrassed Mathews more than murder. He was stopped short. He stared down at the pistol in his lap. It was put up or shut up time.

He stood up and dusted himself off with what dignity he could muster. "You don't have to worry. I will not use the gun. For many reasons, I will not use a gun." He walked toward the doorway and called over his shoulder. "I will swim out past the surf break to be with the whales." Then he stepped out the door.

The fire popped and we sat looking at the flames. After a few moments I spoke up. "You think we ought to see if we can stop him?"

Hannah sat looking at the fire and only said, "He killed her."

Alfred took some more meat off the skewer. He chewed and swallowed.

"Think he's really going to kill himself?" I said.

Alfred Tom nodded into the fire. He wiped his mouth and spoke without turning his head, "Maybe after supper I'll go check."

SIXTEEN

OF COURSE MATHEWS didn't kill himself.

After supper we walked down on the beach and found him curled in a fetal position, naked, at the surf line. Two-thirds of us were in favor of leaving him there to fertilize the intertidal zone, but I picked him up and brought him back into the bunker, where he remained shivering and silent.

We slept near each other and close to the fire. By morning the weather had calmed down. The clouds were low with a slight wind blowing from the northeast. The seas were a rolling blanket of smaller chop. We stood on the point and waved our coats as Alfred's uncle's boat came in close to shore. I had a feeling he had not simply stumbled upon our location but was looking for us. He was able to bring a small rubber raft to shore and as he hit the beach, Alfred walked up to him and they spoke very quickly in low voices.

The boat was an old cabin cruiser that had been built for use on a lake but was now rigged for trolling. It had an ancient outboard motor that ran quietly. Every inch of the inside was covered in dried fish slime and his fishing tackle was in coffee cans and buckets tucked all over the boat. We slung the man in the snakeskin boots into the fish hold with his feet dangling out. We hung the deer carcass in the rigging away from harm. Mathews stayed silent and shivering in the forward berth. Ashamed, I suppose, but it was hard to tell.

On the trip in, Hannah stood next to me for a moment in the stern. She turned, facing into the wind so that her hair brushed back into my face.

Past the small wheelhouse, Alfred's uncle's hand came out the port and dropped the revolver over the side.

I didn't ask any more questions about Potts or Louise Root. Now there was only curiosity and curiosity can turn you inside out. No one would be able to pick up all the pieces.

When we got to the dock Mathews walked up the ramp without speaking and went to a pay phone. He must have decided that instead of killing himself, he'd get a lawyer.

Alfred and his uncle said they would clean the boat and take care of the deer. They would wait for the cops to come down and take care of Pick.

Still curious, I watched Alfred say goodbye to Hannah with a friendly handshake.

He looked at me steadily. "I was telling my uncle about it and he threw the gun away. Said he didn't want it around."

The uncle stood next to him, his pants tucked into his boots and his shirt untucked from his dungarees. He simply nodded. I nodded back.

"Okay. I'll see ya," was all Alfred said and then the boat pushed off from the dock and left a small widening wake as they headed for their harbor slip.

I waited by the phone booth. Mathews had his hands cupped around the telephone's mouthpiece and he was shaking his head vehemently. I gathered he was bickering about legal fees. He slammed down the receiver and walked past me as if I were invisible and strode up the street still wearing his damp exposure suit. He stopped suddenly when he saw a Sitka policeman standing at the corner, motioning with his index finger for Mathews to step forward. Standing next to the cop were the blond woman and her black dog. Mathews hung his head, and moved slowly forward.

I used the phone to call the cops about Pick, and the body under the tank. I explained about Doggy's shooting and the footprint and a little, but not much, about the background. I told them Pick had drowned out by the cape and was now in the hold of Alfred's uncle's boat. They were a little confused but agreed to go take a look. They asked me to come in for a statement.

I called the hospital and asked about Doggy. Once I found out he was okay, I just left a message that the explosion had occurred but there was no need to pick up the pieces. The first thing he needed to do when he had the strength was to get Phil Dominic out of jail. The nurse took the message without comment, but from her tone I suspect the news hit the gossip network of Sitka as soon as the receiver was down.

It was late afternoon by the time I walked down Katlian Street and I saw Toddy standing outside our house. He waved and I reflexively raised my hand and waved back at him like a little kid who is just coming home from summer camp. Toddy shifted from foot to foot and when I stood next to him he put his hand on the front of my shoulder.

"Hello, Cecil. You okay?"

"Yeah, I'm okay."

I gave him what I had intended to be a brief manly

hug with lots of backslapping, but instead I held him close and we rocked back and forth in the middle of the street.

"Cecil, I've made an arrangement with the people at Social Services and they said that we can work on a probationary status for my permanent living situation as long as you can . . . stick with the guidelines and can provide a stable living environment for me." He was showing off, smiling.

"Stable is the thing, Todd."

I went in the house, took a shower, and taped my head and my thumb. I put on clean clothes and hurried downstairs where Todd was still standing. He and I went up to Jake's house to get Nelson out of the freezer.

Jake's freezer had been on the fritz and it was lucky we came back when we did because just as we arrived Jake had taken the last of his venison roasts up to his friend's freezer and he was wondering what to do with Nelson. He was upset because he had an entire garbage bag of moldy bread crumbs that he was going to have to throw away and I took it from him to calm him down. Todd looked frightened when I came out of the front door with the black plastic bags covered with frost. He didn't talk to me as I walked down the stairs and he didn't ask about the parcels.

We started walking up the road when Dickie Stein and Hannah drove up in Dickie's rusted station wagon. Dickie had an open beer wedged in between his legs. He stuck his head out the window.

"Jake's been freaking out 'bout when you were going to get that thing."

"Yeah, well, we got it. I guess we better take care of it."

He jerked his thumb to the back and said, "Whaddya want to do?"

"I don't know. But I think you got some business walking toward your office. Mathews needs some local counsel. My bet is it could be a way into the bank, maybe some headlines."

He thought about it for a moment, considering whether to turn around and head to the office.

He said, "We better take care of Nelson. I got a cooler, a knife, and some other stuff in the trunk."

Todd and I started to get into the back but Hannah jumped out and motioned Todd to sit in front. She pulled herself in beside me. The car clattered up the street. Todd stuck his head out into the wind. He kept looking forward and sliding his glasses up his nose.

She pressed her head close enough so I could hear. She put her hand into mine.

"I've been kind of a pain in the ass, haven't I, Cecil?"

She looked down at my palm where the two-inch knife wound was scabbing over. She held my hand and spoke down to it.

"You're a hard case, you know. I don't regret it. I'm glad I bottomed out with you." She smiled. "But I want to be in control of my life now."

I rubbed her thumb with the tip of my index finger. She looked at me again and said, "Can I call you and talk about it sometime?"

What I wanted to tell her was, I couldn't talk about a controlled life. I didn't know who controlled life. All I wanted was to go back to the hotel in Craig, set up a tab with room service, then eat and laugh and make love until we were absolutely full and empty of all the things to be controlled.

But as I looked at her I felt a weight in my stomach telling me that it would never happen. So, I offered: "Yeah, we can talk about it."

She drew away from me on the seat but left her hand in my lap. She stared out the window, the wind blowing her hair back into my mouth. She reached up and rubbed Todd on the back of the shoulder. They both looked out their own windows.

We drove out the road to a sharp curve and a pullout with a trail down to a gravel beach. When we got to the beach I took the bag of crumbs out and laid it on a stump. Dickie came down the hill, bringing the cooler. Then I went back to the car get the bag with Nelson in it. Toddy was looking down at the bag.

"Cecil, do you think he didn't like being dressed up? Do you think that was why he ran away?" Tears were tracking down his face. I put my arm around his shoulder.

"No, buddy. Nelson was smart enough not to be bothered by your dressing him up. He didn't run away. He just got someplace where he couldn't get back."

Hannah stood close to me as I tore open the bag to look at the partially defrosted body of the black Labrador. Sitting on top of Nelson's body was a packet wrapped in freezer bags. Hannah reached in and picked it up. There were the letters and documents she had taken out of Louise Root's pack.

Hannah said, "I knew you wouldn't look in here until you

were strong enough to face it. And I knew no one else would. I slipped them in there that first day after you got arrested." She folded the papers into the inside pocket of her jacket. "I'll give them to Doggy."

Toddy started a fire on the beach and I skinned the old boy out. We laid the hide and the skull out on the rocks and we looked at them. Toddy wasn't sentimental about the body. He didn't cry as I laid the hide out but just watched with interest as I first cut up the quarters and then the ribs, taking all of the meat off the bones that I could. Dickie worked with the fire to get it hot enough to burn the bones. Hannah brought the cooler down from the car. She got a beer out for Dickie, hesitated, then looked up at me.

"There's a beer in here if you want it," she said, and looked away from me quickly.

"I'll get one if I want."

I turned and held out the bag of bread crumbs to her. Hannah walked to the edge of the water with a beer and the sack dangling in her hand. She threw handfuls of bread out on the water and then on the beach.

The gulls came and the ravens came, in squalls of black and white feathers. A heron circled from the north in its slow curving flight and landed thirty feet from us. Then the eagles came and we threw strips of the meat out onto the rocks and the water. Some of the meat sank and some was caught in flight by the gulls or the eagles. Crows hopped on the outer edge and snatched at the pieces of food. They fought with the bigger birds. The air was a rush of feathers and sounds that drifted down in the flurry of screeches, squawks, and ragged calls. Birds of all sizes worked the air and swept the busy atmosphere with their wings, trying to get to the meat.

Toddy had his glasses on and he bobbed his head in dazed happiness. He delighted in the birds and the sounds. He rocked back and forth murmuring, "Catch a bird, Nelson. Catch a bird."

They curled above him and behind him, gulping down the flesh. It was Nelson in the air and in the calls. It was Nelson in the water and in the tiny feathers that drifted down on us in the way we dreamed our lives would be: pitiless and so sweet.